She'd been right. He was gorgeous...

Oh, that mouth. Those lips. Mmm.

Lark didn't know if it was all the talk of sex today, or if Shane was simply the most desirable man she'd ever seen in her life.

Oh, yeah, she suspected he was even better naked. Long, lean and luscious, he'd know what to do with his body. Better yet, he'd know what to do with *hers*. She'd bet he could do things she'd only read about in those sexy romance novels.

It wasn't against the rules to look, and he looked even better up close.

Her heart beat a little faster, her breath shaky as she offered him her best smile. "You'll have to try our sugar cookies. Everyone loves them. They're soft and sweet, but everyone says they get a guy hard—"

Holey moley. The heat that'd been stirring in her belly climbed its way up to coat her cheeks.

She'd just offered the sexiest man she'd ever met a copulation cookie...

Dear Reader,

One of the things I love about September is the change it brings. To the weather, to our clothing choices and most of all to my footwear. Out with the sandals, in with the boots. Yay. So I had change on my mind as I wrote *A SEAL's Temptation*. Not only was it fun to contrast the difference between the states of Idaho and California, but it was also fun to play with what Lark and Shane *think* they want and what their actual wishes change into.

Even more fun, for me, was exploring the world of pottery and ceramics through Lark. It's an art I've always admired and, well, lusted after, to be honest. For fun, I'll share a few of my favorite pieces of pottery I've gotten over the years on my blog this September. I hope you'll stop by and check them out, as well as the fun contests and sexy hunks I'll be featuring.

Wishing you a wonderful autumn, and if any changes come your way, I hope you embrace them as Lark and Shane did. Visit me at tawnyweber.com or find me on Facebook at TawnyWeber.RomanceAuthor.

Happy reading,

Tawny Weber

Tawny Weber

—

A SEAL's Temptation

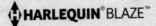

HARLEQUIN® BLAZE™

ISBN-13: 978-0-373-79863-6

A SEAL's Temptation

Copyright © 2015 by Tawny Weber

Recycling programs
for this product may
not exist in your area.

The publisher acknowledges the copyright holder
of the additional work:

Hard Knocks

Copyright © 2014 by Lori Foster

Printed in U.S.A.

CONTENTS

A *New York Times* and *USA TODAY* bestselling author of over thirty books, **Tawny Weber** has been writing sassy, sexy romances since her first Harlequin Blaze book was published in 2007. A fan of Johnny Depp, cupcakes and color coordination, she spends a lot of her time shopping for cute shoes, scrapbooking and hanging out on Facebook.

Readers can check out Tawny's books at her website, tawnyweber.com, or join her Red Hot Readers Club for goodies such as free reads, complete first-chapter excerpts, recipes, insider story info and much more. Look for her on Facebook at facebook.com/TawnyWeber.RomanceAuthor and follow her on Twitter @TawnyWeber.

Books by Tawny Weber

HARLEQUIN BLAZE

Blazing Bedtime Stories, Volume VII "Wild Thing"
Nice & Naughty
Midnight Special
Naughty Christmas Nights

Uniformly Hot!

A SEAL's Seduction
A SEAL's Surrender
A SEAL's Salvation
A SEAL's Kiss
A SEAL's Fantasy
Christmas with a SEAL
A SEAL's Secret
A SEAL's Pleasure

Cosmopolitan Red-Hot Reads from Harlequin

Fearless

To get the inside scoop on Harlequin Blaze and its talented writers, be sure to check out BlazeAuthors.com.

All backlist available in ebook format.

Visit the Author Profile page at Harlequin.com for more titles.

A SEAL'S TEMPTATION

Tawny Weber

With heartfelt thanks to Pat Jones for her brilliant gift with ceramics and pottery. I so appreciated all of the insights you shared, and, of course, all of the lovely pieces gracing my home. I love you.

Prologue

"Hey, Lark. We need two double-whipped, triple-caramel mocha lattes."

"And one of those passionflower tarts." The woman leaned so close she was bent over the counter, then said in a faux whisper, "You know, the ones Heather makes. She told me the ingredients in one of those is enough to make a girl irresistible to any man."

"Heather said what?" Lark Sommers stopped in the act of ringing up their order to stare.

"You know, that the baked goods here are aphrodisiacs," Cassia said with a wide grin.

"Hey," Sara O'Brian whispered at the same time, smacking her cousin on the shoulder. "I thought you said that was a secret."

"Right, like Lark doesn't know that Heather's making her aphrodisiacs for the coffeehouse," Cassia said, rolling her eyes.

Lark frowned at two of her favorite customers turned good friends, then blinked. First at the curvaceous redhead, then at the kewpie doll blonde. The cousins looked nothing alike. Cassia was as sassy as Sara was sweet. And both were usually pretty perceptive.

Sure, Heather baked for the coffeehouse. Lark's aunt also baked for the market, for the high school and for three local restaurants. She provided everything from cupcakes to croissants to half the town. So why would Cassia think the tarts were a turn-on?

Before Lark could ask, Cassia continued.

"Look, I haven't had sex in eight days. That's more than a week. At this rate, I might forget my best moves." The busty redhead sounded as if she was about to cry.

And knowing Cassia, Lark Sommers figured she probably was. The only thing Cassia Moore loved more than herself was sex.

Still…

"C'mon, Cassia, you know better than to listen to Heather's crazy talk," Lark chided, not caring that she'd just thrown her aunt under the bus. That's what Heather got for trying to stir everyone's imagination.

"Then they aren't real?" Cassia huffed, slamming her hands on her hips so hard her bracelets jangled like bells. "But I need sex. Soon. Today. Now. Otherwise, I'm going to lose my mind."

"Oh my God, hush," Sara hissed, hunching her shoulders before looking right, then left to see if any of their fellow caffeine addicts had overheard. Color washed her sweet face from her dimpled chin to her pale blond roots. "Do you think everyone in The Magic Beans wants to know that you're desperate?"

"Desperate? You go a week without sex and see how you feel."

It only hurt for the first thirty weeks. But Lark didn't figure sharing that little tidbit of knowledge would help, so she kept it to herself. As the cousins bickered, she tried to remember what went into a double-whipped, triple-caramel mocha latte—and what was up with multiples? And why wasn't regular coffee good enough for people?

She slid a quick glance toward the counter, with its old-fashioned cash register, antique metal tin of honey sticks and vintage cake servers, one piled high with tiny yam scones under the domed glass, the other with a variety of muffins.

Lark bit her lip, and as soon as she was sure that the two women were totally engrossed with their debate, she slid her laminated cheat sheet out from its hiding place tucked between a commercial coffee machine that looked as if it should be on a spaceship and the midnight-blue wall.

After a quick glance at the ingredients and steps, she began measuring, whipping, mixing and stirring. While she did, her friends debated the reality of magical tarts and if it was fair to use them to get a guy into bed. As she so often did over the past year, Lark felt as if she'd fallen down a very dark rabbit hole.

She pursed her lips, studying the only part of the café that felt like her—a half wall of shelves holding ceramic cups, bowls, mugs and dishes. It seemed like a lifetime ago that she'd made them for her mom when the older woman had decided to open a coffeehouse. Scattered around the place on high shelves and display cabinets were a few bigger pieces that she'd shipped from her studio in San Francisco. Guilt pieces, she called them, because she'd sent them instead of taking time out of her busy life and dream career to visit her mom's new home in Idaho. And now they were all that was left of Lark's dream life. Just like the coffeehouse was all that was left of her mom.

Knowing if she thought about it too long, she'd sink into a funk that would inevitably have her drinking chocolate syrup from the bottle, she blocked the thoughts. Instead, she carefully chose two of her favorite style, the tall fluted ceramic cups a rich blue glaze dripping over teal.

"Lark, if you did believe in magic, would you think it was okay to use it to get a guy naked?" Sara asked as Lark filled the mugs with the mocha-caramel-caffeine mixture.

Once upon a time, Lark had believed in all sorts of magic. In positive energy and thinking good thoughts and wishing on stars. But that was then—she frowned—and this was now.

"Nope. I'm not getting between the two of you." Grabbing the whipped cream dispenser, Lark shook her head. When a single strand of hair, black and silky, slid out of her French braid, she blew it out of her way. She'd missed her last two hair appointments because she was too busy to leave the café. And maybe, just maybe, because she couldn't work up much enthusiasm for her haircut at a place called Budget Cuts—the only salon in Little Lake, Idaho—population ten thousand—that didn't sport a barber pole.

"Okay, fine," Sara said, shooting her cousin a sideways look. "How about this question. Do you think it's okay to talk about your lack of sex in public?"

Lark held up a shaker bottle of mocha magic, a chocolate dust her aunt made for the drinks. When both women nodded, she shook a dusting over each mountain of whipped cream and considered the question.

"I think it depends," she said with a shrug, relaxing now that they were served. She leaned one hip against the counter, trying not to yawn. This getting up at five in the morning thing was for the birds.

"Depends on what?"

"On whether the discussion is between good friends or virtual strangers. On if it's held in quiet, considerate tones or put out there loud enough for the guy in the corner to hear."

The three women glanced across The Magic Beans. The café was on the small size so they didn't have to strain their eyes. Seated in the corner at a table made of a tree stump was a man who looked older than the dirt the tree had grown in. Grizzled and Grumpy, Lark had nicknamed the café's regular. But he wasn't paying any attention to them, so obviously the sex talk hadn't reached his hairy ears.

"But most of all," Lark added when the other two women turned to face her again, "it depends on if one of the friends is getting sex and the other isn't."

"Ha, there you go." Cassia did a little happy dance boogie that did get Old Joe's attention. He sent them a scowl and a growl from his corner before snapping his newspaper. Cassia gave one last defiant hip wiggle, then she poked Sara in the shoulder. "See, it's okay to talk about how devastating it is that I haven't had sex in over a week."

"Devastating?" Sara rolled her eyes. "I haven't had a date, let alone sex, in three months."

"Boo-hoo to both of you," Lark said with a laugh, taking her bottle of iced lemon water from under the counter to sip. "I've been in dry dock for seventeen months, eleven days and—" she glanced at her watch "—nine hours."

"And you're not stark raving crazy?" Cassia shook her head and eyed Lark as if expecting her to burst into maniacal laughter or run around the cozy café, screaming her head off.

Or worse, curl up behind the counter and cry. Which, Lark acknowledged with a sigh, was a possibility that grew stronger every day.

But not over sex.

Before she had to admit that, or react to the pitying look on her friends' faces, the door chimed.

"Well, well, what have we here? Three lovely ladies and coffee. What more could a man want?"

"Eww," muttered Cassia.

Sara pulled a face.

Lark barely managed to keep her smile in place as Paul Devarue approached the counter. The banker's pale gray suit did nothing to disguise his bulk, nor did his carefully styled hair hide the fact that he was balding.

Lark told herself not to hold any of that against him. Nor should she blame him for his ongoing campaign to convince her to sell her mother's coffeehouse so he could demolish Raine Sommers's legacy to put in a minimall. As he so often said, that was only business.

Yet, no matter now often she told herself all of that, she simply couldn't stand the guy.

"Good morning, Paul," she said, grimacing when he subtly nudged Sara and Cassia aside. Before Cassia could nudge him back, Sara grabbed their mugs by the thick handles, shoved one at her cousin and gave Lark a little finger wave.

"What can I get for you?" she asked. "Your regular? Black coffee, large, and a banana hazelnut bran muffin?"

The kind that came from the bakery. Not from Heather's creative kitchen. Not that aphrodisiac-laced treats would work on a guy like Paul. Lark's mom had always said that the first tenet of magic was imagination.

"Coffee and a muffin sounds just right. The perfect start to the day."

Lark glanced at the funky clock on the wall, a mosaic of coffee beans with spoons for hands, and gave a fond thought to the time in her life that she'd called 10:00 a.m. the start of the morning.

"Did you want it to go?" she asked, lifting the lid of the domed dessert dish and, remembering to use a napkin, grabbed the largest muffin.

"Here is fine. With business so slow, I'm sure you can keep me company for a while."

Oh, goody. Lark filled a rich purple mug etched with stars with coffee and tried not to grimace. That sounded about as fun as being kicked in the gut by a scary clown during a tax audit.

Or barring that, having a pity party over her nonexistent sex life.

"I HATE THAT GUY. He's such a jerk." Her eyes narrow with suspicion, Sara watched the smarmy banker lean forward, damn near climbing over the counter to shove his capped-tooth smile in Lark's face. "Look at how he's getting in her space. That can't be good. A guy like that, he'll smudge her aura."

"You're a goofball," Cassia said, shaking her head. But she twisted in her chair to check it out. "Quit worrying. It's not like he's hitting on her."

"Worse. He's nagging at her. And if he keeps at it long enough, she'll cave and sell him The Magic Beans. If she does, she'll move away and then we'll lose a good friend. A good friend with a great wardrobe that she lets you borrow. Then what?"

Misery was what.

Misery for Sara, that was.

She'd lose her best friend. The coolest person she'd ever met. Lark was everything Sara wanted to be. Sophisticated yet bohemian. Clever yet sweet. She had a degree in Fine Arts, she'd owned a chic apartment in San Francisco and worked in a fancy art gallery and attended fancy art shows there featuring her own pottery. She'd had it all.

And she'd given it up for family. Lark had come to Little Lake, Idaho, a year and a half ago because her mom was sick. When Raine Sommers's flu had turned out to be cancer, Lark had stayed. First to take care of her mother, then after Raine passed, to take over running The Magic Beans.

Sara thought Lark was the strongest woman she knew.

"Well, she's not happy," Cassia pointed out. "She puts

on a good face and all. But she's working her tail off to keep this place going like if she doesn't her mom's gonna come back and kick her ass."

Sara winced and resisted the urge to look over her shoulder. If ghosts where real—and she was sure they were—talk like that would earn a good haunting.

"She promised Raine that she'd keep it going."

"Lark shouldn't be miserable just because she made a deathbed promise." Cassia shook her head. "That's, like, medieval."

Sara hummed instead of answering. She knew Lark was sticking around for more than her mom's legacy. Raine's insurance hadn't gone very far, so Lark had sold her San Francisco apartment and taken out a second mortgage on the coffeehouse in the hopes that something—anything— would change the prognosis.

The bottom line was that Lark couldn't afford to leave. But Sara wasn't telling Cassia that.

"And speaking of medieval, can you believe she hasn't had sex in eighteen months?"

"Seventeen months, eleven days and nine hours," Sara corrected. Then, frowning, she added, "Maybe ten by now."

"No wonder she's unhappy. I mean, can you imagine going that long?" Cassia gave an exaggerated shudder, but the horror in her eyes was real.

"Well, her heart was broken," Sara pointed out. "Between her mom and that jerk, Eric, she's had a lot to deal with."

Eric had been Lark's sexy San Francisco guy. They'd been practically engaged, and he'd cheated on her the first week she'd been in Idaho. Worse, Lark had found out when a friend posted New Year's pictures on Facebook—one of which was her true love with his lips plastered on a busty blonde's mouth and his hands on her butt.

"That's the answer," Cassia exclaimed, slapping her hand on the table. Sara hissed when everyone, including the woman whose sex life they were whispering about, looked over.

"What's the answer?" she asked when they all turned back to their own business.

"Sex."

Sara blinked.

"Sex?"

"Yeah. You know, the horizontal boogie? The mattress mambo? Riding the—"

"Stop!" In defense against the onslaught of euphemisms, of which she knew Cassia had legion, Sara threw up a hand. "We've already established that I know what sex is. What I don't know is why you think it would help Lark right now."

"Sex helps anything, anyone, anytime," was Cassia's sage response.

"How is sex going to help Lark's situation?" She didn't ask how it'd help Lark personally. She knew what Cassia would say to that.

"Sex will keep Lark from seizing her engine."

"What do you mean?"

Her cousin grinned. "Remember that mechanic I went out with for a while?"

"The one who liked to, um, do you on the hood of his Camaro," she asked. At Cassia's nod, Sara shrugged. "So?"

"While we were doing the hood hop, he rebuilt my engine." Smirking at Sara's arch look, Cassia shook her head. "That way, too, but I mean he literally rebuilt the engine of my 'Vette. Chewed me out for not taking care of it properly, too. Said that an engine has to stay lubricated if it's going to run right."

Confused, Sara lifted her mug to lick the last of the whipped cream from the side. Maybe if the sugar high kicked in, she'd understand.

"Lark needs sex," Cassia explained patiently, pushing aside her coffee mug, only half-empty. "It'll give her a boost. If she's boosted enough, she'll be able to figure out what she wants to do with her life, she'll know how to handle the coffeehouse and, let's face it, she'll feel damned good."

Sara pursed her lips and thought over Cassia's words. Sara was a smart woman when it came to most things, but in the matter of sex, she always bowed to Cassia's greater knowledge. Everyone did. She wanted to suggest Heather's aphrodisiac tarts, but knew better.

"So you're saying if we get Lark some sort of date that she'll stick around? I mean, that she'll be happy," Sara corrected, not wanting to sound selfish.

"It can't hurt," Cassia said with a wicked smile. "Now, let's figure out who to hook her up with."

"He has to be good-looking."

"Better if he's got a rockin' bod. The kind that will make her mouth water and her hormones stand up and dance."

"Someone with a good sense of humor," Sara decided as she nibbled her bottom lip. "Lark's had it rough the last couple of years, so someone who makes her laugh would be nice."

"We want someone with stamina. A guy who can give her a dozen orgasms in one night, and still greet her the next morning with a breakfast boner."

"A breakfast..." Knowing her cheeks were turning pink,

Sara shook her head. Just when she thought Cassia couldn't shock her any more.

"Yeah. Every woman deserves a once-in-a-lifetime guy. He needs to be temp, though. You know, transient. Otherwise Lark will get all emotionally involved and it could mess with her mind. That'd just put her right back where she is now."

"I was thinking a local guy, someone who'd make Lark want to stay." Sara frowned.

"Nah. Lark's been here a year and a half—if there was a guy who appealed to her, she'd have already met him. We need a temporary guy to pop her cork, then once he's gone, she'll be more amenable to looking at the locals."

"Good point," Sara agreed.

Lark's perfect guy, but temporary.

He'd have to be good-looking, fun and nice. Cassia would toss in sexy, so Sara figured that probably mattered, too. Someone who wouldn't screw Lark over like Eric had.

Sara quit nibbling her lip and started sucking on it instead, her mind racing. It could be one of those two birds with one stone deals. She'd help Lark, keep her best friend and fix a few family issues all at the same time. It was a crazy idea, but maybe...

"You thinking one of those online dating services? Because I tried that a couple of times and those guys lie. They tell you they're sporting ten inches and they really got three." Cassia shook her head. "Why don't I check my history book, see if there's anyone in there who'd tempt her."

"Nope." Sara waved a dismissive hand before the sleek redhead had her little black book cleared from her purse. "I've got the perfect guy for Lark. Absolutely perfect."

1

"Report, O'Brian. Did you complete your mission?"

Petty Officer Shane O'Brian stood at attention. Shoulders back, chin high, eyes ahead.

"Yes, sir," he barked. "Completed with resources to spare."

"Is that so. And at any time did the target become aware of your mission?"

"Hell, no." Eyes dancing, Shane grinned. "He's as clueless as a newborn. Which, I've gotta tell you, is totally weird. Of all people, you'd think he'd be suspicious."

"Nice job." Shane's commander, Mitch Donovan, slapped him on the back before dropping onto the couch. Resting his booted foot on the knee of his camouflage fatigues, Mitch laughed. "Gabriel's a wily SOB, but there's no way he'd expect an engagement party. Especially since the bride-to-be doesn't even know they're getting engaged."

"He's going to be so pissed," Shane observed, handing Mitch the list of what had and hadn't been done so far.

"That you accessed his private information, evaluated his actions, went behind his back to report said information and actions, then compounded it by bringing multiple people into it in a way that will, when it comes out, be a huge slap in the face?" Mitch jutted out his chin and considered that, then nodded. "Yup. Seriously pissed."

"I can't wait." Laughing, Shane dropped into the chair

opposite Mitch. Like most everything else in the apartment, the brown furniture was butt ugly, but it was comfortable. Shane figured that's all a person could ask for with base housing.

Both he and Mitch, along with their friend Gabriel—better known as Romeo to the SEAL team—had got the PCS—permanent change of station—to the Coronado base a year ago. The three of them had bunked together until his buddies had hooked their perfect women. After they'd moved out, Shane hadn't seen any point in looking for other quarters—or in replacing the butt-ugly furniture.

"You're sure he's going to propose?"

Shane simply raised one brow. They didn't call him Scavenger for nothing. There wasn't anything he couldn't find. Supplies, enemies, information.

"Right," Mitch said, shaking his head. "Of course you're sure. Which means he has no clue what you're planning."

"That'd be we, not me," Shane pointed out. "And yeah, I'm sure. Nobody expects a party for getting engaged. Married, having a kid, okay. But for volunteering to hook on a ball and chain?" He gave a pitying shake of his head. Not over Gabriel landing Tessa, or that Mitch was newly married with a baby due any day. His friends had scored some great women.

But Shane figured the odds of military guys, SEALs especially, making it work long-term? Of finding a woman who got what they did, was okay living their life with a man who answered to Uncle Sam, put his life on the line on a regular basis and kept 90 percent of what he did to himself? Pretty much zilch.

Hell, he'd experienced issues himself in his family alone. His own mother was so pissed about his career, she refused to acknowledge it. To keep her happy, the entire family pretended he was a traveling salesman. It'd been funny for a while, but over the past couple of years it'd started getting to him. He'd got to the point that he rarely went back home to Little Lake, Idaho, and since nobody acknowledged his career, none of the family had ever visited him here in Southern California.

Shane frowned, taking the list from Mitch. He was better off without any more emotional crap in his life.

Maybe his buddies would do better. But he doubted it. Mitch had actually walked away from a shot to join the elite Special Mission Unit, DEVGRU. Sure, he said it was because he preferred training and wanted to stay with his team, but given that it'd happened about the same time as he met Livi, Shane had his doubts. And now Romeo was getting ready to pop the question. He'd already started making noises about extended training, taking on things that would keep him stateside instead of hot zones.

Shane got it. He understood why his friends were making those choices. But those weren't the kind of choices he wanted to make.

So he'd make damned sure he didn't get himself in a situation that would call for them.

"Any thoughts on the ETA?"

"Not yet." Shane glanced over his list again. "He's bought the engagement ring, but you know Romeo. He's going to want to set the scene, make it something special. He's leaving on maneuvers in the morning and he'll be gone for the next two weeks, though, so it won't be before that."

When the front door swung open, neither Shane nor Mitch had to school their expressions. They were experts at keeping their faces blank.

And in came Romeo, in all his glory. But if you knew to look, you could see a hint of smug terror in his eyes. Yeah, he deserved this party. Shane casually folded the list into a neat rectangle and stuck it in his pocket as if he hadn't just been planning on going behind the man's back.

"Yo, Scavenger."

"Yo, Romeo?"

"Mail for you." Gabriel tossed a couple of envelopes on Shane's lap on his way into the kitchen. "You got beer?"

"You're in uniform," Mitch pointed out, ever the stickler.

Gabriel simply lifted his hand, showing the gym bag he carried.

"I've got twelve hours before I have to report for maneuvers. Tessa's meeting me for dinner at Zappatos since it's halfway between here and our place," he said when he came back with his unopened beer. Just one, since Mitch and Shane were still in fatigues, too. "So I'm using your shower."

Flipping through the envelopes, Shane waved to indicate he do whatever he wanted.

"Shit."

"What?" Mitch leaned forward.

"A letter from home."

Knowing Shane's family situation, Mitch gave a sympathetic grimace.

Shane stared at the flowery handwriting on the pastel envelope for a second, then with a sigh, tore it open. After all, Sara wouldn't risk their mother's wrath by addressing a letter to an FPO unless there was a really good reason. And she usually took care to make the three-hour drive to Boise to mail her letter. But this one had a Little Lake postmark.

Affection, irritation and resignation all tangled together in his belly as Shane unfolded the paper. As he scanned his little sister's letter, his gut tightened.

"Well?"

"Huh?" He glanced at Mitch with a frown.

"The letter. What's wrong?"

They'd served together, been through too much together, for Shane not to answer.

"Drama. Sara's upset about the family rift. She wants me to come home for her birthday. Apparently she'll be miserable and her entire year ruined if I don't."

Shane frowned at Mitch's snicker.

"Go ahead, laugh. You're an only child. You have no idea what this means. I have five sisters. If one blames me for her misery, they all will."

"So? You're what? Eight hundred miles or so away. They don't even acknowledge you're here. And it'd take a hell of a lot for them to storm the base and get to you."

Shane didn't laugh because he could imagine them doing just that. Women were scary. His sisters scarier than most.

"Maybe I can volunteer for a mission. Something far, far away," he muttered.

"Or maybe you can take some of that leave you have built up and go home," Mitch suggested. "Watch your sister blow out the candles, keep her from being miserable, fix the mess with your mom."

Just the thought of it tightened his gut.

"I'm already working on an assignment," he said quickly.

"An assignment that's on hold for the next two weeks. Take a few days. Go home." Mitch waited a beat, then smiled. "Consider it an order."

"So, HANDSOME...WANNA join the Mile High Club?"

Damning Mitch for making this an order, Shane peeled his eyes off the book he'd been trying to read. He didn't turn his head. He just slid a glance to his right in hopes that the whispered question hadn't been aimed at him.

But the big-haired blonde's hungry smile dashed those hopes all to hell. And in case he'd been too dim to catch a clue, she skimmed her fingers up his thigh, those lethal nails skimming uncomfortably close to his goods. He wanted to shift away. He *really* wanted to move her hand. But he'd been trained to never blink first.

Shane was a SEAL. He'd faced down terrorists, shot down enemy combatants and answered to cranky Admirals. He'd once jumped from a burning plane with a wounded soldier in his arms and a parachute on his back.

And he'd done it all with nerves of steel.

But faced with a predatory woman and he froze. He specialized in communications, but he was lousy at this kind of thing. He didn't have Romeo's flirting skills. Nor did he have the social ease that Mitch was known for. Added to that, women generally either hit on him or wanted to take care of him. Both of which always confused the hell out of him.

"I'm Kathy, by the way." The lush blonde gave a low growl when she leaned closer to press her ample breasts against Shane's arm. "Mmm, you have such an impressive body. I'll bet you work out a lot, don't you? I'd love to see more of those muscles…"

"Whoa." Shane clamped down on the hand that was about to test his *muscle*. "Sorry. I'm going to have to pass."

He hated turning women down. Even ones who looked as if they could send the plane into a tailspin during a Mile High bounce. But the thrill of being hit on for reasons that often baffled him had long since passed. The thrill of easy sex, easy women and easier times walking away had faded, too.

"Now why would you do that?" Kathy fluttered her

lashes, giving him a wicked smile. "Don't you like adventures?"

Shane laughed. He couldn't help it.

"I live for adventures," he deadpanned, figuring there wasn't any point in telling her he'd scored his Mile High wings years ago, when he'd still been riding that thrill. She'd likely dare him to prove it. "I appreciate the offer, though."

As soon as the words were out, he mentally cringed. *Appreciate the offer.* As if she'd just suggested he take the window seat and enjoy the view. God, he was lousy at this stuff. Put him in uniform and he had no problem with communication. But when it came to witty repartee, clever conversation or easy dialogue with anyone he hadn't known for a while, he choked.

Shane didn't consider himself shy.

Shy was for girls and toddlers.

And it wasn't that he didn't know how to handle women. He was damned good when he put his hands on one. He was simply a quiet man who preferred to get the lay of the land, to get a feel for a person, before he opened up. A private man who believed fiercely in walking the talk. Since he didn't like people prying into his life, into his thoughts, he didn't ask questions. He figured if someone wanted to share, they would. Damned if most people didn't share way more than he could imagine anyone wanted to know about all sorts of things.

As if proving his point, Kathy the blonde took his refusal in good stride. Instead, she dived into a stream of chatter. Resigned, Shane tucked his book into the seat in front of him and gave her the semblance of his attention.

But he was only half listening. The rest of him was making the mental adjustment from his life in California and his job as a SEAL with its military mindset to dealing with whatever was waiting for him when he got off this plane.

Since she hadn't returned any of the messages he'd left, he didn't know if Sara told anyone he was coming home or not. Either way, it wasn't going to be pretty. All warning would do was give his mom time to stew.

It'd been rough enough when his dad had died in a skydiving accident when Shane was seven. He'd left behind a grieving wife, two sons and five daughters. Then in Shane's senior year of high school his brother, Mike, the oldest of the O'Brian siblings, had been killed in a drag racing accident.

Molly O'Brian was a strong woman. She was a loving mother. And she was the best cook in the world as far as Shane was concerned. But the loss of her husband and her oldest son had devastated her. She couldn't handle the idea of her second-to-youngest child, her only remaining son, living in danger.

And Shane couldn't set his dream aside. Not even for his mother. When he'd joined the navy right after graduation, she'd had a meltdown, but eventually, with all of his sisters persuading her, she'd dealt with it. If overcompensating by sending care packages that had to be delivered by forklift, insisting he call her every week he was in port and sending him job clippings from the local paper was dealing. But his joining the SEALs five years ago had been too much. This would make his third trip home since she'd issued the ultimatum that he choose between his career and his family.

By the time he'd shaken off the blonde, deplaned and made his way through the Boise Airport to baggage claim, he figured he should have argued harder with Mitch for a dangerous mission instead of this trip. Sara would have understood.

"Shane!"

A few inches taller than most of the crowd, he easily saw his sister on the far end of the row of chairs. His height was always an advantage, but probably not necessary this time since Sara was jumping up and down.

Damn. A weight he hadn't even realized he'd been carrying lifted. There was a lightness in his chest, a sort of joy he barely recognized.

Then, because he apparently wasn't moving fast enough, Sara plowed through the crowd to throw her arms around him.

"You look so good. Oh man, I missed you," she gushed once she'd released the stranglehold enough to lean back and grin.

Shane grinned back.

Damn, his little sister had grown up pretty.

Although Sara was as blonde as all of the O'Brian sisters and Shane's hair was dark brown, nobody would mistake them as anything but siblings. From their bottle-green eyes to the squared chin, the O'Brian genes ran strong.

"Did you bring a suitcase?" she asked.

It took him a second before he remembered that yeah, he did have a suitcase. It was rare that Shane actually booked a flight. One of the perks of traveling as an active duty SEAL was flying free if he was willing to go standby.

"We'll grab it, then head back. I'm so excited you're here. It seems like forever, doesn't it?" Sara babbled, tucking her arm through his as they moved toward the baggage carousel. "Was it a safe flight? Easy? No turbulence?"

He wanted to say that he'd flown through lightning storms and dived out of a Seahawk into the raging ocean, so it was stupid to think he couldn't handle a few bumps on a commercial airline.

But he knew hearing that would freak her out, so he shrugged instead.

"It was a quick flight."

"Oh, Shane. I'm so, so happy to see you. You'll be here through next weekend, right?"

"I'm here for your birthday," he said. There was no point reminding her that his welcome was thin at best. Pushing the length of his visit past its purpose was pointless.

"But my birthday party is in two days. And on a Tuesday. Celebrating in the middle of the week is so lame. I want another party. A big one with dancing, music, fun. That means the weekend." She leaned her head against his arm and slanted him a look through her lashes. "You will be here to celebrate with me, won't you?"

Shane wanted to close his eyes against the beseeching look in her eyes. He was a SEAL, he reminded himself. SEALs didn't show weakness.

Nor did they have to keep reminding themselves of that. He scrubbed his hand over his hair. Damn, he wasn't even technically home yet and he was already acting like a dumbass.

"What did mom have to say about my visiting?" he asked instead of committing himself.

He didn't need to hear her response. Her face said it all. Downcast eyes, a pouty lip and flushed cheeks. Dammit.

"Sara—"

"Don't be mad," she said, her words spilling out in a breathless rush. "It's going to be okay. I've got it all planned. I've got a place for you to stay until my birthday, then you'll pop in like the best present of my life. Mom will be so happy to see you that she won't have time to get upset."

He'd flown home. He'd met with his sister. He could pull a fifty out of his wallet, tell Sara it was her birthday gift and grab the next flight home. Technically, he'd followed orders. He could get away with it.

And—he looked at Sara—he couldn't do it. His family ties were tenuous at best. He couldn't break them with the only person in the family who didn't pretend he was a traveling salesman.

"Do you have anything that will inspire lust? You know, like magical Viagra that can be slipped into a drink or sprinkled on a plate of spaghetti."

"Have you considered a little lace chemise? Maybe add in candlelight to go with the wine and meatballs."

"Lark!" The tone danced somewhere between a whine and a laugh as the woman on the other side of the counter lifted a pink striped shopping bag to wave it back and forth. "C'mon, you know I've already covered the basics. I need oomph, though. A little guarantee."

Lark wanted to point out that nothing in life came with a guarantee, but she knew the pretty brunette wouldn't listen. The only thing Jenny wanted to hear was the magic phrase that would get her into Dave White's tighty whities. But Lark didn't have magic, nor did she feel right encouraging Jenny sneak into Dave's underwear.

"Jenny—"

"C'mon, Lark. Nobody's here, to hear us. Besides, everyone knows The Magic Beans sells special treats. Heather says all those exotic ingredients she uses have a special kick." Her elbows on the cherrywood counter, Jenny leaned forward and added in a persuasive tone, "Your mom would have something for me."

Lark clenched her teeth so tight, she thought she heard cracking. Then, because she knew from experience that the nagging wouldn't stop, she angled her head toward the glossy frosting of the brownies under the dessert dome.

"Chocolate is reputed to be an aphrodisiac," she said, trying to make her voice sound mysterious. "From the time of the ancient Aztecs, it's been fueling passion-filled nights."

So had cheap beer in recent times.

But Lark kept that to herself, preferring to hurry Jenny on her way with two huge brownies and a pound of freshly ground dark roast.

The horny housewife hadn't been gone ten minutes before the source of Lark's frustration came sweeping through the front door, her lavender hair curling over her wide hips and a trio of crystals dangling from her ears. In her plump arms was a large purple bakery box and on her face was a loving smile.

Lark wanted to scream, but that smile stopped her.

"Darling, I had a baking epiphany after my morning meditation and had to try a new recipe. Sesame mango cupcakes with almond frosting. What do you think? Will your afternoon crowd like them?"

"Heather, you have to stop—"

"Stop?" Heather interrupted, setting the box on the counter and lifting the lid. The scent of fruit and almonds filled the air. "Would you ask Mozart to stop composing? Van Gogh to stop painting? I'm an artist, darling. I must create."

"Fine, then create edible art instead of rumors."

"Rumors?" Heather's brows, as black as Lark's own, rose to meet her pastel hair.

"Aphrodisiacs."

"Well, darling, many of my ingredients have been reputed to have desire-invoking results. Just look it up on the internet."

Lark closed her eyes, wishing for the millionth time that

she had her mother's patience. But, nada. Fortunately, she did have her sense of humor.

"Did you know the internet claims that Elvis is alive, living on Neptune partying with Freud?"

"Well, that'd be a trick, wouldn't it? Especially as I heard that Elvis was in Brooklyn imprinting his profile on toast."

Lark burst into laughter. She couldn't help it. Heather was too sweet, too fun and too much like her sister for Lark to stay mad at her.

"Please stop," she asked, pulling a glossy red ceramic tray off the highest shelf. "It's bringing in the crazies. Last week, Mrs. Bell from the post office asked if I could sell her cookies for the nursing home. Apparently the residents are bored."

"Are they? Well, I'll have to make a batch and drop off a few dozen."

"No," Lark exclaimed, throwing up one hand. "I mean it. The last thing I need are more customers with a sweet tooth looking for the easy way to get lucky."

"Magic isn't a cure-all," Heather agreed, bustling around the counter to unbox the cupcakes, arranging them neatly on the tray. "It's more a boost, a little extra help. You know that."

"No." While Heather arranged cupcakes, Lark began putting freshly washed mugs back on the shelf. "I know that things can happen, sometimes, because of the power of suggestion, subliminal messaging and luck. Not magic."

"Your mom believed in magic," Heather insisted, jutting out her chin as she refilled the coffeemaker in preparation for the busy afternoon crowd.

Her own jaw tight, Lark kept her eyes on the mug-lined shelves, carefully inspecting them for chips or dings. Her mom had believed a lot of things. She'd thought dancing in the rain brought good luck, she'd believed in magic and she'd been sure that positive energy and clean living could keep her healthy, that a shaman with his herbal tea or the healer with her glowing crystals could beat cancer.

Lark had believed all of that, too.

Turns out, they'd both been wrong.

"If you'd just believe, just have faith, you'd be happier, Lark."

"I'm happy enough."

"You could be happier."

"Sure," Lark agreed, refilling the whipped cream dispenser. Most of the afternoon crowd considered their drinks as a segue to dessert. "Maybe if I was planning for a weekend of naked games and wild sex, I'd be happier. But I'm not."

"You could be," Heather said. "If that's what you want, you could eat a cupcake, open your mind to that power of suggestion and make it happen."

With who?

Lark had spent over a year in this little town and had yet to see a man who gave her the tingles, let alone one who made her think of all-night-sexcapades. No amount of positive energy or suggestive powers were going to change that.

"I'd be happier if you'd quit trying to convince my customers that your desserts will get them great sex. I'm starting to feel like I should be wearing a purple pimp fedora to sell cookies."

"A lot of them are asking for special treats, are they?"

"Way too many." Lark rolled her eyes.

"New customers?" Heather asked, her voice muffled because her head was in the supply cupboard.

"Absolute strangers, people who've never come in before. Last week a busload from the ski resort stopped in.

It's crazy." Lark took the stack of paper to-go cups from her aunt, waiting for the other woman to get to her feet before adding, "It's like you took out an ad or something."

She stopped talking when she saw the triumphant look flash across Heather's face.

"What?"

"So my fun with baking is helping your business. Even better than an ad, I'll bet."

Sara dropped the cups on the counter so her hands were free to slap on her hips.

"You did that on purpose? Why?" She waved her hands in the air. "No, no. Don't tell me why. Just tell me why you didn't tell me in the first place."

Heather frowned, blinked, then shook her head.

"What?"

Lark rubbed her hand over her hair as if the move would soothe her frazzled brain.

"You apparently put the word out that your baked goods were laced with an extra dose of come-do-me. You obviously did that to bring more business into the coffeehouse. Which I appreciate." Didn't she? Lark scrunched up her nose, then decided to mentally debate the merits of higher sales versus the irritation of having a slew of people asking if caffeine would dull the sexual buzz. "I don't understand why you didn't tell me what you were doing, though."

"You'd have told me to stop," Heather said matter-of-factly as she took over putting the to-go cups in their place.

"Of course I'd have told you to stop." Unable to stand still, Lark turned to pace, then realized that there was no room behind the counter. "We sell coffee. Not happy hard-ons."

"Here, refill the straws," Heather suggested, handing over a box.

Lark dumped them in the glass jar by the self-serve

station, then, box in hand, started pacing. It wasn't until her second turn that she realized her aunt had sent her out here so she could walk through her thoughts.

"Why?" she asked, stopping midstride to turn to face Heather.

"You're not happy here," her aunt said quietly. "As much as I want to keep you here with me, I know it's not your place."

Lips trembling, eyes burning, Lark stared at the wall of mugs until she was sure she wouldn't break down.

"It was Mom's place," she finally said.

"Yes, for as long as it would have lasted." Heather waved her hand to indicate time flying by. "Raine was a butterfly. She'd landed here and might have stayed for a while. But before here she was in Seattle. Before that in San Francisco. Before that…well, you know all of those befores because you were still living with her."

"Itchy feet," Lark murmured. Because her own feet were feeling a little shaky, she dropped into a chair. "I went to fourteen different schools before applying to the Academy of Arts."

"Proudest day of Raine's life was when you graduated with those degrees in Fine Art and Ceramics. She used to say she was glad to see all those years of making mud pies to serve with your porcelain tea set were put to good use," Heather said, her tone making it clear that she'd been just as proud. Then her features shifted from fond to stern. "So you know that your mother would want you to still be putting it to good use."

Lark had to swallow twice to get the words past the lump in her throat. But finally, she said, "And selling baked goods with sexual properties is going to do that?"

"Well, it can't hurt," Heather said, tapping the display case. "And if that doesn't do it, I'll step it up. I found some lovely silicone bakeware in the shapes of busty breasts and well-endowed penises."

"Oh God." Lark dropped her head into her hands. "I'm going to need a fur-lined trench coat to go with the pimp hat."

2

HEATHER'S WORDS WERE still playing through Lark's mind when she closed the coffeehouse at six. She'd been obsessing over their conversation, replaying it in her mind for the past few hours. But she still didn't know how she felt about it.

It was sweet of her aunt to try to help out. And the increase in customers had definitely impacted the bottom line. But that didn't mean that Raine would have wanted Lark back in San Francisco, hobnobbing with the artsy crowds, throwing clay for a living and attending gallery galas to celebrate her latest ceramics show.

As she cleaned the coffee and tea machines, she tried to imagine herself living that life again. But she couldn't see it. In part because her circle of friends there not only included her ex-boyfriend, his new wife and, of course, the three good friends who'd *just had to* send Lark pictorial proof of Eric's infidelity.

More, because she didn't feel as if she fit in that life any longer. But Heather was right—she didn't really fit here, either. She felt like a square peg wandering around a world of round holes.

But fit or not, she was stuck in this round hole for however long it took to climb out of the financial hole she was in. Or, since there was no way she was selling the coffeehouse to Paul to tear down, maybe she could find a buyer who would pay what it was worth and keep her mom's dream alive. Lark moved on to wiping down tables, her shoulders drooping a little as she tried to imagine where she'd go, what she'd do.

But her imagination wouldn't cooperate.

Because underneath it all was the simple fact that when she left The Magic Beans, when she moved away from Little Lake, she'd be saying goodbye to her mom. Again.

And she wasn't ready for that.

She was wiping down the last table when she heard a tapping on the glass.

"Sara," she exclaimed as she unlocked and opened the door. She was surprised to see her since the younger woman knew the coffeehouse closed early during the week. "Did we have plans that I forgot about? Or are you jonesing for an after-hours caffeine fix?"

"Neither. I'm here about the apartment. The one upstairs next to yours. You said I could put something in it this week, remember?" Sara's words were as upbeat and bouncy as her movements as she danced into the coffeehouse.

"Yeah, sure," Lark said, exchanging her sponge for the broom. The second floor housed two fully furnished apartments. Lark had taken one for herself when her mom died. The other was usually rented out, but the tenants had moved the previous month and she'd yet to find anyone new. "What are you storing?"

"My brother."

Lark almost bobbled the broom.

"Your what?"

"Shane. My big brother."

"You want to put your brother upstairs? Why not at your mom's?" Then she narrowed her eyes. "Is he alive? Because I draw the line at storing dead bodies."

"Of course he's alive." Sara laughed, starting to help

with the cleanup by grabbing a bag out of the trash can. "I dropped him at Sam's for a beer."

Lark glanced out the window toward the corner sports bar with a mild sort of curiosity. Over the past year or so, she'd met all of Sara's family except the secret brother. This should be interesting.

"He flew in for my birthday," Sara continued as she emptied the rest of the trash cans. "Isn't that sweet? But I want to surprise my mom, so I need a place for him to stay until Tuesday."

"Is this your brother's first visit since I moved here?"

"Yeah. He's, um, super busy with work and stuff."

Lark could hear the tension in her friend's voice. It took a second before she remembered that there were problems between Sara's mom and her brother. What those problems were, Sara had never said.

But apparently it was enough to keep the talkative woman quiet, since Sara had only mentioned her brother a couple of times. From her description, he was a cross between a philosopher, a Greek god, Einstein and a Boy Scout with a degree in psychology. What she didn't know was what he actually did for a living.

Whenever she asked, Sara sidestepped, shrugged or sighed. Which was probably the issue their mom had. Maybe they were ashamed of his job. Lark frowned, trying to think of a job worth being ashamed of. But all she could come up with was male stripper.

Hmm…

"How long is your brother visiting?" Lark asked, grinning a little as she imagined Sara's reaction if she asked if her brother danced in a G-string. She'd better keep it to herself, though. Otherwise Heather would have him dancing in the corner while she hawked penis-shaped brownies.

"He said he's only staying for a few days, but I'm hoping it'll be a week." Sara's shrug echoed her pouty tone as she piled the trash bags by the door to the backroom.

"He has to get back to work?" Maybe he was a headliner at one of those fancy strip clubs.

"Yeah, something like that," Sara said. As if she were eager to avoid answering questions, the pretty blonde grabbed the tray of dirty mugs and carried them into the back.

As much to finish her chores as to tease Sara about her brother's stripping career, Lark followed.

The back room was so small it barely held the two of them and the dirty mugs. The purple walls were stenciled with her mom's favorite motivational quotes, like, Do It With Happiness, the floor-to-ceiling shelves were filled with supplies and the sink and industrial dishwasher were tucked under the window overlooking the stairs to the apartment above.

On one shelf was a picture of Raine, her arms wrapped around Lark and a wide smile on her face. Lark would never admit it to anyone, but sometimes when she was alone back here, she talked to the picture. Thankfully, it never talked back.

"So," Lark said, loading the mugs into the dishwasher, "you never told me what your brother does for a living. Or is it top secret?"

One of the ceramic mugs slipped out of Sara's hand, plopping in the sinkful of watery bubbles. The blonde squealed, Lark cringed and the mug floated to the surface without a crack.

"Whew, sorry about that," Sara said, handing over the mug.

Wincing, Lark carefully placed the delicate cup in the dishwasher. Maybe she should give teasing Sara about her brother a rest. At least until the other woman wasn't handling her mugs.

"Um, yeah. Shane's job is sorta top secret, actually," Sara said, her voice carrying a fake edge. "He's not supposed to talk about it, so maybe do me a favor? Don't ask him while he's here. He'd feel awkward, and it kinda upsets our mom."

Wow. He really must be a stripper.

Or worse.

Before Lark could figure out what a mother would consider worse than a stripper, the chimes on the door tinkled.

Sara let out another loud squeal, tossed the sponge at Lark and ran out of the back room. Figuring it was the stripper—no, no the brother, she corrected—Lark took her time finishing up before heading out to meet Shane and decide if he had the body to justify her stripping theory.

Oh my.

He was gorgeous.

Wasn't he gorgeous?

She thought so, but the room had taken a nice, slow spin, which she was sure accounted for the sudden dizziness filling her head and the odd tightness in her belly. Resting her hand on the door frame, Lark blinked a couple of times so she could see him more clearly.

And oh boy, was she glad she did.

Because she'd been right. He was gorgeous. Sara hadn't exaggerated—he definitely had a little Greek god in there somewhere.

Tall, close to a foot over her own five-four, he had a swimmer's build. Broad shoulders, a slender waist and long, long legs. The kind of body that would look mighty sweet naked but for a gleaming coat of oil.

His dark brown hair was cut supershort, the top spiked in a way that looked as if he'd run his hands through its thickness while it was wet and left it at that. Unlike Sara's round sweetness, her brother's face was narrow, with slashing brows and a full mouth.

Oh, that mouth. Those lips. Mmm. Lark wet her lips while imagining doing the same to his. She was pretty sure she could spend hours nibbling on that bottom lip of his and still not be satisfied.

She'd bet if he were doing the nibbling, her satisfaction would be guaranteed. She didn't know if it was all the talk of sex today, or if he was simply the most desirable man she'd ever seen in her life. Either or both got credit for the images flooding her mind.

The two of them, naked. Oh yeah, she'd bet he was even better naked. Long, lean and luscious, he'd know what to do with his body. Better yet, he'd know what to do with *hers*. She'd bet he could do things she'd only read about in those sexy romance novels.

"Lark, hey," Sara said in a bouncy tone, her arm hooked through her brother's as she pulled him across the room. "I am so excited. I finally get to introduce you to my favorite person in the whole world."

Lark hurried over to the checkout counter, hoping it'd be enough to prevent her from jumping him while his little sister was in the room. Jumping a guy before they were actually introduced was just rude.

And, she remembered as her stomach sank into her toes—taking a good chunk of her happy lust with it— jumping friends' brothers was against the rules.

Dammit.

"This is Lark," Sara said as she and the hunk of gorgeous sexiness reached the counter. "She runs The Magic Beans. Best coffee in Idaho with the greatest baked goods. The muffins I brought to the airport were from here. Shane loved them, Lark. I'll bet he's going to be in here all the time, drinking coffee and eating goodies. Is that great or what?"

It took a moment for Lark to realize that the younger woman had run out of verbal steam. She ran a mental replay of the babbling, but only remembered every other word.

"Great," Lark murmured, anyway, unable to tear her eyes off the man in front of her. It wasn't against the rules to look, and he looked even better up close. Her heart beat a little faster, her breath shaky as she offered him her best smile. "If you liked the muffins, you'll have to try our sugar cookies. Everyone loves them. They're soft and sweet, but everyone says they get a guy hard and horny."

It wasn't her own words that clued her in to what she'd said. It was the expression on their faces, Sara with her wide-eyed shock and Shane's arched brow, that made Lark realize she'd quoted Cassia's take on the cookies out loud.

The heat that'd been stirring in her belly climbed its way up to coat her cheeks. Holy crap. She'd just offered the sexiest man she'd ever met a copulation cookie.

She tried to think of something, anything, to say to make up for it. But her mind was terrifyingly blank.

Thankfully, Sara jumped in.

"Like I said, this is Lark. She's my BFF and she's going to be your landlord for the next little while. Hopefully the next long while if I have anything to say about it," Sara said, the words flying out of her mouth so fast Lark was surprised they didn't have smoke behind them.

Shane smiled, those full lips spreading to show perfect white teeth and a tiny hint of a dimple in his cheek. Lark wasn't sure if it was because her cheeks were on fire or if it was because the lust was running so hot it was giving her orgasm previews. But she was pretty sure her panties had just melted.

"It's nice to meet you." Shane's voice was as sexy as his smile. Low, a little husky and so, so mellow. Lark had a sudden vision of hearing that voice in the dark. She'd bet his hands would be just as smooth as his words as he slid them over her naked skin.

"It's nice to meet you, too," she said, hoping her hand wasn't wet as she held it out to him.

When he wrapped his fingers over hers, her only thought was gratitude that her hand had actually been dry. Otherwise the electricity sparking between them might have caused some pain.

She bit her lip, studying his face. Did he feel it, too? His friendly expression didn't look as if he'd been plowed down by lust, so maybe it was just her.

Disliking that idea, Lark slid her hand from his. She didn't take her eyes off his face, though. It was just too yummy.

"Lark?"

His eyes were the dreamiest green, with thick lashes and a look of intensity that promised he'd give anything he did his full attention. She gave a delicate shudder as she imagined what it'd be like if all that attention was focused on her body. On their pleasure. Oh, baby.

"Lark."

Her eyes skimmed down that sleek face, with those high cheekbones and full lips, over shoulders made for holding on to during wild sex and a chest that just begged to be cuddled against. It was all Lark could do to keep herself from stepping back so the counter didn't block her up-close view of what he had to offer below the waist. If the rest of him was anything to go by, she'd bet whatever he had behind that zipper was an amazing treat.

"Lark!"

"What?" Lark blinked. She shook her head as if waking from a very hot dream, then she blinked again. Oh my God. She wanted to groan. Better yet she wanted to run for the nearest cold shower—to ice down the desire and to cool her blazing cheeks. Horrified, her eyes shot to Sara's, hoping her friend would give her a hint how long she'd spent staring like a lust-struck man-meat groupie.

"Sorry to be a pain," Sara continued as if she hadn't just yelled for Lark's attention. But her eyes were dancing. "Are you done closing up? I want to show Shane where he's staying. You know, get him settled so I can run to the store, pick up some food. I didn't want to get groceries early in case he changed his mind about coming."

At her brother's arch look, Sara threw her arms in the air.

"It could happen. You know it could. And if it did, what was I going to do with a bunch of man food? It's not like I can take it home or anything."

Lark's brows rose. Not just at the reference to their family issues—which she'd thought were off-limits—but at Sara's confrontational tone. Her gaze shifted to Shane's face. Instead of looking upset, he was grinning. Obviously he must be used to his sister's babbling and lack of tact.

"Apparently Sara thinks I'm incapable of finding food on my own." He slanted his sister a rueful look, then shook his head as if to say *go figure*. "It's a wonder I survive without you."

"As if." Sara swatted him on the arm. "I just want to spoil you a little. I know you don't get spoiled where you're at. And I hardly ever get to see you. So the least you can do is let me have fun with it."

"Then why don't I show you the apartment," Lark said before the banter could continue. As an only child, she was never sure if siblings were teasing, arguing or both.

"It's a studio, so it's kind of small but it's comfortable," she continued as she got her keys from the drawer under the counter. "I'm in the apartment next door, so if you need spoiling and Sara isn't around, just knock."

Holy shit. Had she actually said that? Lark gave a mental groan.

"I mean, if you need coffee or a snack and we're closed down here," she said quickly, afraid she'd start babbling like Sara soon. "I can help with that."

But apparently Shane was as sweet as he was sexy. His eyes danced, that hint of a dimple winking again.

"I'll do that. From what Sara said, your coffee is great. If it's as good as this place looks, I'm sure she's right."

Lark looked around at the funky, fun space as she came around the counter.

"Thanks. My mom always wanted her own coffeehouse. Once she'd saved up enough, she decided to open it here so she could live near my aunt." Lark hesitated as pain, swift and familiar, gripped her heart. "I joined them a year or so ago."

"So it's a family business. That has to be interesting." His tone made it clear he wasn't sure if interesting was a good thing or not.

Clearly picking up on that, his sister elbowed him with a huff.

"He says it like that because he'd run screaming into the night before he tied himself to forty hours a week with any of his own family," Sara said, heading for the door.

"I would," he said, offering Lark a serious nod. "I really would."

Delighted that his sense of humor was as sexy as his body, Lark grinned.

"That makes you very brave to spend a whole week here, surrounded by family," she teased.

The light in his eyes dimmed a little before he gave a one-shouldered shrug.

"Sara hopes I will. More likely, I'll run screaming for the airport after the party Tuesday." His lips twisted into a grimacing sort of smile before he headed for the door.

Lark followed a little more slowly as her mind and body did battle.

Her body argued that he was hot. Easily the sexiest guy she'd ever met. She was single; she hadn't had sex in eighteen months, two days and—she glanced at her watch—twelve hours. He was single and he knew how to laugh.

Her mind countered with the fact that he'd be here for a week, maybe less. He was as temporary as a guy could be. And, again, it was against the rules to fool around with the brother of a friend.

Besides—her mind tossed with a victorious glee—he was probably a stripper. Sex with a stripper was all kinds of tacky.

"Upstairs?" Sara asked, all but clapping her hands with excitement.

"Upstairs," Lark agreed, gesturing Shane ahead of her as she locked the door. She blew out a breath, then followed them along the wraparound porch to the stairs at the back of the building.

Which gave her a perfect view of Shane's butt, encased in khaki cargo pants.

Mmm. Those little fingers of lust tickled again so her thighs trembled a little and her belly tingled.

To hell with the fact that he was only here for a few days, that he was her friend's brother and that he might make his living wearing a tear-away cowboy costume.

All she wanted was that body.

WATCHING HIS SISTER all but bounce her way up the outside stairs that led to his apparent home away from home, Shane gave himself a moment to assess the situation.

Sara's friend was seriously hot.

Dark eyes and darker hair gave her a sultry look, her full lips and lush lashes cementing that impression. She made him think of a gypsy. Not so much in looks since her hair fell in a sleek line to her shoulders, the edges jagged and choppy. But the dozen bracelets jangling on her wrist and the hoops hanging from her ears were big enough for a baby's fist to fit. And then there was the way she looked at him, as if she could not only see into his mind, but all the way to his dreams.

But he was only here for a few days. A week if he gave in to his sister's nagging. He was supposed to be spending time with Sara, maybe mend fences with his mother.

So getting a major hard-on for a small town girl who was besties with his sister was on the no-go list.

Even if she was seriously hot.

Once he was sure he had a handle on his reactions—and his body's response to the luscious Lark, Shane followed the women up the short flight of stairs.

As he went, he mentally cataloged the terrain. Cool weather with a clear sky meant good visibility. The coffeehouse was located at the corner of Main Street, the second floor offering an easy view of downtown. Minimal noise as businesses shut down and locals went home for the day. The stairs creaked; he stepped harder on the next one and deemed them safe enough. And Lark Sommers was seriously hot.

He shook his head, forcing his attention back to recon.

Except he wasn't on duty. And this wasn't a target zone.

That didn't mean he was off the hook for paying attention to details, evaluating locations and gauging risks. No that estimating the distance from the apartment windows to the ground below was more important than appreciating the way Lark's hips swayed as she walked.

And what a sway she had. His eyes traced the curve of

her butt. Her backside was just as sweet as her front. So why not enjoy himself while he was here? If Lark was interested, there was no reason not to see how far that interest he'd seen in her eyes could go.

It didn't have to be an issue.

Did it?

Sara's laugh burst out like happy bubbles floating through the air. Shane smiled as her exuberance lifted his mood. Damn, he'd missed her. Hearing her cheerful voice made him realize how much he tended to block out thoughts of his family. Because of his mom, sure, but also because of his job.

As they reached the landing, Sara shot him a bright smile and set his mind straight. The situation between their mother and him was hard enough on Sara. She didn't need to deal with her best friend pissed off at him, too.

Which put Lark right back in the off-limits category.

He stepped into his temporary quarters with his resolve in place and looked around.

"What do you think? It's great, isn't it? Not too big, not too small." Sara moved through the room like a bumblebee, flitting, landing and flitting again.

Because watching her was making him dizzy, Shane glanced around at the space instead.

Approximately five hundred square feet, the floors were polished wood, the walls a soft blue and the furniture looked comfortably lived in. A small kitchenette stood at one end, a door that led to what he assumed was the bathroom at the other.

Scattered everywhere were pottery and what he thought might be porcelain. A long, slender vase the color of a stormy ocean stood next to a sculpture of an owl so detailed he could see each feather. A wide-lipped bowl covered half the kitchen table and the open kitchen shelves housed almost as many pottery mugs and cups as he'd seen downstairs.

"As you can see, it's pretty self-explanatory." Standing in the middle of the room like a centerpiece, Lark gestured to each feature with an elegant hand. "Living room slash kitchen slash bedroom here."

Lark lifted the couch cushions to show him the pull-away, her silky-looking purple blouse gaping as she bent over. Her bra matched, just as silky and bright as her top.

Shane's mouth went dry.

Damn.

There was nothing sexier on a woman than matching undies. His eyes skimmed down to her denim-covered hips. Did the rest match, too? Then he noticed that her short fingernails were the same shade of purple. Yeah. Her panties matched.

Damn again. She'd just gone from seriously hot to the sexiest woman he'd ever seen. Shane didn't usually fall into instant lust, but he was more than willing to make an exception in this case.

"The bathroom's through that door." Lark pointed to the one next to the kitchen. Then she opened the door of the one he'd assumed was the bathroom. "This is storage. Sorry it's full."

He walked over. More to get closer to the sexy brunette than because he cared about her storage habits.

Then he saw the various pieces of pottery and ceramic sculptures scattered around the small space. Damn. It was like getting hit in the face with the vast variety of colors, shapes and styles. Under all the color and fun, all he could see a lot of imagination.

"Impressive." When he stepped in for a closer look, his arm brushed Lark's.

Whoa. Instant hard-on. Shane knew he should step

aside. Or at least get control of the lust pounding through his system. But it felt too good.

So he took a breath, reminded himself that he was a highly trained operative with nerves of steel. He could handle a little lust-gone-wild.

"Where did it all come from?" he asked, keeping his tone light and easy. "Do you collect it? Sell it? What?"

"She makes it," Sara said, balancing one hand on Shane's arm as she stepped on tiptoe to see over his shoulder. "Isn't it great?"

"You made all of this?" Impressed, Shane looked in the room again. The pieces ranged from a vase big enough for him to stuff his sister into on down to some smaller than his hand.

"I did. I mostly use the pottery wheel, but I occasionally do slip casting and hand build sculptures," Lark said, following his gaze toward the richly colored stock on the shelves. Her expression echoed her tone. Easy, comfortable pride. "All of the ceramics in the coffeehouse are mine. The mugs and plates and decorations. I used to have a studio but now I mostly supply to a few wholesalers and a couple of decorators contract pieces from time to time."

"She's great, Shane," Sara chimed in. "You should have seen this piece she did for some fancy spa last year. It was a nude, all glossy and sleek."

A nude.

Unable to stop himself, Shane's gaze shifted from the sensual arch of Lark's mouth to travel down the tempting curves of her body. The color of crushed grapes, purple and bleeding, the long sleeves of her dress were tight to the wrist, the top cupping breasts full enough to make his mouth water before draping loose over hips just the right width for his hands. He wished there was a little less fabric, so instead of hitting her calves to show off black boots that laced to the knee, he could see her legs. The only thing that got him hotter than a nice set of breasts was a pair of long, sleek legs.

He lifted his gaze to meet hers and had to mentally adjust that long-held belief. Because those dark eyes were getting him pretty damned hot, too.

For the first time in his life, Shane wished a woman would hit on him and hit hard. At least, he wished it if that woman was Lark.

That was the only way he was going to get her naked, he realized with an unfamiliar surge of frustration. If he did the hitting on, he'd have to get to know her first. That's just the way it was. He'd have to learn more than her name before he asked her to strip down naked. That meant he'd have to tell her more about himself. Because once *he* stripped down naked, she'd see the scar riding low on his hip. And despite what his mother liked to tell people, he didn't figure a woman as savvy as Lark was going to believe he'd taken shrapnel while installing phone systems.

And that wasn't going to happen for two very good reasons.

One, word would get out, which would piss off his mother, which would launch yet another round of drama. Then his sisters would all join in the nagfest, every one of them singing the same ole familiar song, with a dozen choruses of why he should leave the military, how he should find a safe job and when was he going to move back home where they could watch over him.

Which led to reason number two. Shane would never, ever, live under the eyes of his family again. He loved them just fine, but loved them more at a distance and in small doses. Which meant hometown girls with connections to his family were off-limits.

"Hey, do you guys mind? I'm going to run down to the

car and get a few things. Be right back," Sara said. Before he even turned his head, he heard her rush out, leaving him alone with Lark.

"So…" His mind raced, desperate to find a topic that didn't make him think of seeing her naked. "Is that what you mostly do now? In pottery? Cups and plates and things?"

Nice, O'Brian. He gave himself a mental slap upside the head.

Lark didn't seem to mind, though. She just gave him a long, considering look. He knew that look. It was the one women used when they were wondering what he looked like naked.

His body stiffened, more than ready to show her that it was a pretty good view. Then she blinked and the look was gone.

"I can do almost anything with clay. Pottery is my passion but I really enjoy sculpting, too. Hang on." She smiled and held up one finger, as if he'd turn heel and leave the minute she turned around.

Then she did just that, sweeping into the storage room and bending low to get something from the bottom shelf. And Shane knew it'd take an explosion to get him to move.

Because that was one sweet view.

He watched the way the fabric of her jean skirt clung to what looked to be a Grade A ass, then had to shove his hands into his pockets to hide his reaction.

As Lark came back with something in her hand, she gave him a smile that carried a hint of embarrassment, but unless she could read his mind, he didn't know what she had to be embarrassed about.

"You might like this," she said quietly, wetting her lips before holding out her hand, palm up.

On it was a small, whimsical dragon. Wings unfurled, it looked as if it were smiling.

"You made this?" Awed at the way the colors bled from red to gold to purple, he rubbed one finger over the tiny, detailed scales of the dragon's back. "It's great."

"He's a guardian dragon," Lark said, touching her finger to the cool ceramic, close enough that all he'd have to do was shift his hand to touch her. "You might like one of your own. I can tell Sara worries about you."

Shane grimaced at the idea of his baby sister telling people—especially sexy female people with eyes like midnight—that he needed protecting. Better to change the subject than comment on that.

"It takes a lot of talent to make something this intricate," he said, waiting until her gaze met his to slide his hand over hers. He felt her fingers tremble even as he saw that spark heat. Her lips looked so soft as she puffed out a soft breath before tugging that full bottom cushion between her teeth. He wanted to do that for her, just nibble there for a little while.

"I'm good with my hands," she finally said, her words so low they were almost a whisper.

How good? he wanted to ask, just before he dared her to prove it.

Before he could give in to the temptation, Sara came back into the room.

"This is a great apartment, Lark. Shane, you're going to love staying here. It's so comfy and cozy," she said, her voice bubbling with enthusiasm. "I'll put groceries in this cute little kitchenette, then we'll go get dinner, okay? Anywhere but the sports bar."

Her words trailed off, then she giggled.

"What'chya guys doing?"

Lusting, dammit.

Shane blinked once, then shoved aside the knife-sharp

edge of frustration, calling on his years of training to yank himself back under control.

"Nothing," they both said at once.

"Uh-huh." After a brief silence, Sara asked, "Lark, do you want to join us for dinner?"

Lark slowly shifted her gaze from Shane to his sister. She pressed her lips together, taking a deep breath that did amazing things for her lush breasts.

"Thanks." Before Shane could decide if spending more time with her was good or bad, she shook her head. "I've got a lot to do tonight. Besides, I'm sure the two of you have a lot of catching up to do."

"Are you sure?" Folding the canvas grocery bag, Sara tucked it between the counter and the refrigerator before joining them. "I'd love for you to join us."

With an unreadable look on her face, Lark gave Shane a long look again.

"I'd better not," she said quietly. She took the key ring out of her pocket and slipped one key off. "This will get you back in later. Why don't you guys go eat? I'll set out the bedding, towels and such."

He'd rather stay.

Which is why Shane didn't object when Sara tucked her hand into the crook of his arm and called a goodbye to her friend.

He shot Lark one last glance on his way out the door. Not because he wanted to remember what she looked like—her image was etched on his brain. He just wanted to see if she was looking.

Damn.

She had the sexiest smile, standing there with that dragon in her hand. The one she'd made by fondling a long tube. Sure, the tube was clay, but he'd bet she was good enough to extend that talent to tubes of flesh.

And she was off-limits, he reminded himself as he fol-lowed Sara down the stairs. It was just as well that Sara had sideswiped his making a move on her friend.

His mind agreed.

His dick, however, called it pure bullshit.

3

GRABBING THE GROCERIES from the back of her Scout, Lark glanced at the back stairs of The Magic Beans building. Nerves danced in her stomach as she eyed the door to the apartment next to hers.

She must have gone over the bend into crazy.

What other reason was there for her blah, bland and boring behavior the day before? Instead of flirting or acting interested when she met the sexiest man in the world, she'd babbled about pottery.

Why else would she spend an entire night with her ear pressed against the adjoining wall just because she was fantasizing about the guy on the other side?

Where was she ever going to meet another guy with the perfect combination of a gorgeous face, a body hot enough to dim the sun and a personality that made her want to curl up on the couch and talk for hours?

When would she get another shot at a little fun to break up the miserable monotony that had become her life?

Yet, she'd blown it.

At first, she'd tried to excuse her behavior by reminding herself that Shane was Sara's brother, so the standard dating rules were in effect. But somewhere around midnight, she'd remembered that oft-used loophole in the rules—that if the sibling never found out and it wasn't a big deal, then the rule didn't count.

Shane was only here for a few days, a week at the most.

Despite his family, he clearly had no strong ties to the town. And she'd been without sex for over a year and a half. All of which, she'd decided, qualified her for the loophole.

But somewhere between her middle of the night fantasies and produce shopping, she'd made a vow. She wasn't going to wimp out next time she saw Shane O'Brian.

Excitement danced in her belly as she reached the landing. Was Shane in the apartment? She wondered if he'd slept okay. She could stop in and ask. That was totally nonwimpy.

Maybe she should offer him some muffins or cookies from downstairs. She suddenly wished for some of Heather's reputedly sex-inducing passionflower tarts. Or, she glanced at the cloth bag in her arms, at least something more exciting than granola.

Boring snack or not, checking on him was the neighborly thing to do. The fact that he was the sexiest, most appealing man she'd ever seen in her life had nothing to do with it.

But he *was* the sexiest, most appealing man she'd ever seen in her life. He might be quiet, but he was well-spoken with that deep, husky bedroom voice. And even though the idea of hooking up with a male stripper had its drawbacks, she figured it meant he had to have some seriously incredible moves—on *and* offstage.

Because she was so ready for hot, wild sex. The kind that came without commitments. The kind that came with multiple screaming orgasms.

She wanted to experience a wickedly wild affair.

And she knew exactly who she wanted to experience it with.

Because not only did he look as if he would be amazing

in bed, but Shane O'Brian was the kind of guy she could get seriously hooked on.

She was halfway to his door when her feet stopped all by themselves and it hit her. She'd been hooked before. And she knew that hooked meant hurt.

Her eyes lingered on his door for a long moment, but she didn't step forward to knock. Instead, she turned left and unlocked her own apartment.

As homes went, the place wasn't very big. But it was hers.

She'd painted the walls a dusky blue leaning toward indigo and kept the windows bare. She'd sold most of her furniture when she'd given up her apartment, only keeping the pieces she loved most. Her purple velvet chaise lounge. The brass floor lamp with its dangling crystal shade. Her bedroom set, with its ornate brass headboard and etched armoire. And, of course, her art supplies.

Which was why she used the tiny second bedroom as a living area and had turned her living room into her art studio. Her pottery wheel held the place of honor in the center of her small living room, shelves of supplies lined the wall under the window and her kiln was in the kitchen.

She'd no sooner set down her grocery bags than her cell phone range. Grabbing it from her purse, she took one look at the display, cringed and let it go to voice mail.

Before she'd finished unpacking her cucumbers, a text signaled; Answer your damned phone. Two seconds later, it rang again.

"You are so pushy," she said in lieu of hello.

"Darling, how does one get what they want unless they are willing to push?" Carlo Franconi said, as always his heavily accented voice sounding romantically impatient. "Are you still in that little state? The one east of California? Iowa?"

"Idaho."

"Right, right. Wherever you are, you're not here where I can drop by your studio. As if that isn't bad enough, you don't return my emails. So I must call."

"I haven't turned on my computer in a week or so." The phone tucked between her ear and shoulder, Lark put her cucumbers, along with the rest of her groceries, in the refrigerator.

"Are you living in the dark ages? Does your cell phone not check email?"

"Sorry. I never look at my phone unless it rings." Wrinkling her nose, Lark put her dry goods on the shelf over the stove.

"If even then." Before she could defend her preference to avoid everyone and anything from her previous life, Carlo continued. "Considering I'm calling to offer you the deal of a lifetime, you should be more than sorry."

Lark had to bite her lip to resist the urge to hang up.

"Bellissimo has been contracted to do redesign of decor in the Palace Hotel," he continued, his English suffering in his excitement. "I do everything, top to bottom. Lobby, suites, right down to toilets."

Lark had to sit. She didn't bother pulling out the ladder-back chair, but dropped her butt on the table instead, only half listening to Carlo's recitation of his extensive redecorating plans for one of the biggest hotels in the San Francisco Bay Area. The other half of her was panicking.

She knew what he was going to say. There was only one reason he'd call, only one reason he'd be telling her all of this. Only one offer that he'd term *the deal of a lifetime*.

She knew what she was going to say.

No.

There was nothing else she could say. Not with the workload she had here. Not with the equipment she had here. She glared at the small electric kiln, then at the plastic bin she'd modified into a wet box.

Yet, she couldn't find it in her to cut Carlo off. She had to hear it all. Had to hear about the custom urns he wanted by the pond and the unique sculpture he wanted in the lobby. Finally, she couldn't take any more.

"Carlo, I have to go. My phone is about to die," she interrupted with a lie.

"Fine, fine. I will email you a tentative outline of the pieces I'll want, the budget I'm allocating and time frames. You reply, yes."

Lark wanted to say yes. She wanted it so bad she could taste it. But she knew she couldn't.

Yet, she couldn't quite get the word *no* out of her mouth.

"I'll look at it," she promised before hanging up.

And she would. What was life without a little self-torture.

With that in mind, Lark tossed the phone into her purse, where she'd hoped it'd be buried so deep, she'd never hear it ring again.

She didn't open her laptop, though. She didn't need anything else adding to the pressure weighing down on her head.

Instead, she turned to the only solace she had. Her escape from reality. Her pottery wheel.

After a second's debate, she opened the front door, but left the screen closed. Not because she was hoping to hear Shane or anything. It's just that it got stuffy in here, bent over damp clay. It'd be nice to work with a little air circulating.

And that, Lark realized as she pulled on a light canvas apron over her T-shirt and jeans, was a lie of the wimpy.

But wimpy or not, once she'd cut off a slab of clay and worked the air out of it on her wedging table, she was in her element. When her fingers were in clay, her head in a project, she could forget everything else.

Worries, fears, even joys faded.

But apparently, with all of those emotions out of the way, lust was free to take over. As she worked the malleable mud, the image of Shane's smile flashed through her mind. His laugh echoed through her head, making her smile a little. He was so sexy.

She set the clay on the throwing bat and carried it over to her wheel. Sitting on her stool, she flipped the switch, then using the foot pedal, started forming the clay with her hands.

A man with hands like Shane O'Brian would know how to use them. Lark knew just how they'd feel as they skimmed over her bare skin. Like rough silk. Soft enough to entice, hard enough to excite. She'd want to be naked the first time they made love. Both of them bare so they could slide over each other's bodies. For all that gentlemanly air he had going on, she'd bet he wasn't a strictly missionary kind of guy. What was his favorite position? she wondered. Maybe they'd take turns showing each other how they liked it best.

Lark sighed, the heat in her belly spreading high and low so her nipples tingled and her panties grew damp.

Nothing like a sexy little fantasy to get a girl through the day, she decided as she let her fingers dig deeper into the swirling clay.

A harmless one, she reminded herself. It wasn't as if she was going to act on it.

Was she?

A new kind of excitement tingled in her belly at the thought. She'd only been with three men, and all of them had waited way longer than the requisite three dates before seeing her naked. Not because she was a prude. It just took her that long to feel comfortable enough for the intimacy of sex.

"Hey."

Lark's fingers spasmed, putting an unexpected groove in the pitcher.

Nerves danced with excitement in her tummy as she looked toward the sexy man on the other side of the door. She stayed hunched over her wheel, figuring it seemed more casual than jumping to her feet, running across the room and throwing herself into his arms.

Because, oh, baby, he looked good enough to jump on. Roll on, lie on, ride on.

"Hey, back." Oh God. Did her voice sound too choked? She added a friendly smile just in case. "How are you doing today?"

"Good."

Lark waited, but Shane didn't say anything else.

He didn't walk away, either.

Did he want to see her? Because he was, like, interested? Was there a problem with the apartment? Or did he want to ask something about Sara?

Why wasn't he talking?

Nerves shimmied down her back.

She wished he'd say something. Anything.

"Would you like to come in?" she asked when the silence started itching.

"Sure."

"Do you mind getting the door?" she asked. Straightening, Lark lifted her clay-covered hands to show him why.

He stepped inside, carefully closing the screen so it didn't bang. And stood there in silence, inspecting her space.

"I hope you like the apartment," she said, as much because she wanted him to be comfortable over there even as the intense way he was looking around was making her nervous.

She should have kept her mouth shut.

Because now he was inspecting her with that same intensity. His gorgeous eyes, that misty green, seemed to peer right into her soul. She wondered if he could see her hopes, her fears. More importantly, her lust.

Figuring he was doing it so she might as well, too, Lark looked right back. He was dressed as casually as he had been the day before, this time in light denim jeans that hugged his long legs and a button-down shirt the color of the ocean. Her fingers itched to sweep across those broad shoulders, to test those muscles to see if he was as hard as he seemed.

She wet her lips.

She'd bet he was.

"The apartment is nice," he finally said, his deep voice so sexy she'd bet just the sound of it from the pillow next to her would inspire an orgasm.

God! What was with her? She never lusted after men like this. And certainly never mentally consigned one to the role of sex object before. Somewhere between shocked and horrified, Lark tried to reroute her thoughts. Glad her apron covered her puckered nipples, she grabbed the hand towel from its hook on the edge of the wheel.

"I'd like to pay you for letting me use it, though. I know Sara said you were cool with the favor, but I don't feel right unless you let me give you something in return."

She could think of about three dozen things she'd like him to give her, but most required them both to be naked and none were appropriate.

"We can call it my birthday gift to Sara," she said after clearing the lust from her throat. "She's so excited to have you here. She talks about you all the time."

"Does she?"

"You sound surprised." Lark laughed a little at his shocked expression.

After a moment's consideration he shrugged.

"I guess I am."

Lark waited for him to expand on that.

Then she remembered Sara's comments about the rift between Shane and their mother and realized it was probably a touchy subject.

She winced, worried that she might have made him feel bad.

"Can I get you a drink or a snack or both?" she offered, hoping to smooth over the awkwardness.

He hesitated for a second before nodding.

"Sure. A drink would be nice. Thanks."

A man of few words. Smiling, Lark tossed the towel over the clay and got to her feet. Her insides hummed when his gaze swept down the length of her body.

She waited a second, but when he didn't start taking off his clothes, she gave a mental sigh and headed for the kitchen. After washing her hands and slicking them with lotion, she pulled open the fridge.

"Juice or soda?" she asked, holding up one of each. "Or we can go downstairs and I can whip you up triple-mocha caramel whipped latte."

She grinned at the horror that flashed over his face.

"Is that something people drink?" he asked, crossing the room to take the juice.

"Unfortunately." Lark put the soda back in the fridge and grabbed a juice for herself.

"Whatever happened to coffee? You know, black or with cream and sugar?"

"I ask myself that every day." Lark twisted the cap off her drink before toasting him with it. "Of course, if that's all people wanted, The Magic Beans' customer base would plummet. You'd be amazed at how many people justify a thousand calories in the name of getting their caffeine fix."

He gave a slow shake of his head before tipping back his own bottle. She watched his throat work as he swallowed. She pressed her own bottle against her cheek to cool her skin. She didn't know why the act was so sexy, but watching him was getting her excited.

Since she didn't know what to do about that—she'd never made the first move in her life—Lark figured it was a sign to cool her libido.

"I know it's weird but my living-room furniture is in here," she said, gesturing toward the spare room.

"Makes sense. It looks like you've used every inch of the living room."

"A girl's got to have priorities," Lark said with a laugh. She led the way into her faux living room.

"Why don't you get comfortable?" She waved her hand toward the chaise.

He glanced at it, looked around.

Admittedly, there wasn't much else. A long table covered with sculpture, framed photos and a thriving pothos, its green leaves draping their way toward the floor.

"Where are you going to sit?"

"The pouf," she said, reaching behind the chaise for the stuffed footstool. A rich brocade of emerald green, it hit Lark's knees when she set it down. "It's comfy, really. At least it is for me. My legs are a lot shorter than yours."

She hadn't meant her words as an invitation, but a little tingle curled low in her belly when his eyes skimmed down to her legs.

Then she saw the heat flare in his eyes. An answering flame sparked low in her belly. Lark's thighs trembled, her nipples pebbling against the lace of her bra. She sat so ungracefully that the pouf wobbled, almost sending her to the floor.

After a second, he sat sideways on the chaise, showing considerably more grace than she had. He was so big, though, he made her elegant lounge chair look like a miniature.

While Shane glanced around the room, Lark tried to settle the nerves in her stomach. It'd been a long time since she'd been involved with a man. Even longer since she'd dated. She was out of practice dealing with men. Maybe that's why she couldn't read him.

"Did you get over to see your family yet?" she blurted out, hoping conversation would help her figure him out. "Or are you waiting until the birthday party to surprise everyone?"

"I'll wait." After a second, he added, "You'll be there, won't you?"

"You say that like you won't know anybody at the party," Lark said with a laugh.

Something flashed in those green eyes. Hurt, maybe? Frustration or anger, she couldn't tell. And in a blink it was gone.

"We can go together. Like a date or something," she heard herself saying. Before she could grab the words back, Shane grinned.

"That sounds great."

She opened her mouth to warn him of all the crazy ideas people would get if they went together. But instead of saying anything, she clamped her lips back together. Because she was hoping that some of those ideas might turn out to be right.

"Sara's talked about you from time to time, but somehow she's never mentioned what you do," Lark said, relaxing enough to tuck her feet under her tush and get comfy.

Shane took another long drink, draining the bottle before answering.

"I'm in communications." His words were so smooth, so easy, that Lark didn't know why she didn't quite believe him.

"Communications?" she echoed, tilting her head to one side as she studied him. "That sounds interesting."

"It has its ups and downs."

Who knew a man of so few words could be so sexy.

"Sara is hoping you'll stay for at least a week. Where are you visiting from?"

He hesitated for a second, glanced at the bottle in his hand, then shrugged.

"I'm based in California."

"Based?" It was like trying to pry state secrets from a special agent or something.

"Based, because I travel a lot." He gave a ghost of a shrug and added, "I guess you'd say I troubleshoot."

His words were easy and his expression didn't change, so Lark wasn't sure why she thought saying that bothered him. Wasn't traveling troubleshooter better than stripper? Giving in to temptation, she skimmed her eyes over that gorgeous body again. She pursed her lips. Of course, it might depend on what kind of trouble he shot.

"Traveling must be fun," she said. "My mom had what you'd call itchy feet, so we moved around a lot when I was growing up. Do you enjoy it?"

"It's just what I do."

Lark waited, but that was it. He didn't add anything else to the statement.

And she'd thought Sara was reticent about his job? Lark racked her mind for a different conversation topic. Since she figured asking him about his favorite sexual positions and edible body oil flavors were out, what was left? The weather?

Had it come to this? Eighteen months in a small town serving coffee instead of basking in the glow of the Golden Gate with her hands in clay and she became completely lame with men?

Then Lark caught the look in his eyes. Not distance.

Shyness.

Her heart melted a little.

Suddenly every bit of social awkwardness fled as determination took hold. Her smile bloomed, spreading over her face as her mind raced. One way or another, she was going to make him comfortable. Whatever it took, she wanted the sexiest man she'd ever met to feel good.

SHANE WONDERED IF Lark knew how expressive her face was. Those big dark eyes had gone from friendly curiosity with a hint of sexual awareness before flashing irritation. And then, with a single sweep of those thick eyelashes, her expression shifted to one he'd seen on women's faces hundreds of times.

A nurturing sort of sweetness. Her eyes softened. Her lips curved in an encouraging smile. She leaned forward a little, resting her forearms on her thighs, as if to show she was there to listen.

Usually when he saw that look he made a split-second decision. Ride it all the way to bed or run like hell.

Shane leaned back in the weird chair, getting comfortable. Because he wasn't about to run.

Yesterday he'd felt as though he'd taken a fist to the gut when he'd walked into the coffeehouse and gotten a good look at the sexy brunette. He'd spent the night hoping he hadn't looked as stupid outside as he'd felt inside when she'd smiled.

But if that expression was anything to go by, he was fine.

"Have you lived here long? You must have come to Little Lake after I moved away." And after he'd stopped visiting. Because there was no way he wouldn't have noticed her if she'd been here.

Hell, given the sexual sparks arcing between them, he was pretty sure he should have felt her the minute he'd crossed the city limits.

"My mom moved here about four years ago to be near my aunt." Her eyes filled with grief for a moment before she smiled. "Heather Sommers? Do you know her?"

Despite his curiosity over what had caused that sadness in her eyes, Shane grinned.

"Heather is your aunt? She was my middle school basketball coach. Is her hair still orange?" Not carrottop, but true orange. She'd added blue streaks for the play-offs to match the school colors.

"It was blue for a long time, but it's lavender now." Lark leaned forward with eyes wide and brows arched. "So tell the truth. Were you one of the kids who freaked out over having a female coach?"

"Me? No way. I saw it as a way to psych out the opposing team." He gave his preteen self a fond pat on the back. "Besides, I grew up with five sisters. Believe me, I know women can do anything."

Lark gave an admiring shake of her head.

"I can't imagine having five siblings."

"Six." Pain jabbed his heart, so familiar that Shane barely noticed it. "My brother, Mike, died about seven years ago."

"Oh, I'm sorry." Lark's slight wince was quickly replaced by an apologetic grimace. "I knew that. Sara said he died in a car accident?"

"Drag racing. Another car lost control, rammed him,

sent them both into the wall." Shane had been on tour in Afghanistan when it had happened. It had taken over a week for word to get to him, then another one before he could fly home. By then his mother's grief and fears had been so firmly entrenched that Shane had known that even if he'd left the navy, moved back home and lived in his childhood bedroom, she'd still have freaked over his safety. So he'd done the only reasonable thing he could. He'd lived his life.

"It's hard, losing someone," Lark said, her words quiet and filled with understanding.

"Your mom?" At her surprised look, he shrugged. "Sara mentioned it at dinner last night when I said that I was surprised to see someone with your artistic talent pouring coffee."

As soon as the words were out, he realized how obnoxious they sounded.

"I mean—"

Her grateful smile interrupted his attempt at a lame apology.

"No, that's awesome." She reached over to lay one slender hand on his knee. Her touch sent a shaft of heat straight up his leg. "I love that you think I'm talented. And you're right. Pouring coffee isn't really my thing."

She pressed her lips together, then gave him an impish look.

"Wanna hear a secret?"

"Definitely." Especially if it involved whipped cream, naked dancing or sexy water games.

"I don't even drink coffee," she said in a husky whisper.

Shane grinned.

"So why ceramics?"

"My mom blamed it on mud pies." Lark laughed, the sound wrapping around Shane like a warm hug. Which shouldn't have been a turn-on, but somehow was. "But, really, I just loved pottery."

"That's good. It's important to love what you do." That's how he felt about his career. "So you work the coffeehouse and do pottery now?"

"No." Shane frowned at the pain that flashed in her eyes. "The coffeehouse takes most of my time. Pottery has become more of an occasional hobby than a main focus."

"That's too bad. You've got a gift." At her questioning look, he admitted, "I couldn't sleep last night so I took a closer look at some of those pieces next door. They really are excellent."

At the mention of sleep, her smile took on a little of that heat he'd seen earlier.

"I'm good with my hands," she finally said, her words so low they were almost a whisper.

Shane's gaze skimmed over her body, his body tightening as he noted the pebbled bump of her nipples against the soft cotton of her T-shirt.

"How good?" he asked just as quietly.

"I can make a long, hard tube of clay soft and malleable," she told him, her eyes locked on his. "I can make it into whatever I want. Whatever brings me the most pleasure."

Damn.

Shane's dick did a happy dance at the image.

Ready, desperately ready, to see just what she might make it do for her pleasure, he slid his gaze to her lips.

Soft, full, welcoming.

And ready for his mouth.

He watched her slender hands as she twisted them around the bottle, her fingernails a dark orange today. His gaze scanned her purple T-shirt and he wondered if her bra was the same color as her nails. He'd bet it was. And unlike his seatmate on the plane yesterday, he wouldn't mind those fingers tiptoeing their way to his jewels.

Stop thinking about her hands on your dick, he warned himself. Not only was it rude, it was going to be rudely *obvious* in another second or two.

Not for the first time, Shane wished he had some of Romeo's talent with handling women. Somehow, the guy had been able to juggle one-nighters, quick-bangers and relationship hangers with an easy smile as he sent them on their happy way with nary a complaint. If Romeo had been faced with a seriously sexy woman like Lark while under a gag order about his career and the inevitable awkwardness of family expectations, he'd have still found a way to have Lark naked a dozen times before she happily waved goodbye at the end of the visit. But Romeo was getting married, and sadly hadn't passed on his skill with the ladies despite no longer needing it.

Shane had spent a lot of years watching Romeo score. He'd never tried to emulate the guy because, hey, he had plenty of scores of his own. Besides, he'd have felt like a total idiot trying to act like someone else.

But maybe he could recalibrate a few of his buddy's moves, try to drum up a little charm and see if he could fan that spark in Lark's gaze into a flame.

What could it hurt?

With that in mind, and more tension in his belly than he usually had jumping out of a plane into enemy territory on a pitch-black night, he slowly got to his feet.

Lark jumped when the kiln timer dinged from the other room.

Ready to put those moves into action, Shane crossed to stand in front of her. She rose, too, making him smile that she was so in tune with him. Talk about encouraging.

"This was fun." He kept his voice low, his eyes locked

on hers, letting himself imagine that he was poised over her body, his muscles sliding over the silken softness of her bare flesh.

He watched as her midnight eyes blurred and the pulse pounded against her throat.

"I appreciated the drink." He took a step closer, watching her hand as she stroked it up, then down, then around the bottle. Heat surged behind his eyes, his entire body going on full alert.

"Uh-huh." Lark's expression didn't change. The desire in her eyes didn't even flicker.

"Maybe I can return the favor sometime." He reached out to skim his finger over her face, reveling in silky softness before sliding a jagged strand of hair behind her ear.

"Mmm." Her gaze shifted from his eyes to his lips, her mouth rounding into a soft O as if she were imagining it on his.

"I should go," he said, his fingers moving down the side of her throat before wrapping around the chain of her necklace.

"You should?"

She sounded so disappointed that Shane had to grin.

Then she leaned into his hand, making his smile vanish.

Need pounding through him, desire demanding satisfaction, Shane slipped his hand behind her neck, rubbing lightly with his thumb as he focused on her mouth.

Those full pink lips, just waiting for him.

"You know if I kiss you, I won't stop."

Her gaze jumped to his, surprise clear in those dark eyes. Then she smiled. A slow, inviting smile that he felt through his entire body.

So he did the only thing he could think of.

He accepted the invitation.

4

LARK'S WATER BOTTLE banged against his head with a thunk.

But that wasn't why Shane's head was spinning.

It was Lark. Her intoxicating flavor. Her deliciously ad-dicting shape. Her magical mouth. Damn, he thought as his tongue dived deeper, her mouth was amazing.

He didn't know how it happened.

One minute he was standing there talking, watching Lark stroke that bottle. The next, he had his hands on her ass and his tongue in her mouth.

He'd had plenty of women corner him for a cozy grope, but he'd never been on the flipside. He squeezed her butt, pulling her closer. He had to bite back his groan when her soft curves fit perfectly against the harder planes of his body. And the ever-hardening length of his dick.

Control, he thought desperately as it spun out of his grasp. He needed to hold on to control. Then Lark's hands slid off his shoulders, skimmed down the small of his back and returned his grope.

Heat, sharp and demanding, slammed through him. His brain shut down as soon as her hands touched him. His body took over. And his body wanted satisfaction.

His tongue plunged, deeper, harder, faster. His hands raced over her curves, sliding under her shirt, delighting in the smooth silk of her skin. He slid one hand between their bodies, smoothing his palm over her belly, up her torso until it rested between her full breasts.

When she gave a shuddering breath against his mouth, he almost lost it. His hand shifted to the right, cupping her breast while the other trailed up her spine until he reached her bra clasp. With a quick flick it was open.

Taking the kiss deeper, he swirled his tongue over and around hers as both of his hands slipped under the loosened bra to cup her breasts. God, they felt good. Full and heavy, and so responsive that he could feel her nipples stabbing into his palms.

What did they look like? Were they as luscious as they felt? He had to know. For one moment, needs battled. Finally, he reluctantly pulled his mouth from hers. Lark slowly lifted her lids, her heavy lashes shadowing her eyes, adding to their mystique.

"I have to see you," he murmured.

He was gentleman enough to give her one second to protest before he stripped her blouse off. As the fabric hit the floor, she shook her head so her hair settled again in choppy disarray around that exotic face. Then, her eyes locked on his, she shrugged her shoulders so the straps of her bra slid down and away.

Leaving her bare.

He'd spent the previous night imagining what Lark would look like naked. He'd dedicated some seriously hot fantasies to the kind of body he figured she had under her clothes.

Shane's breath lodged somewhere in his chest. His heart raced, his pulse jangling at the vision in front of him.

A vivid contrast to her black hair and midnight-dark eyes, her skin was porcelain white. So pale that he could see the faint blue of veins beneath her skin. So pale that the rosy pink of her nipples stood out in vivid relief. So pale that she looked delicate, despite those heavy breasts and the sweeping curve of her waist.

He locked his eyes on hers, noting the nerves there beneath the passion. He wanted to tell her how beautiful she was. He wanted to say how much he desired her, how strong his attraction was. He was even willing to admit that he'd never felt anything this powerful, this intense, this overwhelming for a woman.

Shane wasn't much for talking; he simply didn't have the words.

So he set out to show her instead.

He reached out to slowly, reverently cup her breasts in both of his hands, his thumbs sweeping over the tender tips. Gauging her height against his, he dropped to his knees in front of her. Her breasts still filling his hands, he pressed a trail of whisper-soft kisses over her belly just above the waistband of her jeans.

He slowly worked his way up her torso, breathing in her scent. It reminded him of a tropical beach, of pulsing water and shifting sands.

Then his mouth reached her breasts. Shifting his thumb aside, he sipped at one nipple, gently tugging the rigid pebble into his mouth. Lark's hands curled over his shoulders, her nails digging lightly into his skin. The bite of them sent a shaft of demanding heat through Shane, from his shoulders straight down to his throbbing dick.

God, he wanted her.

His mouth working harder now, he sucked on one hard nipple, pinching and tweaking the other so Lark gasped. Her hips pressed against his belly, undulating an invitation that he couldn't resist.

He released one breast to reach for the snap of her jeans. One quick flick, a raspy slide and his fingers were dipping into the lacy fabric of her panties.

Curls tickled his hand as he dipped lower. His mouth

filled with a deliciously engorged nipple, he groaned when he found wet heat. Damn, she was responsive.

And he was rock hard.

Need pounding through him, demanding release, Shane pulled his hand free so he could shove her pants down. The snug denim didn't go easily, so he had to push it down those long, sleek legs inch by glorious inch. When he reached her ankles, Shane skimmed both hands back up the length of her legs, cupping her ass for one second before his hands returned to her breasts.

Slowly, reluctantly, he released her nipple and leaned back. He had to see. His eyes swept down her body, noting the vivid contrast her black thatch of hair made against her pale white thighs. His gaze shot up to meet hers when he felt the trembling, tiny shudders moving through her.

But her expression didn't show fear or even nerves.

She looked hot. Hot and needy, her eyes filled with demanding passion.

"Not fair," she said in a husky voice.

"What's that?"

"I'm naked." To prove her point, she kicked her feet free of her jeans. "And you're not."

"Fair's fair," he agreed, grinning.

Shane got to his feet, his fingers making quick work of the buttons on his shirt. Before he'd reached the last one, Lark reached for his pants, her fingers doing a teasing walk over his erection where it strained his zipper before she unbuckled his belt.

When Shane shrugged his shirt off, her eyes widened. Grinning at the appreciation on her face as she reverently traced her fingers over the muscles of his chest, Shane finished unbuckling his belt himself. His pants unsnapped and unzipped, he looked down. Damn. Boots.

He looked around, grabbed Lark by the elbows and

moved them both over to that weird long chair of hers. He lifted one finger to indicate that she wait before he dropped to the seat and went to work on his boot laces. Military footwear wasn't made for quick and easy sex. At least, not the kind that included actually taking pants off.

While he mentally cursed the delay and unlaced as fast as he could, Lark curled up on the seat next to him, caressing his back, shoulder and arm with delicate hands. As soon as his feet were free, Shane sprang up, shoved his pants and boxers off and turned to grab Lark.

But she shook her head.

"Sit," she suggested.

Eyeing the chair, Shane figured it could handle a rough ride. So he sat.

As soon as he did, Lark slid off the chair, her body skimming his enticingly before she reached the floor. Her gaze was appreciative as she looked him over. Right up until her eyes landed on the scar on his hip. Seeing her frown, he tucked one finger under her chin, lifting her face to meet his kiss. A moment later, her eyes glazed with desire, she knelt in front of him, scraping her fingernails lightly down his thighs before curling her hands around the back of his knees.

Her gaze locked on his, she leaned forward and blew a gentle puff of warm air over the head of his penis.

Shane grinned, both at the sensation and at the fact that she could make sexy fun. Then she leaned closer, swiping her tongue around the tip and his smile disappeared.

Watching her take him in her mouth made the sensation even more erotic. Her hot breath, talented tongue and the occasional scrape of teeth had him clenching his fists.

She ran her tongue along the length of his shaft. Down, then up, then down again before she blew again. Her breath against his wet flesh felt so good.

When she sucked again, she cupped his balls, squeezing gently in time with the movements of her mouth.

Oh God.

This time he couldn't stop from groaning aloud.

His fingers tunneled through the heavy silk of her hair, basking in the sensations building higher and harder toward an explosive orgasm.

Then she shifted her angle. His vision blurred as her mouth closed over him, her tongue swirling before she sucked hard enough to make his eyes cross.

"Whoa." He jackknifed into a sitting position, his hands sliding through her hair to lift her head. At the sight of her passion-blurred eyes he almost told her to keep going. But he wanted to watch her when he came. He wanted to stare into those sultry eyes and see her go over, too.

"No?" she asked, her eyes glinting with wicked desire.

"My turn," he insisted, his voice hoarse.

Hoping he'd make it through all of the pleasures he had planned without exploding, Shane got to his feet. He grabbed Lark's hands to bring her with him.

Unable to resist her glossy, swollen lips, he kissed her again, losing himself in the delight of her mouth. When her hands moved between them to grip his erection, Shane figured time was of the essence. Still, he finished with tiny nibbles of her bottom lip before he stepped back.

He looked around, debating. Then, figuring the floor offered the best range of options, he knelt, pulling Lark down on her knees next to him.

As if a bell had signaled, they both dived for each other. Her hands curled around the back of his neck, pulling his mouth down to hers as he gripped the sweet curve of her ass to pull her tight against his body.

Their tongues danced a teasing dance, their lips sliding together. Light-headed, throbbing and getting viciously close to desperate, Shane ended the kiss and gently laid Lark on the floor.

Then, figuring it was as good a time as any to put his earlier fantasy to work, he grabbed the poofy footstool she'd sat on earlier and pulled it over. He slid his arm under the small of her back, lifting her hips high enough to slide it under her.

Shane looked down at Lark. She was a work of art— erotic art, that is. With her hair spread out around her in a halo of midnight, her eyes watching him as if he were the answer to her every sexual dream. Her breasts rose, full and lush before her body angled upward, her feet flat on the floor and her knees loose.

He didn't know what the hell was going on.

He might have horndogged around in his early days in the navy, but despite the multitude of women throwing themselves at him—or rather, at his uniform—Shane was a man of honor. He didn't sleep with women until he'd known them for a while—more importantly, until he was sure they could handle the realities of his career. Lark didn't even know what his career was. They were practically strangers.

But he couldn't resist Lark.

Not her smile.

Not her personality.

Not her body.

But most of all, he couldn't resist the unfamiliar emotions demanding his attention. He felt as if he'd known her his entire life. As if he could share anything with her and know she'd understand, that she'd be there for him. He felt a connection between them that he didn't understand, didn't quite trust.

And none of that mattered.

Not now. Not with Lark's body spread out in front of him, waiting for his pleasure.

Tossing aside the concern, ignoring the questions, Shane got down to what he should be focusing on.

Lark.

Her body.

Their pleasure.

With that in mind, Shane smiled a slow, wicked smile. He kneeled at her feet, loving the view for one long, erotic second.

Then he gave in to the hunger and feasted.

MY, OH MY, OH MY.

Her body so sensitized that she thought she'd explode at any second, Lark watched Shane wrap his long fingers around her ankle. Those dreamy eyes locked on hers, exciting her all over again. Kneeling, he lifted her foot to his mouth to skim his tongue over her toes.

She shivered, pleasure coiling deep in her core, her nether lips tingling as he sucked one toe into his mouth before sliding his tongue along the arch of her foot. He pressed soft kisses over her ankle, then angled her leg higher so he could slide his tongue over the back of her calf.

A wave of vulnerability poured through her. All of a sudden she felt even more naked than when he'd stripped her clothes away. She waited for the embarrassment to follow, but it didn't come. Instead, the heat in his eyes, the deep appreciation on his face, turned her on even more.

When his lips brushed over the back of her knee, Lark drew in a sharp breath, her hands fisting on the floor beside her. Needing more, her body tightened with a desperation for whatever was just over the edge, beyond her reach. Heat coiled, tight and edgy, low in her belly. Her heart raced, the sound of it pounding in her ears as she shifted her hips higher.

Clearly reading the invitation, Shane grazed his palm up the inside of her thigh. His fingers stopped short of her damp curls, making Lark whimper. Then his mouth followed the path of his hand and she didn't have enough breath left to make a sound.

Soft kisses, hot breath.

Her fingernails dug into her palms, her teeth clamped on her bottom lip as he gently traced his tongue along her sensitive folds.

Oh. Her body tightened, pleasure pounding through her as he worked magic with his mouth, sipping, licking, nibbling. Then he slid his tongue inside her and Lark felt that heady pop of delight as the orgasm washed over her in huge, delicious waves.

"Mmm," she murmured. She started to reach for him, but apparently he wasn't done. She'd have called him greedy if she had enough breath to speak. His tongue swirled, stirring heat again, making Lark realize she was the greedy one.

Because she wanted more. Lots and lots more.

As if he'd read her mind, Shane upped his game.

His eyes were reverent, his expression sweet as he lifted her other leg, hooking both over his shoulders before he bent his head again. The angle gave him better access, his tongue sliding over her G-spot faster and faster.

Lark's thighs shook. Her elbows dug into the floor and her hands fisted in her hair. Her body arched as she tried to press herself tighter against that magical tongue.

Then his fingers joined the party, his thumb drumming against her bud as his fingers tightened against her mound. Passion coiled tighter, winding through her, more intense than anything she'd ever felt before. His tongue stabbed, his fingers teased.

Then she felt his hand on her breast, his fingers teasing, circling, tweaking her nipple.

That's all it took to send her flying over the edge.

Ohmygod, ohmygod, ohmygod.

Lark's entire body tingled, tiny climactic aftershocks rippling through her in delicious waves. Her breath burned her throat, her chest heaved and her mind spun.

She was spinning too fast to realize he'd lowered her to the floor until she felt the nubby texture of the carpet beneath her feet.

Then Shane moved away, leaving her alone, naked and vulnerable. Her flesh immediately chilled, missing the heat of his body. She wanted to roll to the floor or at least climb onto the chaise. But her bones had turned to mush so she couldn't move. Maybe, after the sexual haze cleared from her brain, she'd figure out a way to move.

But not yet.

Not until she figured out what had just happened.

Not the orgasm part. That part she had a really good handle on. Heat swirled in her belly again at the memory of his tongue inside of her.

What she wasn't sure of was how she'd let it happen.

Sure, she'd justified wanting to act on her attraction to Shane as a loophole in the rules, but that was beside the point.

Even as tiny orgasmic aftershocks rippled through her, Lark tried to pinpoint the moment that she'd consciously decided that she was going to have sex with a man she'd only met the day before. Way back in her dating days, she'd had a firm three-date policy before even considering getting intimate with a man. With Shane, she hadn't even held out for three kisses.

The only excuse, no, not excuse. The only *reason* she could think of was that she'd never felt this way before. Had never experienced this instant, overpowering sexual attraction to a man. Maybe it was because she knew he was only here for a short time that she'd let their relationship jump over a few steps. Okay, so it was closer to a few dozen.

But there was something special about Shane. He made her feel again. Desire, yes. Orgasmic pleasure, definitely. But more than that, he made her feel good. Alive and happy. Like herself again.

Not sure what that meant, or how she was supposed to deal with it, she pressed her fingers against her closed eyes.

Then she felt Shane return.

Lark gingerly lifted her fingers a smidge, just enough to see him. Once she caught sight of his body, she forgot her doubts. She practically forgot to think as she dropped her hands to her side to stare at him.

"You're gorgeous," she murmured.

"That's my line." Shane's smile didn't dim the heat in his gaze as his eyes meandered slowly down the length of her body.

She returned the favor, starting with those dreamy eyes, sexy smile and firm chin. She moved on to his strong, broad shoulders and muscular arms, sighing at the sculpted beauty. When her gaze dropped to the flat, sculpted planes of his six-pack, Lark pressed her lips together to make sure she wasn't drooling. The man didn't have a spare ounce of fat on him.

Her eyes slid lower.

Oh my.

He was so big.

Lark wet her lips, remembering how good it had felt to have that long, rigid length in her mouth.

Her body, still loose from the orgasms, tightened, heat curling low in her belly as she imagined him inside of her, thrusting, hard and powerful.

Breathless, she tore her gaze away, forcing herself to look up and meet his eyes.

"Where'd you go?" she asked, not really caring, but needing something to say to distract him from the fact that she was eating him up with her eyes.

"Preparation," he said. "I turned off your pottery wheel and closed the front door. I locked it, too."

Lark gave him a slow, appreciative smile, then patted the floor next to her.

"Why don't you c'mere and I'll show you how much I appreciate your thoughtfulness."

Shane flashed a wicked smile, then held up a couple of condoms.

"I see you're ahead of me," Lark said, laughing. "I like a man who's prepared."

"That's why they call me Scavenger," he said. "I can find anything, anywhere."

"Scavenger?" Lark teased, raising herself up to her elbows.

Something flashed in his eyes, but before she could decipher it, he dropped to the floor next to her. He tunneled his fingers into her hair, cupping the back of her head to lift her face to meet his kiss.

Need pounded through her, her body suddenly aching and desperate for him. She reached out to skim one finger over the rigid perfection of his pecs, reeling in how good his skin felt, how good he made her body feel.

She welcomed his thrusting tongue, sucking it into her mouth and making him groan low in his throat. He palmed her breast, working his hand in tiny circles until her nipple was rock hard. Desire spiraled tighter, coiling deep in her belly while sending a spark of surprise through her at the same time.

She'd never experienced excitement so fast so soon after an orgasm, especially one as intense as Shane had given her. But when he tweaked her nipple, rolling it around between his fingers, that beckoning heat pooled between her thighs again.

Then he shifted, skimming whisper-soft kisses over her cheek, her chin, down her throat until he reached the breast he'd already teased so deliciously. He took it into his mouth, his tongue and teeth working her nipple while his fingers slid down her belly, taking a brief dip into her belly button before moving on. Lark's breath shuddered when he slipped a finger inside of her, testing, swirling, making sure that she was ready.

She couldn't hold back her moan when he slipped his finger inside again, sliding in and out one more time before moving up her body in one slow, smooth motion that sent shivers through her. He paused for a brief second, the sound of ripping foil sharp and exciting.

Then Shane was back. He took her face in his hands, kissing her crazy with such intensity that Lark felt her head spin in dizzy delight.

Shane braced his hands on either side of her head, his legs locked wide beside hers. Lark planted her feet on the floor, knees high and toes curled into the carpet. Slowly, oh, so slowly, Shane thrust his throbbing length into her wet, welcoming heat. She could feel every inch of him as he slid deeper, deeper, oh God, deeper.

Her breath shuddered, her inner walls gripping him tight, squeezing every ounce of pleasure from the feel of him inside her. A tiny voice whispered that this was what it felt like to finally be whole, to finally know ecstasy.

Then Shane moved, silencing that voice and Lark's every thought disappeared.

He slid almost all the way out, one hand moving under her hips to angle her higher. Lark pulled her feet tighter toward her back, meeting each thrust with a tiny whimper. He felt so good. So, so good.

His eyes locked on hers, Shane plunged again and again. Soon the sound of his harsh breaths, her gasping moans and their slick bodies coming together filled the room. Lark's fingers dug into Shane's biceps—the fact that she couldn't even squeeze the rigid muscles turned her on even more.

She could feel the climax tightening low and deep and began undulating her hips to meet each thrust. Her breath came in sobbing gasps as she climbed higher and higher. She wanted to close her eyes, to lose herself in the sensations, but Shane wouldn't release her gaze. His dreamy eyes held hers captive, the look in them as powerful as his rock-hard body.

Without breaking his rhythm, Shane leaned down to take her mouth. Hot and wet, his tongue plunged in time with his body. Once, twice, thrice.

Lark exploded. She cried out as lights burst behind her eyelids. The orgasm poured over her in fiery waves, again and again and again. Shane drove into her, hesitated, then drove again before he came with a guttural moan.

Delighting in how good he felt, how incredible she felt, Lark caressed his back in tiny circling strokes. Her inner walls contracted, milking him dry before Shane heaved out a long breath and collapsed against her as Lark's legs slid, boneless, to the floor.

She wasn't sure how long they lay together, Shane's breath hot on her neck, his arms holding her tight against him. She rubbed slow, soothing circles over his back and shoulders, waiting for her heart rate to settle.

Then Shane pressed an openmouthed kiss against the side of her throat and sent her heart rate soaring once more.

"Again?" she asked, not sure she could so soon. His teeth scraped a fiery path along her neck But she was more than willing to try.

"Soon," he said, his husky words vibrating gently against her throat. "Bed?"

"That way." Her body still too heavy to move, she sorta gestured by lifting one finger off his back.

As soon as the words were out, Shane shifted, jumping to his feet while still holding her in his arms. Lark's brain was still floating on those waves of ecstasy, but she was pretty sure she couldn't jump to her feet at all, let alone do it with someone—something—anything in her arms. God, he was in such incredible shape.

"Mmm," she murmured, sliding her hands around to lock them behind his neck. "Nice."

"Yeah?" He curled her closer to his body, carrying her into the bedroom. "Wait until you see what's next."

5

LARK WOKE SLOWLY, her body resisting every inch of the way. She gave a long, breathy moan as she pried her eyes open just enough to note that it was dark, and if the dim shapes were any indication, she was in her bedroom.

Her body felt amazing. Loose and satiated and deliciously tender.

It took her a few more seconds to realize the reason she couldn't move was because there was a weight lying across her waist.

Carefully, oh so carefully, she lifted her hand, sliding it along the weight.

An arm. A hair-covered, muscular arm. Her fingers tiptoed down, noting the leather watchband.

Holy cow.

Her eyes flew open so wide they almost popped out of her head. She started to squeak, quickly clamping her mouth closed before the sound escaped.

Holy cow, she thought again.

She'd slept with Shane.

No, she corrected, taking a long shaky breath as panic clamped tight on her chest.

She'd had sex with Shane.

Four times.

Then she'd slept with him.

Even as her heart raced, a delighted sort of pleasure poured through the rest of her body.

She'd thought about having sex with him from the moment he'd walked into the coffeehouse.

She'd fantasized about it, dreamed about it and had listed a ton of reasons to talk herself out of it.

Her mind took a deliciously slow trip through her memories of the previous day's fun. Not only was Shane an excellent distraction from her worries, he was as amazing in bed—and on the floor, and in the shower—as he was gorgeous. She'd had no idea her body could feel that good. She'd been clueless over just how good an orgasm could feel.

Oh, she'd had orgasms aplenty in her life. But yesterday, last night, it had been as if Shane had taken the entire concept of physical pleasure and multiplied it by a hundred.

Between exploring each other's bodies and discovering the many ways to give each other pleasure, they'd talked. Lark didn't think she'd ever talked as much—or with such ease—to anyone in her life except maybe her mom.

But that wasn't the point, the panicky voice in her head screamed. The point was here. In bed. The two of them. Lark bit her lip, giving a mental scan under the blankets. In bed together *naked*.

It was okay, she told herself. A one-night stand was okay. Different rules applied to those than relationships. Rules that kept things casual, easy, without strings or ties. Hence, the loophole.

Feeling a little better for having justified herself to her conscience, Lark let some of the tension leave her body. As if he'd been waiting for her to work through the worst of her freak-out, Shane's arm tightened around her waist. Before she could figure out what to say or what to do, he pressed a soft, warm kiss against her shoulder.

Lark melted.

Her freak-out and her fears melted, too.

Suddenly worrying about whether this was right or

wrong didn't matter. He didn't know it, but Shane had been there for her yesterday. He'd been the perfect distraction from her stress about the coffeehouse, from her grief over giving up her career.

As grateful as she was turned on, Lark shifted toward Shane. Accommodating her, he slid his hand from her waist to her butt.

"Morning," he murmured, those dreamy eyes sharp and alert. Whiskers shadowed his cheeks, giving him an air of danger. How could he look even better now than he had last night? Maybe it was the tantalizing hint of scruff on his cheek.

And her?

Lark knew what she looked like in the morning, and it definitely wasn't sexy.

She shoved a hand through her hair, wincing when her fingers found a myriad of tangles.

"You look great," Shane said, his smile seducing her as much as his hands were.

When he leaned forward to kiss her, though, Lark shifted back just a smidge.

"Just so you know, I don't do this—" She waved her hand toward the rumpled bed between them. "This sort of thing."

"No?"

"No," she said, the word exploding in a rush of air. "I mean, I've *done* it before. Obviously. But I don't do it. I mean, not regularly. I mean, I did, but now I don't. And never so fast."

The easy look in his eyes assured her that he wasn't judging. The wandering delight of his hands assured her that he wasn't finished.

"Fast is an issue?" he mused. His hand settled on her breast. "Then how about we do it slow and see how that goes."

"Slow."

"Very, very slow," he said just before his mouth covered hers.

As he shifted through the gears of the vintage International Scout, hard rock pounding through the speakers and cool air streaming through the open window, Shane's body felt loose and easy in a way it never had.

He hadn't realized how much tension he lived with until he'd rolled off Lark's body and out of bed earlier that morning. His work required vigilance, readiness and focus. His friends were all in the same field, most SEALs or Special Ops, his hobbies revolved around improving the skills he needed for his job. He figured even sex, which he rarely did without, was tied to his job. Women hit on the uniform, on the mystique.

Except Lark.

With her, he wasn't a SEAL. He wasn't on duty.

He was simply happy. Happy and satisfied.

"You like?"

Since that question could go so many ways, Shane took his eyes off the road for a brief second and slanted a wicked smile at Lark.

"*Like* doesn't come close to covering it," he teased, remembering the feel of her body over his, of his body in hers and especially the way she'd curled into him in sleep.

Yeah, *like* was a little tame.

"I mean the truck." Lark's laugh was both sexy and sweet, her hand warm as she reached over to slide it along Shane's thigh. "What do you think?"

"I think I actually covet your vehicle. Scouts are rare enough, but I've never seen one with a big block. How long have you had it?"

"It was my mom's. Well, really my dad's. He put the big block in it. Mom got it when he died."

Shane took one hand off the wheel to lay it over hers where it rested on his thigh. Curling his fingers through hers, he offered a comforting squeeze.

"It's a lot of vehicle," he said quietly. "A special one."

"It scared the hell out of me." Lark's laugh broke through the tension like sunshine through the clouds. "I didn't have a car when I lived in San Francisco, hadn't even driven in five years. Then I got here and life just isn't livable without a vehicle. I had to learn to drive all over again in a machine that moves like a tank."

Shane was more familiar with ships than he was tanks, but he figured she had a point.

"How long did it take you to shift from scared to loving it?"

"About ten minutes."

Shane flashed her a grin before he glanced at the old-fashioned analog clock framed in chrome on the dash. His smile faded as he pulled off the highway and headed toward town.

Joyriding time was over.

A couple of miles later, he turned onto streets so familiar he could drive them in his sleep.

As he did with any unpleasant task, be it swabbing the deck or taking aim at a living person, Shane steeled his shoulders and focused his resolve. Ready for whatever was to come, he pulled up in front of his childhood home.

It was amazing how fast sexual nirvana could fade in the face of emotional peril. Just six hours ago, he'd finished lunch with a nooner that had left his body a spent puddle of lust. When he'd regained use of his legs, he'd unpinned Lark from the wall, thinking he'd never felt better.

Stepping out of the car, Shane studied the house he'd

grown up in with the same detached deliberation that he did enemy territory before the launch of a mission. Emotions locked away, reflexes on full alert and his body poised for battle.

The two-story ranch had been painted sometime in the past few years, the pale yellow exterior paired with bright blue shutters. The huge oak was gone, along with his tree house and the tire swing, and the railroad fence framing the lawn was in good repair. He mentally filed the changes to the property, noting all possible escape routes.

"Are you ready to be the best birthday surprise ever?"

He glanced over as Lark got out of her truck, appreciating the contrast of her soft, floaty-looking outfit against the hard black steel of her truck. He'd been impressed—and honored—when she'd offered him the keys to the Scout instead of insisting on driving the two of them to Sara's party.

"I'm not sure I'll qualify as a surprise," he said, jerking his shoulder. "The birthday girl knows I'm here."

She'd arranged the trip, after all. Which—he frowned—made it a little weird that he hadn't seen her since that first day. He hadn't thought about her, hadn't even noticed her absence over the past two days. He'd been too wrapped up in Lark.

Climbing the steps that led to the wraparound porch, he stared at the front door for a second, debating.

Knock, like a guest. Or walk in as he had every other time in his life.

He didn't live here anymore. His mail, his driver's license, his taxes all claimed his address was in Southern California. But he'd grown up in this house. Theoretically, it was home. And he'd be damned if he'd be made to feel unwelcome at home.

Bracing himself for whatever was coming, he stepped

through the front door. Music, voices and laughter assaulted his ears. Damn, he'd forgotten how loud his family could get. It was all he could do not to turn around and leave.

But while he'd walked through gunfire with more enthusiasm before, duty was duty. So he stepped into the fray.

"Oh my God. Shane?" His sister Carly stood in the entry, a drink in one hand and a toddler he'd only seen in photos in the other. "You're here? Oh my God, you're here."

Long blond hair flying, she threw herself into his arms, sandy-haired kid and all.

"What are you doing here? When did you get here? Hey, Lark." One arm still gripping Shane, she leaned over to brush a kiss over Lark's cheek. Then her eyes widened with horror. "Shane, does Mom know you're here?"

"I'm a surprise."

"Uh-huh." Carly's expression hovered somewhere between big-sister-amusement and out-and-out worry. She opened her mouth to either tease or lecture, but before she could do either, the rug rat in her arms started babbling. She frowned, looked at the kid, at Shane, then shook her head. "I have to take Micah to the bathroom. We're at a vital point in his potty training. He's doing so well but if he has to wait he'll have an accident. I didn't bring extra pants, you know, like a show of good faith so he'd see I believe he can do it. So even if it's my fault, he'll think the accident is his fault. That could set us back weeks. Months, even."

Carly babbled all of that while backing her way down the hall toward the bathroom. Hoping to hurry the end of this discussion, Shane waved her away.

"Now there's a welcome home," he said to the silently laughing woman at his side.

"Only three more to go," Lark said, still grinning.

Wincing because she was right, Shane squared his shoulders before making his way into the living room.

In between greetings from neighbors and old friends, he suffered through the same joyous shocked reception from Maura, Barb and Abby, ending with each one of his older sisters looking around the room in a panic in case their mom saw them talking with him.

"What, do they think she's not going to notice I'm here?" he muttered to Lark. It wasn't until they'd made their way to the backyard, where the birthday girl was sitting like a princess on her throne with all of her admirers kneeling at her feet, that he realized his hand was wrapped around Lark's.

Crap. No wonder they'd been getting funny looks in between lectures and warnings. Just as he started to surreptitiously release Lark's fingers he came face-to-face with his mother.

Suddenly he was very grateful for Lark's support.

Molly O'Brian was an older, rounder version of her five daughters. Blonde and fair with a sprinkling of freckles, she had the air of a woman who could handle anything that came her way. Considering everything that she'd had thrown at her over the years, she'd earned that attitude.

Memories, hundreds of them, flashed like a kaleidoscope through Shane's mind. Sunday dinners with his mom at the head of the table. Her pride in her smile when he graduated high school. The look in her eyes the night he'd come home a man. The heartbreak he'd seen way too often—the day they'd buried his father. Again when they'd said goodbye to Mike. And, like a kick in the gut, the last time he'd been home, when he'd told her he wasn't leaving the SEALs.

His training assured him that none of that showed on his face. Instead, Shane offered a neutral smile.

"Mom."

"Shane." Her bottom lip trembled once before Molly lifted her chin. "This is a surprise."

"It's Sara's birthday." He didn't figure there was any point in adding that she'd asked him to come.

"I'm surprised you remembered."

Anger flashed, but before it could take hold, Molly shifted her gaze to Lark.

Her voice a shade warmer, she tilted her head. "Lark. It's nice to see you. How is your aunt?"

Shane could feel Lark's hesitation, could sense her concern as her fingers tightened around his. But her voice was friendly and upbeat when she answered.

"Heather's fine, Mrs. O'Brian. She's covering for me at the coffeehouse today."

"I hear she's doing a different kind of baking for the coffeehouse, as well."

Shane didn't know why, but from his mother's tone and the way Lark stiffened, Heather baking was apparently a bad thing.

"She's helping out as much as she can," was all Lark said, though.

"That's good. Families should help each other. After all, if you can't depend on them, who can you depend on?"

This time it was Shane who stiffened. Before he could respond, because that comment had damned well been aimed at him, Lark moved closer. Close enough that her breast brushed his arm.

"I'm grateful to have Heather's help, but even if she was somewhere else or if she couldn't lend a hand, I'd know I could depend on her. She loves me. Isn't that what family is really for?"

Shane wanted to tell her not to bother. She was setting herself up as his ally and it wasn't worth it. She had to live here; he didn't. Hell, they'd probably never see each other again after this week.

Shane wasn't sure if it was that realization or the skeptical look on his mother's face that made him want to punch something. Whichever it was, he knew there was nothing he could do about it.

"We're going to say happy birthday to Sara," he said, needing to move before he gave into the urge.

Needing space, he shook off Lark's hand, walking away before his mother could respond. He didn't need another ugly memory to add to his collection. He heard Lark murmur a polite goodbye before she caught up with him.

"Are you okay?"

"Why wouldn't I be?" Making sure his expression was surprised, he glanced down at her. "Hey, before I get smothered by my sisters again, I'm going to say hi to a few old friends. I'll catch up with you later, okay."

Something flashed in those dark eyes. Hurt, annoyance, disdain, he couldn't tell. He didn't try to figure it out, either. Because he really didn't want to know.

"Sure. Cassia's waving me over," she said, tilting her head toward a buxom redhead waving her arms. "I'm going to say hi. I'll see you later?"

Needing space, Shane didn't respond. He simply nodded and walked away.

By the time cake came around, he was chill again. In between hugs and babbling from his sisters, he'd managed to shake off the pain of his mom's attitude and was chatting with one of the neighbors he'd grown up with. Twice divorced, Kirk had grown out of his juvenile delinquent stage to become a fireman.

Even as they talked about the good ole days, Shane's gaze searched the room until he found Lark. Curled up on a chair with his sister Maura and the waving redhead, she looked happy and comfortable. But there was something about her that didn't quite fit in. He doubted anyone else could tell, but he knew the signs. After all, he wore them himself.

"Hey, do you mind if I steal my favorite brother?" Wrapping her hand around Shane's arm, Sara pulled him away while smiling her excuses at Kirk.

She steered him toward the dining room. Seeing it full, she redirected them to the only peaceful spot in the house. The hallway.

Used to his sister's oddities, Shane just kept eating cake.

"Sooo," Sara said, drawing the word out to five syllables. "What's going on with you and Lark?"

"Nothing." Shane's expression didn't change. Hell, he wasn't a SEAL for nothing. He'd been trained to pass a polygraph test while lying through his teeth. Scamming his sister should be a piece of cake, no pun intended.

"Nothing, my ass." Sara shook her head and laughed. "You've got something going on."

"And you've got a vivid imagination." Shane deliberately forked up a bite of the cake, absently noting that their mother hadn't lost her touch with chocolate.

"It doesn't take an imagination to see that there's something between the two of you." Reaching over with her fork, Sara stole the pink frosting rose off his plate. Then she grinned and leaned closer to whisper, "It just takes eyes. And my eyes tell me that the something is a relationship."

A *what*?

Shane's mind went blank, except for a vague fizzing sound as if the wires had crossed. For one brief, thankful second, the cacophony of partiers faded. All of the light left the room but for a single pinprick through which he could see his sister's laughing face. The chocolate in his mouth turned to ash, the tasteless texture coating his tongue.

Then, in a blink, it all came back.

Including his stand on relationships.

"Nope," he said, enjoying another bite of the moist cake now that it had flavor again. "Nothing going on."

Sara looked as if she wanted to grab the plate from his hands and smash it in his face. Knowing her as he did, he quickly finished the cake. Just in case.

"So what did you do all day yesterday?" she asked, folding her arms tightly across her chest. "It was Lark's day off. Did the two of you spend it together?"

And there they were... The alarm bells were ringing, loud and clear.

Shane narrowed his eyes.

She'd invited him home on purpose. And that purpose wasn't to be here, standing in their mother's living room eating his favorite cake.

She was trying to hook him up with her friend. Not only had he not seen the sneaky plan for what it was—even after she moved him in next door to Lark—but he'd actually fallen right in line.

Even as a part of him admired her stealth skills, the rest held a firm stand on manipulation. As in, he wanted nothing to do with it.

"Lark?" he said, screwing his face up in a confused frown. "How would I know her schedule? I spent the day waiting for you."

The day, two minutes. Close enough.

"You spent yesterday alone?" Sara sounded as if he'd just told her he'd skewered a few puppies on his way over.

"You'd know what I did if you'd come by." At least, she would if she'd walked into Lark's bedroom. Or living room, kitchen or shower.

"I had to, um, you know." She waved her hand over her

head to indicate the living room. "Party stuff. I had to get things ready and help out and stuff."

"Uh-huh."

"Whatever," Sara said with a scowl. Then her face cleared and she pointed her finger at him. "Wait a minute. You came together. And don't tell me it's because you needed a ride. We aren't that far from the coffeehouse, but you rode over with Lark. And you were holding hands when you walked in."

"She was dragging me inside because I'd changed my mind and wanted to leave," he lied with a perfectly straight face.

"Uh-huh." Sara tossed his response back at him with a smile of satisfaction that only an annoying little sister could pull off.

Well versed in strategy and the art of tactical retreats, Shane simply shook his head and went to get more cake. When he found himself automatically looking around for Lark again, he realized that Sara's little game was working.

His chest tightened, the faint buzzing in his ears sounding in time with the churning in his stomach. The feelings were so unfamiliar that it took him a moment to realize it was panic.

Whoa.

He took a deep breath, reminded himself that he was in charge here—no matter what games his sister played—and tamped down the sensations.

He wasn't hooked on Lark.

He might be—temporarily—hooked on the sex, because it was pretty freaking incredible. But that was physical. No emotions involved.

To prove it, he spent the rest of the party ignoring Lark. Ironically, pretty much the same way his mother was ignoring him.

Which meant the drive back to the apartment was on

the quiet side. It wasn't until they made their way up the stairs behind the coffeehouse accompanied only by the dim light of the waning moon that Lark spoke.

"That wasn't so bad, was it?"

"Who said it was going to be bad?"

He glanced over in time to see Lark roll her eyes and realized she'd read him well.

"Oh, I don't know," she said as she unlocked her door. Neither of them questioned that he'd be joining her. "Maybe it was the expression on your face that made me think you were dreading going to the party."

"I'd have to be a sad kind of person to dread a party," he sidestepped. Then, because he didn't see any point in discussing it—and to prove to them both that it was simply physical—he slid his hands around her waist, slowly pulling Lark against his body. "There's something I've been wondering about."

"What would that be?" Lark asked as her hands slid down to cup his butt, her belly pressing against his burgeoning erection.

"I've noticed that you tend to color coordinate your underwear to your clothes and your nail polish." One hand still on her waist, he slid the other under her blouse and tiptoed his fingers up her spine until he reached the strap of her bra.

"You noticed that, did you?"

"I did. Which brings me to the subject of my wondering." He leaned back enough to slide his hand around her bra to the front, where he cupped her breast. "What color will your panties be if your skirt is blue and your blouse pink?"

"Turquoise and fuchsia," she corrected, her words a little breathless.

"Huh?"

"My skirt is turquoise, my blouse is fuschia."

"And your panties?" The tip of his finger slid along the lacy edge of her bra, teasing them both by not dipping deeper.

"I'll show you if you answer something I've been wondering about," she said flirtatiously as she rubbed her thumb over his bottom lip.

A warning bell rang loud enough to cut through his sexual haze. What did she want to know? He wasn't talking about his career, no matter how tempting her underwear was. Or worse, what if she wanted to discuss feelings. The birthday cake felt like a rock in his stomach. The only feelings he was willing to talk about were feeling tired, feeling hungry, feeling horny.

"What do you want to know?" was all he said, though.

"Nothing much." She wet her lips, her eyes filled with a dozen unasked questions. "I was just curious about whether or not you'll be staying for Sara's club hop on Saturday."

He had no idea.

If not for Lark, he'd be on his way to the airport right now, his duty fulfilled.

He looked at her sweet face, her full lips smiling, her dark eyes filled with sexy invitation.

He'd never imagined wanting to stay in Little Lake instead of heading back to base. Especially not with his mother still fighting her personal cold war.

But now he couldn't imagine leaving Lark. Not yet. Not until he knew what this was between them.

So instead of saying no, which was the correct answer, he brushed her hair back behind her ear and gave her a wicked smile.

"Convince me."

6

LARK WOKE SLOWLY, her body resisting every inch of the way. She gave a long, happy sigh as she peeled one eye open to gauge the time. Early, since the sunshine wasn't tilting through her window yet. Mmm, good. More time in bed.

Both eyes comfortably closed again, she lay there reveling in the unfamiliar sensations in her body. Her lips felt swollen and her nipples tender. Her skin tingled and her thighs felt as if she'd done a major workout.

As, indeed, she had. Lark gave a breathy giggle, then ran her hand along the weight on her waist.

Her eyes flew open and her smile shifted into a frown. She patted the weight, then squeezed. That wasn't an arm.

She wiggled her shoulders. All she felt was air. No broad, manly chest.

Her frown dangerously close to a scowl now, she threw the weight away, realizing it was the rolled-up edge of one of the blankets. And that alone.

"Shane?"

Nothing.

She tossed the blankets aside, grabbed her robe from the chair by the door and wrapped it around her as she stepped into the living area.

"Shane?"

Again, nothing.

Maybe he'd gone for a run. Or for an early breakfast.

Her brows drew together when she glanced at the clock on the kitchen wall. Some people ate breakfast at 5:00 a.m., didn't they?

Except the door was locked from the inside.

Dread swirling low in her belly, she stepped back into the bedroom. As she suspected, his duffel bag was gone.

Even as tears burned her eyes, she told herself to get over it. It wasn't as if they were in a relationship. He didn't have to check in with her when he went somewhere, or even when he left. Sure, she'd started to fall for him, to believe that they had more between them than a few dozen orgasms. But that was her fault. She knew the rules. She knew better than trying to turn a one-night—or two-night in this case—stand into more.

Then she noticed the note propped on Shane's pillow.

Gripping the robe so tight against her chest that her fingers were numb, Lark slowly approached the bed.

She didn't want to read it.

After all, she knew what notes like that said.

Eric had left her one. Granted, his had been on personalized cream stationery, written in what she'd recognized as the blue fountain pen she'd given him for his birthday. This one was on what she recognized as her own sticky notes.

Somehow that made it more personal. Of course, it was hard to get any more personal than standing here all but naked, her body still lax from Shane's lovemaking.

Taking a deep breath to stave off the pain, Lark lifted the note. Absently admiring how neat and precise his handwriting was, she read the sparse words.

Got a call. Had to go. I'll be in touch.

His note was just as reticent as he was.

A part of her wanted to believe he'd be in touch. That

this was just his style of writing. After all, he wasn't talkative at the best of times—why would he be any more so in writing?

Lark squashed that optimistic little voice before it even got going. She'd got her hopes up too many times before. When she'd temporarily moved to Idaho to care for her mom, she'd hoped Eric would wait, just as he promised. When her mom had been diagnosed with cancer, she'd hoped Raine would beat the odds. And when she'd lost her mom, she'd hoped that she'd be able to return to her old life, pick up the pieces and move on.

She didn't realize she was crying until a tear splashed on the note.

Yeah. She knew better than to hope.

So she'd do what she had every other time her heart had been crushed. She'd get up, get dressed and get on with her day.

It took her an extra hour to get ready, but that, she told herself as she walked into the coffeehouse, was why she'd called for reinforcements.

"Good morning, sweetie," Heather called through the crowd at the counter.

"Hey, Lark."

"Good morning, Ms. Sommers."

Lark returned the greetings, kept her smile in place and dived into her day. Heather had the counter covered, so Lark bussed tables, filled dispensers and chatted with customers.

All in all, she decided as the late-morning rush waned, she was proud of herself. Nobody had suspected that she was crying like a baby inside.

"Okay," Heather said when Lark stepped out of the back room with fresh mugs. "Spill. What's wrong?"

"Wrong?" Shifting mugs from the tray to the shelf,

Lark scowled. She might as well have not bothered with the cold pack and extra makeup.

"You look upset." Heather stepped closer, her heavily lined eyes peering at Lark's face. "I haven't seen you this upset since…"

Her voice trailed off, devastation flickering in her eyes before she took both of Lark's hands in hers.

"What's wrong?"

Not willing to drag Heather into a puddle of misery with her, Lark quickly shook her head.

"Really, nothing's wrong." Since nobody knew she and Shane had been a thing, she racked her brain, then almost did a happy dance when she remembered the offer from Bellissimo. "I'm just stressing a little. One of my old clients called a couple of days ago. They're decorating a hotel and offered me a huge commission. Lobby art, pieces for the bigger suites, that sort of thing."

"Oh, sweetie, that's fabulous. I'm so happy for you. You do such beautiful work, that hotel will be lucky to show it." Heather released her hands to pull her into a tight hug. "Now, tell me why this stresses you out instead of making you happy?"

"It's a lot of work," Lark admitted. Work that she'd have been thrilled to have two years ago. "Added to that, they have a tight deadline for what are some very complex designs."

Challenging designs that she'd love to get her fingers into. But they'd require both a soda kiln and a gas kiln, neither of which she had anymore. She'd have to work full-time on the pieces to meet the deadline and she couldn't do that while running the coffeehouse.

"Well, I've never known a harder worker than you," Heather said. "You'll find a way to make it happen."

Doubtful.

But Lark didn't tell Heather that, or the fact that she'd told Carlo to keep looking for someone else.

"So that's what's wrong? Are you stressed about taking this account?"

"Yeah." Sure. Uh-huh.

"You'll make it work, sweetie. I know you will."

And thankfully that was enough for Heather. Ten minutes later, the older woman gave Lark another hug before waving goodbye.

To avoid more concern, Lark made a concerted effort to put on a happy face. By two o'clock in the afternoon, her cheeks hurt from all the fake smiling.

"Your face is going to freeze like that and you'll never have sex again," Cassia murmured when she came in for a latte.

Grateful for the excuse to let the smile drop, Lark did just that, rubbing her aching cheeks as she did so.

No big deal, she told herself. Shane hadn't broken any rules; he hadn't lied or led her on. So she had no reason to be angry or upset.

She was. But she had no reason.

As soon as she'd got over the disappointment of missing all that great sex and fun, she'd be fine.

An hour later, she was still working on believing that little mental pep talk when the bells over the door rang.

"Hey, Lark," Sara called, her voice bouncing across the room ahead of her. She waved in reply to the various greetings she garnered as she strolled over to the counter. "I've been meaning to stop by all day, but it's been crazy. My mom went nuts after you and Shane left. It took me, Carly and Sandra to calm her down."

Lark tried to find her fake smile again when Sara rolled her eyes, but couldn't quite manage it. The younger woman didn't seem to notice as she barreled on.

"I need a large sugar-free vanilla soy milk latte on ice. No, make it an extra-large. And maybe a couple of Heather's chocolate crunch pecan cookies. I need sustenance after all that drama." She puffed out a breath before looking around the coffeehouse. "Where's Shane? Is he upstairs? I'm going to make him go deal with this."

"Did you want the drink for here or to go?" Lark asked, forcing the words past the knot in her throat.

"Definitely here. It'll take me a while to talk Shane into talking to mom."

Taking a deep breath, Lark pulled the note out of the drawer, slid it onto the counter, then turned toward the mug shelf. She grabbed one at random and, not bothering to hide it, pulled out the recipe cheat sheet and started blindly mixing.

"So Shane claims that there's nothing going on between the two of you," Sara said, her words still bubbly and upbeat. "I know he's lying. He never took his eyes off you last night. Hey, maybe you can come, too. You totally diffused things when he and Mom started sniping at each other. That'd come in handy…"

Lark pressed her lips together when Sara's words trailed off. She sucked in a sharp breath through her nose when she heard the gasp. And when Sara growled, all she could do was close her eyes.

"That jerk. I can't believe he did this. He knew I wanted him to stay all week. What a wienie. Instead of manning up and fixing things with Mom, he runs off to play soldier again."

In the middle of pouring the soy latte over ice, Lark frowned, finally looking at Sara.

"What?"

"I said my brother is a jerk."

"No. What did you mean, he ran off to play soldier?"

Her eyes horrified, Sara opened her mouth, then closed it again. She grimaced, then shook her head.

"Sara?" Lark held the drink just out of reach. "Spill it or no latte. And no cookies."

At the mention of cookies, Sara's face crumbled. She huffed and worked her way through every expression of angst that Lark had ever seen.

Finally, she tilted her head toward the booth closest to the counter.

"Can we sit and talk?"

The knots in Lark's stomach sank down to her toes. All conversations that required sitting ended up sucking. Of course, the day sucked already. How much worse could it get.

Figuring she was about to find out, she handed Sara her drink. She grabbed a bottle of water for herself, put a half-dozen cookies on a plate, then because the look on Sara's face was freaking her out, added two brownies.

"So what's the deal?" she asked as soon as they were seated.

Sara took a long drink, pulled a napkin from the dispenser and put a cookie on it. She lifted the cookie, inspected it from all sides, then put it back on the napkin.

"Sara…"

"Okay, well, here's the thing. You have to keep this to yourself. I mean, it's not like nobody knows, but if people talk about it, it'll make my mom mad. She's already upset, and when she hears Shane left without saying goodbye, she's going to be a mess. So people talking will just, you know, make it worse."

Not even bothering to sigh, Lark just waited. She'd known Sara long enough to know that babbling was par for the course.

"So, um, do you remember me telling you about my dad and Mike?"

"Mike? Your older brother?" Lark frowned. "You lost him and your dad both when you were really young, right?"

She and Sara had bonded their friendship over a couple bottles of cheap wine and laments about losing loved ones.

"Yeah. My dad when I was eight and Mike a while later. My mom fell apart when Mike died."

Even though she wanted to scream that Sara get to the damned point, Lark reached across the table to squeeze her friend's hand.

"So, like, my dad had been in the navy. You know, before I was born and stuff, but while he and my mom were married. She sorta hated it, with him being away all the time and stuff. But Shane, he loved it." Her voice trailed off as Sara stared over Lark's shoulder for a second. Then she shrugged. "All Shane wanted to do was be like our dad."

Lark nodded. He'd said that himself after she'd told him about losing her mom. It had been just one more thing she'd idiotically thought was proof that they were perfect for each other.

"Mom always figured Shane would get over his crush on the navy. That he'd settle here in town, get married, have kids and stay safe."

"But he didn't?" Lark prompted.

"Nope. On his eighteenth birthday, he drove over to the recruiting office in Idaho Falls and joined the navy. He left right after graduation."

Was that where he'd gotten the scar on his hip? The water churned uncomfortably in Lark's stomach. Granted, she and Shane hadn't spent a lot of time together—and yes, during most of it they'd been having sex. But you'd think somewhere in there he'd have found a second to mention that he was in the military.

Unless…

"Did he leave the navy? Is that why your mom is so upset over his career?"

Sara gave a bitter sort of laugh.

"Oh, no. She tolerated it okay for a while. And by tolerated, I mean she sent Shane weekly care packages, worried herself sick when he was on submarine duty and nagged him to pieces when he was home on leave."

"So she's still mad that he didn't give up the navy?" Absently taking a cookie and breaking it into pieces, Lark tried to imagine that. Her mom had been bummed when Lark had chosen to stay in California and pursue her career instead of moving to Idaho. But she hadn't pressured, and she definitely hadn't nagged. What was it like to deal with that sort of burden? She'd feel sorry for Shane if he hadn't broken her heart.

"Actually it's a little more than that."

"He's in the navy and he's a male stripper?"

Lark's guess garnered a snort of laughter from Sara before the younger woman shook her head.

"Mom might take that better, actually. But, no. A few months before Mike died, Shane applied for BUD/S." At Lark's blank look, she expanded, "Basic Underwater Demolition. You know, the SEALs."

Lark's brows shot up and a tingle danced down her spine. To give herself time to figure out what the tingle meant, she twisted the lid off the water bottle and took a drink.

"Those are the elite forces, right?" she asked, her voice just a little shaky. "The ones who do all those secret missions?"

"Dangerous secret missions. Shane was accepted to the SEALs, then Mike died. Mom freaked, big-time. She asked him, begged him and then ordered him not to join."

Dangerous.

Being shot at dangerous. Jumping out of perfectly good airplanes and helicopters dangerous. Blowing things up and running through explosions dangerous. Scarring his body dangerous.

Tiny dots danced in front of her eyes.

Suddenly Shane's disappearance from her bed took on a new significance. It didn't make it any better, but now she had a whole layer of terror over the heartache.

"But he did? He joined the SEALs, anyway?" Suddenly she had a great deal of sympathy for Molly O'Brian.

"Yeah, and Mom stopped talking to him. She said if he was going to spend his life trying to get himself killed, she'd make it easier on everyone and just consider him dead already."

"No…" Enough horror washing over her to rinse away some of the gut-wrenching fear, Lark's mouth dropped.

Sara nodded.

"Yep. She regretted it right afterward, but the deed was done. Shane joined the SEALs. He came home a few more times, but by then Mom had dug in. Abby says she's projecting her grief from losing Mike and Dad onto Shane. Carly says it's because she's feeling guilty. I think she's just stubborn." Sara sighed, her eyes sad enough to make Lark cry. "Reasons don't really matter, though. You saw them. It's not good."

"And you all go along with it?" Trying to focus on that instead of thinking about Shane's job, Lark grabbed a cookie and took a big bite. Maybe it was because she'd been an only child, that it had just been her and her mom for most of her life. But Lark couldn't imagine not speaking out over something like that.

Then again, she couldn't imagine how painful it must be to love someone who lived in danger. Her stomach rolled.

"We had to go along or move away." Sara wrinkled her nose as if considering it, then tilted her mug toward Lark. "But you know, if Shane were to come around more often, I'll bet Mom would mellow. There's no way she could hold out against that sweet face if she saw it on a regular basis."

The cookie turned to sawdust in Lark's throat when she saw the younger woman's hopeful look. She had to gulp down water so she could swallow. Even then, she couldn't get the words out. It was so hard to find a polite way to scream *oh hell no*.

Yesterday she'd have been ecstatic at the idea of Sara approving of her and Shane together. Approval negated all the rules. But now she couldn't imagine seeing Shane on a regular basis. Not with all the feelings for him she had trying to take root in her heart. Of course, if he was around, maybe those feelings would grow in him, too. Or better, hers would fizzle out.

"If he's stayed away all this time, what makes you think he'll start visiting on a regular basis?" she finally asked.

"Well…"

Well, what? Lark studied Sara's face. Then a bell went off in her head. Sara thought she could somehow convince Shane to come around more often. Yeah, right. The man had sneaked out of her bed like a john skipping out on payment.

"Don't look at me," she said, shaking her head. "I have no influence over your brother."

"But wasn't there…" Sara bit her lip. "Um, I kinda had the impression that there was something going on between the two of you."

Watching her finger trace circles in the condensation, Lark considered Sara's comment.

Was there anything between her and Shane?

Well, there had been sex.

Lots and lots of mind-blowingly incredible, unbeatable, fantasy-shattering sex.

Long, naked talks while wrapped in each other's arms. Shared jokes, whispered secrets and a pint of Chunky Monkey ice cream. Granted, most of the talking, joking and whispering had been her. But Shane had been there, so attentive and sweet, that she hadn't realized it until after she'd read his note.

It sounded stupid, even in her own head. But she'd been falling in love with him.

Finally, she looked up and gave Sara as close to a smile as she could manage.

"Sorry, but I can't help. There's nothing between your brother and I."

SHANE LEANED BACK against the wall of the helicopter, waiting for the warm metal and rumbling vibrations of the Black Hawk engine to lull him into that mindless meditative state he used to prepare for a mission.

But he couldn't clear his mind.

Not of his thoughts. Not of his guilt.

God, he had to be the world's biggest asshole.

He shouldn't have left Lark the way he had.

He'd had to leave, that he felt fine with.

But he should have woken her before he did.

He should have said goodbye.

He'd thought about it. Even while he wrote her that note, he'd told himself to go in and say goodbye.

But he hadn't.

When the call had come in, he'd been floating in that foggy place between sexual exhaustion and sleep. It'd taken him a few seconds to recognize the ringing as his cell. As soon as he did, training clicked in, the fog dissipated and he'd instantly rolled out of bed, careful not to wake Lark. Clothes in hand, he'd stood naked in her living room reading the text.

Leave recalled. Report immediately to the Idaho Falls Regional Airport for transport.

He'd had his pants on and his shoes in hand before it hit him exactly what reporting immediately would entail.

For the first time since he'd earned his trident, he'd resented his orders.

Not just because they meant he'd have to leave Lark. But because they meant he'd have to tell her why he was leaving. Somehow, in all their hours together, in all the time they'd spent totally absorbed in each other, he'd never told her what he did.

He'd never explained what he was.

He could use his family issues as a defense. He could claim that he was so used to pretending he wasn't a SEAL when he was in Idaho that the habit was ingrained.

He could justify his silence by remembering how much trouble it was to be a SEAL and be in a relationship. Women either wanted sex with the uniform or dibs on the paycheck, or then went the other way and freaked out, unable to handle the danger or the separations or the secrets.

He wasn't sure which category Lark would have fallen into, although from what he knew of her, he was pretty sure it wouldn't be the former. She wasn't the type to go after a guy for his money. And despite the intensity of their relationship and how much of it had been spent having sex, he'd got to know her really well. Well enough to know that sleeping with him after such a short acquaintance wasn't the norm for her.

So he had enough justifiable excuses for not telling her that he was a SEAL.

What he didn't have was an explanation for the intense guilt he felt about it.

It shouldn't matter.

It wasn't as if they'd made a commitment. They weren't even in a relationship. Hell, he didn't even know her last name.

Which put those fifty-nine hours and twenty-two minutes in one of two lights. Either he was a sloppy man whore who had no respect for himself or the woman he'd slept with. Or he was a complete chickenshit who'd run away from the most intriguing, sexiest, sweetest woman he'd ever met.

Shane clenched his fists on the knees of his jump pants, bouncing his head a couple of times against the metal wall in the hope a better choice would shake loose.

But, nada.

Man whore or chickenshit. Those were his only choices.

"Five minutes."

Shane ground his teeth when he heard Romeo's words. The Chief Petty Officer was taking lead on the dive, a quick jump from the helo into the churning waters of the Pacific Ocean. There, the eight-man squad would split into pairs. Shane was partnered with Mr. Wizard to take point on hostage rescue while the rest of the team demolished the oceanfront property and cut off pursuit.

Lives were at stake. The hostages, the teams. His own.

He needed his head in the game.

As if hearing his thoughts, Romeo got to his feet. The rest of the team immediately tuned in. Eyes opened, books closed, chanting stopped. Everyone came to attention.

"Conditions are ideal," Romeo said, automatically checking the straps on his pack while the rest did the same. "We're looking at a rocky entry in ten-foot waves under a dark moon."

Most of the team snickered.

In other words, possible death to the average diver.

Romeo didn't waste time going over the mission plan again. He didn't need to. They'd spent the past three days on practice runs, but they trained regularly for missions just like this. Their team had been called in because they were familiar with the terrain, having run a similar mission a year back to rescue a fellow SEAL.

They had it down.

That didn't mean they were cocky about it.

They were simply the best.

Along with the rest of the team, Shane got to his feet. He adjusted the pack holding his parachute, double-checking the buttons on the dozen pockets of his pants, all filled with a variety of tools of the trade.

He turned to Mr. Wizard, aka Taylor Powell, to see if he was ready.

"Yo, Scavenger, you ready?" The Wizard's question was pitched too low for anyone else to hear it over the engine.

"Getting there."

"Slower than usual."

Crap. Shane's hands fisted on his straps, self-condemnation pounding through him. He was here to do a job. Lives depended on him doing it, and doing it well.

He might be a chickenshit man whore, but he was still a SEAL. So he did what his training demanded.

He blocked it out, putting all of his attention where it belonged. On the mission at hand.

Ready to rock, he listened to the pilot announce their bearings, then gave Mr. Wizard a slap on the back.

"Ready to rock," he said, letting his partner know he was at 100 percent.

"Men." His goggles resting on his headgear, Romeo put one hand on the bay door, the other out, flat.

Shane, along with the six other men, placed theirs on top of his. Together, they chanted;

"Stay low, Go fast.
Kill first, Die last.
One shot, One kill.
No luck, All skill."

Then, pulling his night vision goggles in place, Romeo grinned.

"Let's go earn our tridents, men."

With that and a cocky salute, he was out the door and down the ramp. One by one, the rest of the team followed.

On his turn, Shane stepped up to the door, his feet poised on the edge, his mind already focused on the task at hand. He counted down, and on his mark, he ran down the ramp and jumped.

His last thought as he dropped through the cold night air toward the churning ocean was of Lark.

7

HUNCHED OVER HER WHEEL, Lark tried for the third time to form an elongated vase. She shouldn't have told Heather about the Bellissimo offer. Once her aunt had got the idea in her head, she'd insisted on doing everything in her power to make sure Lark made it happen.

She'd offered to work half of Lark's shifts at The Magic Beans. She'd come up with a dozen different promotional ideas, all aimed at bringing in more money. And, unfortunately, she'd developed a brilliant talent for nagging.

Once upon a time, Lark had loved nothing more than spending time alone, just her and her clay. But now it was simply too much. Working in the coffeehouse was draining. Between the still-unfamiliar work, the early hours and the stress from dealing with people all day, every day, Lark had missed her pottery time.

But not anymore. Up here, it was just her, the clay and her thoughts.

And all she could think of was Shane.

Sexy, gorgeous, fun, sweet Shane with his quiet voice and his incredible body.

It'd been five days and she missed him so much, and she hated that she did. She should be angry, as she'd been when Eric had cheated on her, and then ditched her. She should be numb, as she'd been after she'd lost her mom. Instead, she was hyperalert, all of her senses focused on Shane as if they were waiting for him to walk into the room.

She'd spent hours on the internet after Sara's bombshell, reading anything she could find on the navy SEALs. She'd watched two movies, read four books and hyperventilated three times thinking of what he did for a living. But even as she'd freaked out about it, so many things had slipped into place.

That body—oh, that body—was military made. He was in such good shape that he hadn't got winded, even during their wildest sexy times.

His demeanor. He projected a cool, controlled strength. Even during the stressed-out drama at his mother's house, he'd remained composed and calm.

And, of course, his reticence. From everything she'd read and seen, almost everything he did was secret. His entire career was top secret. To say nothing of the fact that from what she'd read, SEALs traveled all over the world, were gone a lot of the time and lived in danger.

It'd be crazy to think she could have a relationship with a guy like that. Especially when the guy had left her with just a freaking note.

Still...

Running her knuckles inside the vessel, she slowly pressed outward, widening the bowl as images of Shane flashed through her mind.

His smile. His laugh. The curve of his back where it met that sweet ass. And the note he'd left on her pillow.

Just before he left her.

Her thumb dug into the clay, leaving an ugly gouge in the neck of the vase. Clenching her teeth against the frustration, Lark tried to smooth it out. But instead of smoothing, the clay folded, the walls collapsing on themselves. She tried to reform them, her fingers carefully pulling the pieces apart so as not to break them. When the kiln timer dinged she jumped, her fingers squishing the delicate walls into the base of the vessel. Devastated beyond reason, Lark stared at the mess. Then she dropped her face into her hands to keep from screaming.

It took a second before she realized the pounding she heard wasn't the blood rushing through her head. Some-one running up her stairs. Lark looked up just as that same someone beat on her door. Before she could blink, the doorknob rattled, turned and the door flew open with enough force to bounce it off the wall.

"Lark. Oh my God." Sara ran into the room, her face blotchy and swollen, wearing what appeared to be pink flannel pajamas under her coat and mismatched tennis shoes. "Lark, you've got to help me."

"What? What's going on?" Already on her feet, Lark opened her arms just in time to catch the sobbing woman.

Sara babbled something, but the words were swallowed by her sobs.

"Come on, sit," Lark said, leading her into the living area. When Sara's calves hit the settee, she dropped into it, letting her purse fall to the floor while she threw her arm over her eyes.

Lark would have been amused at the high drama if she weren't so worried about Sara hyperventilating.

Running back into the kitchen, Lark grabbed a bottle of cold water from the fridge, then hurried back. Sara let her head fall back on the pillow as she drew in a shaky breath.

She frowned at Lark through swollen eyes.

"Did you know you have clay on your face?"

Lark absently brushed at her cheek, grimacing when she encountered the hardening mud flecked all over her skin. Ignoring it for now, she focused on her friend.

"Can you tell me what happened? Are you hurt? Is your family okay?"

"I got a call. This morning. Um, on my cell."

Because the younger woman was crying again, Lark

pressed the bottle of water into her hands. After gulping it down, Sara took a shaky breath and tried once more.

"The navy called. Shane put me down as his emergency contact person."

The room spun. Black dots danced in time to the roaring in her ears. Lark tried to breathe, but her brain wouldn't function. When her knees gave out she simply sank to the floor.

"Sh—" She wet her lips, swallowed and tried to breathe before trying again. "Shane?"

"He's hurt. They didn't say what happened. They wouldn't tell me anything. Not how bad he's hurt, nothing. All they said was that he'd been admitted to the hospital and would be going in for surgery this afternoon." Sara broke down again, silent tears rolling down her cheeks.

Shane was alive.

Lark closed her eyes and sucked in a deep breath to her air-deprived lungs. The miserable knots in her stomach loosened as she tried to focus her thoughts.

Shane was hurt. Hurt bad enough for the navy to call Sara. Did that mean the surgery was major? Was there minor surgery in the military? Her brain raced through all of the things she'd read about the SEALs since Sara told her what Shane really did.

Lark got to her feet to pace. Sea, air and land. Guns and parachutes and explosives. Images, each one scarier than the last, flashed through her mind.

Even if she couldn't have him, even if he didn't want her, she had to know he was okay. When that afternoon did he go in for surgery? How long would it last? Would they let Sara know when it was over? What if it didn't go well? Would they tell her that? Shoving her hands into her hair, Lark tugged at her scalp. She couldn't stand it. There was no way she could sit here waiting and wondering without freaking out.

Turning to the sobbing younger woman, Lark reached out to take her hands and pulled her to her feet.

"C'mon, we're going to deal with this," she said. "You go home and pack. I've got to let Heather know she needs to take care of the coffeehouse, make a couple of calls and get my stuff. I'll be by to get you in about a half hour."

"Why?" Her voice hoarse from crying, Sara rubbed her hands over her face.

"We're going to California."

Sara's jaw dropped.

"California?"

"Your brother is having surgery—you need to be there." *I need to be there*, Lark thought. "You're in no shape to go on your own, so I'm going with you."

Sara blinked a couple of times before nodding.

"Thank you," she murmured. Then, as she headed for the door, she called over her shoulder, "Don't forget to wash the clay off your face."

FLOATING ON AN ocean of happy drugs, Shane tried to navigate his way through tranquil waves and figure out where he was.

The last thing he remembered was grabbing hold of Cowboy, as the team called Alex Tanner. While rappelling up the side of the cliff where they'd hitch their return ride, the Petty Officer had taken a bullet to the shoulder and lost his grip. Shane knew he'd caught Cowboy before he fell. He was pretty sure they'd made it to the top of the cliff.

Then what?

Fighting against the waves as they tried to take him under again, Shane clenched his fists, using the feel of his knuckles' contraction to help him focus.

He'd taken a bullet.

Damned sniper had got him in the leg. Shane's brow

creased. Right leg, lower thigh. A good half foot from his pride, so to speak. Easy enough to field dress.

So why was he doing the backstroke through a sea of narcotics? He tried to open his eyes, but they refused to co-operate. He could hear a low humming, intermittent beeps and, from a distance, the murmur of voices. He sucked in a long breath through his nose, noting the smell of anti-septics and rubber.

Damn. Hospital.

Panic grabbed him in its unfamiliar grasp, squeezing his guts and clogging his throat.

How bad was he? Had he lost his leg? He tried to feel it, tried to move his foot, to shift his hand to check if it was there. Nothing. Dammit, he couldn't fucking move. He could feel his heart racing as he struggled to rise above the drugs, to rip his brain out of the fog.

Nothing.

Then a new scent registered. Soft and earthy, like flowers in the forest. He unclenched his fists, his body relaxing inch by inch. The panic faded, serenity taking its place. Wherever he was, whatever the reason, he was good.

Because that was Lark's scent.

Lark was here.

If she was here, everything was fine.

Riding on that, he let himself drift again.

FLOATING OUT OF the safe comfort of oblivion, Shane felt as if someone had beaten him all over with a pickax. He knew he was in the hospital. But how bad was he hurt?

"He looks so pale."

"They said he's fine. The damage wasn't as severe as they'd thought and the surgery went well."

A huge wave of relief coursed through the haze of drugs,

loosening the fist fear had held over his subconscious. He was fine. That meant he'd be able to return to duty.

"He could have died."

"He didn't." The voice was firmer now.

Damn. Shane would have smiled if he could. His guardian angel was a hellcat. Her adamant insistence that he'd fully recover dispelled every vestige of lingering worry. His body relaxed again; his mind drifted.

When the whisper-soft glide of soft fingers skimmed over his cheek, Shane shifted his face into that touch. Warmth coursed through him, easing the pain, erasing the worries. All that was left was emotions. An entire sea of them, all unfamiliar, all terrifying. But none as terrifying as the idea of losing this comfort. Something hot and wet dropped on his cheek only to be wiped away.

"Rest," a sweet voice whispered. The order was followed by a kiss so gentle it barely skimmed his lips. Sighing at how right it felt, Shane did just that.

He slept.

SHANE DIDN'T KNOW how much time had passed when he surfaced again. Eyes closed, he did a mental scan of his body. His feet—both of them—moved on command. His right leg ached but he welcomed the pain. Everything seemed to be in working order. He did another scan of his brain, reciting name, rank and serial number in his head before reviewing the events as he knew them.

It'd started out as a textbook mission.

They'd extracted the hostage, disabled the enemy and retrieved the weapons cache. Everything was moving according to plan when it'd all gone to hell. Whether the villager with sniper training was employed by the militants or just had a hard-on for helicopters, he'd opened fire, putting a hole in the Black Hawk. The team had instantly shifted to plan B, moving to higher elevation for an easier retrieval Mr. Wizard had taken point with Romeo covering their rear.

That's when the rifle-toting idiot had targeted the team.

Shane had grabbed Cowboy, then Cowboy had grabbed him. As always, every man on the team had the others' back. They'd made it to the top of the cliff; he remembered that. It'd been rough going because the rocks were so slippery. His blood, he realized now. The bullet must have hit an artery. Everything was a blur after he'd heaved himself over the cliff, though.

He scoured his mind for what had happened next, but all he came up with were impressions of the hospital. Irish's voice ordering him to heal fast. Romeo cussing—which was weird because Romeo never cussed. And Lark.

He'd dreamed of Lark.

He'd smelled her. He'd heard her voice. He'd felt her touch.

Damn, these must be good drugs.

Ready to return, needing to get back to normal as quickly as possible, Shane slowly peeled his eyes open. Without moving his head, he looked around.

He'd been right. He was in the hospital.

The room was dim, a pale light coming from somewhere to the left giving just enough illumination for him to make out the sparse furnishings, medical equipment and—his gaze shifted to the left—a person.

Shane turned his head sideways on the pillow and squinted at the body curled up on a chair.

Lark?

Here?

He wanted to reach out, to touch her and reassure himself that she was real. To make sure that he wasn't still floating on a sea of drugs.

He watched her shift and mumble in her sleep. Something clicked in his chest, as if his heart had just settled into place.

Then, as if an alarm went off, she lifted her head.

"Hey, you're awake."

That was definitely Lark's voice.

She unfolded herself from the chair, getting to her feet to reach out and take his hand.

His fingers curled around hers, assuring himself that yes, it was Lark's touch.

"Hey," he said, surprised to hear how rough his own voice sounded.

"How are you feeling? Should I call the nurse?"

Since the nurse meant more drugs, Shane shook his head. He wasn't sure how Lark had got here, had no clue how she'd found out he was here, and was seriously clueless why she was looking at him with such sweet concern instead of smacking him with his own pillow.

"You're sure? They said it was natural that you'd have pain when you woke."

"I'm fine." As if the answer to instant healing was hidden there somewhere, he gazed at her face. Her eyes were shadowed, worry creasing her brow. But her hand was warm in his and her fingers gentle as she skimmed them over his forehead as if checking for fever.

"No pain?"

Totally weirded out by the fear in her eyes, Shane lifted her hand to his mouth.

"I'm fine," he said again. When her expression didn't lighten, he put on his best put-upon sigh—thinking that for once having five sisters came in handy. "Although…"

"You are hurting. How bad? Should I call the nurse?"

"It's not that bad," he said, making it sound just the opposite. He pointed to his mouth. "It hurts right here."

The worry on Lark's face shifted to amusement.

"You poor thing," she said. She leaned down to brush her lips over his. Shane sighed at the touch of her mouth. Because it felt incredible, yes. But also because the feel of her hand on his chest, of her tongue sliding along his bottom lip, stirred some interest from down south, assuring Shane that his injury was, indeed, minor.

"Better?" she asked when she lifted her mouth from his.

"A little. I think I need more of that, though." Shane reached up to cup his hand behind her neck, pulling her down again. This time he took charge of the kiss, his tongue plundering deep and hard into her welcoming mouth.

His head spun, sensation after sensation washing over him in pleasurable waves. His fingers tangled in her hair while he lifted his other hand to cup her breast. Her soft moan against his mouth felt so damned good.

Before he could slide his hand under her shirt and see if he could elicit another sexy moan, the spinning in his head did a reverse three-sixty.

As if she knew, Lark slowly pulled back. Her midnight eyes were blurred with desire, her lips swollen from his kiss. He was a little confused as to why she had two heads, but hey, she was so gorgeous that gave him more to enjoy.

Then he realized that he'd lost enough blood that having it all pool in his lap was enough to make him feel as if he'd been on a three-day drinking binge.

"More," he murmured, willing to take the hangover if he could taste her again.

"Sleep first, then you can have all you want," she said, her words so soothing that Shane felt himself doing just that.

As he slid into sleep, he tried to remember why he'd left her. Whatever the reason was, it'd been a dumbass mistake. Because he was pretty sure he couldn't live without her and her magical lips.

THE NEXT TIME Shane woke, the room was bright.

He'd dreamed of Lark. Except it wasn't a dream. She'd been here. She'd looked so good. Tasted so good. His chest felt odd, something there warming over the idea of seeing her again. Wanting another taste, he turned his head toward the guest chair.

His expectant smile dimmed a little when he saw the female form curled up in the chair this time wasn't Lark. It disappeared completely when he recognized just exactly who it was.

"Oh, hell," he muttered.

"Yay, you're awake." Sara bounced out of the chair and practically skipped over to the bed with enough enthusiasm to make Shane want the drugs again. "You're okay. You're alive. I was so worried."

"I'm fine."

"That's what Lark said, but I had to see for myself. But I gotta say, big brother, that all I've seen so far is you snoring."

"Sorry to bore you." Then, because she'd mentioned her first, he asked, "Lark was here?"

"Yeah. When she saw how upset I was, she insisted on coming with me so I didn't have to fly alone. And nobody would tell me how bad you were hurt. Just, you know, that you needed surgery." Her words coming to an abrupt halt, Sara took a shaky breath and blinked fast to clear the tears from her eyes. "I was afraid."

Before he could say anything—before he could even figure out how to respond—she lifted her wobbling chin.

"Nope, I promised Lark I wouldn't fall apart on you." She pressed her fingertips against her eyelids, did a little dance in one place, then shook her head.

"Lark said no tears?"

"Yeah. She said you'd been through enough already

without a bunch of emotional drama. She said you hated that kind of thing and if I got soggy it'd set back your recovery." She bit her lip, then shot him a teasing smile. "She said it would set it back because you'd jump out of the bed and go running from the hospital like your ass was on fire."

"She didn't say that." Shane laughed.

"Oh, yes, she did." Sara pointed her finger at him. "She totally gets you."

Remembering his sleep-fogged thoughts from earlier, Shane wasn't sure how he felt about that. Wanting a woman who understood him so well was good. But one that he felt he couldn't live without? That might be a mistake.

"How'd you find out I was here?"

"I'm your emergency contact, remember."

Shane frowned. He'd actually forgotten. He'd have to get that changed as soon as he could.

"We got here just after you were taken into surgery and even though I'm your, you know, emergency contact and all, they wouldn't tell me anything. Not how you'd been hurt, not what you'd hurt, not even how long the surgery would take."

He knew her sniff was supposed to be disparaging, but he could see she was trying not to cry.

"I was going to throw a fit, and as you know, I can throw a good one. But then Lark stepped in. She was all reasonable and stuff. She asked if your commanding officer was on the premises and then had him paged. Yowza, he's a looker. Of course, the rest of those guys were, too. You know, the ones we met in the waiting room."

Shane lifted his hand to stop her.

"Lark had Lieutenant Donovan paged?"

"He said to call him Mitch."

"And the two of you met my team?"

"I don't know if we met the whole team." Sara frowned.

"Let's see. There was Gabriel and Taylor and Cade and Alex. They were there the whole time. Dominic and Aiden stopped by but had to leave, though they said someone named Brody would be by today. Oh, and Blake was there. He's so sweet. When he saw how upset I was, he called his wife. Alexia's the one who took me to the hotel. She tried to get Lark to go, too, but no go. I didn't realize Lark could be so stubborn."

Feeling overwhelmed for the first time since he'd woken in the hospital, Shane pressed his fingers to his eyelids. He wasn't sure if his eyes were actually reeling around in his head or if it just felt like it.

"Are you okay?" Sara asked, rubbing her hand over his arm. But the move couldn't erase the barrage of words pounding against his head. Finally, Shane dropped his hands and gave her a steady look.

"So to recap, you, along with Lark, who was there for support, talked your way into a military hospital waiting room, met the majority of my team, cried all over my commander's wife and you think Mitch—who has a newborn baby girl and a great wife, by the way—is hot. Is that everything?"

"Um, that depends."

"On?"

"On if you're upset about all that other stuff. Because if you are, then yes, that's everything."

For one brief second, Shane wanted to fly back to that village and beat the sniper with his own rifle for making this conversation possible.

"Let's say I'm not upset."

Sara gave him a narrow-eyed look that said she knew he was playing with words. He figured she'd be the expert on that since she used way too many of them. He saw the stubborn expression in her eyes and sighed. Apparently in this case, words were going to be hard to come by.

"What else?" he asked tiredly.

"Well, I had to do it. I mean, if something had happened to you and I knew about it and hadn't done it? Oh my God. Can you imagine?" Sara shuddered. "So I did it even though I know you're going to be mad. Maybe I should have waited, like Lark said, but I couldn't. I was too scared."

Since the last was said in a shaky voice accompanied by a quivering chin, Shane took that part at face value. The rest he had to decipher. It wasn't his time as a cryptologic tech that clued him on to what she was trying not to say. It was having grown up with five sisters.

"You called Mom."

Her eyes locked on his face, she slowly nodded.

"And?"

"You're not mad?"

"I'll decide after you finish telling me."

"And nothing, really. Lark told me to wait and find out what the actual situation was before I said anything. You know, because Mom's such a basket case about what you do. So I did, I waited until we were here to see if you were, you know, on death's door. Then I called her. She wigged at first, but you know Mom. She pulled herself together, asked if she could make it in time to see you before surgery."

"Right." Shane rolled his yes. "Like Mom was going to come to a military hospital to see me after I was hurt in the line of duty."

"She was. I think she's kinda figured that she's gonna have to be the one to budge, because you obviously won't. She said she'd rather have her son taking stupid, crazy risks than not have a son at all."

Before Shane could process that, the sound of rubber hitting linoleum interrupted them.

"Good afternoon, Petty Officer O'Brian," called the nurse in a syrupy tone. "It's the end of visiting hours, so your friend will have to go."

"But he just woke up a few minutes ago. I've barely had a chance to do any visiting," Sara protested.

"Visiting hours are over," the nurse repeated, this time without the scary smile.

"Fine." Pouting, Sara leaned over to give Shane a kiss on the cheek. "I'll go call home and let everyone know you're okay. I'll come back as soon as I can."

With that and a glare at the nurse, Sara flounced out.

Shane eyed the nurse, hoping she'd follow suit.

"Time for your medication."

"No, thanks."

The burly blonde was the size of a linebacker, but Shane was pretty sure he could take her. His injury might slow him down a little, though.

"I feel fine," he insisted, shifting the bed into a sitting position in case he had to make a run for it. "I don't need more pain meds."

"Good, good," she said in that same upbeat voice. "You go ahead and walk yourself over to the bathroom. As soon as you're done, we'll see if you say that."

Watching her the same way he'd watch a suicide terrorist on a rampage, Shane gave a slow, friendly nod.

"So all I have to do is walk in there, do my thing and come on back? I do that and you'll take your pills and needles and drugs and go?"

"Mmm," she hummed absently, as if she were too busy checking his chart and adjusting the bedside table to use real words.

"Good. Because I've already used the head twice."

"Is that so?"

The look she gave him reminded Shane of one of the drill instructors he'd had in boot camp. The guy had smiled just like that before ordering the entire squad to do fifty push-ups. He wasn't sure he could handle more than twenty, but he was willing to give it a go if it would get rid of her.

Before he had to try, there was a commotion at the door. Shane and the linebacker both looked, the view making Shane grin. The linebacker's expression didn't change.

"Yo," Shane said, laughing at the sight of a huge bouquet of flowers shaped like an anchor with a ribbon that read Break a Leg. He couldn't tell who was carrying it because it was so big all he could see were the person's camouflage pants and brown leather boots. "Look. It's the flower fairy."

"Don't make me beat you with my wings," joked Romeo's voice from behind the posies.

"We're here to debrief Petty Officer O'Brian," Irish told the nurse. "You'll have to leave."

"But—"

"Dismissed."

The four men watched a wave of red fury wash over the nurse's face. But seeing as this was a military hospital and Irish was sporting an oak leaf on his collar, she had no choice.

"Thanks," Shane said after the linebacker left with one last glare.

"No problem." Taking a seat, Irish stretched his legs out in front of him and gave Shane a baffled look. "But I think I figured out why you're so quiet."

"Huh?"

"If your other sisters are anything like Sara, I figure there weren't any words left in the house for you to use."

He shook his head. "I've never met anyone who could talk like that."

Shane laughed.

"So tell me more about her friend," the Wizard said, settling on the window ledge. "She single?"

"No." The word was out before Shane even realized he'd answered.

"Too bad. Pretty lady like that might enjoy spending time with a good-looking guy like me. Entertaining conversation, smooth dance moves and a body like this?" Mr. Wizard flexed, then gave his bicep a kiss before grinning at them. "She'll dump whoever she's with for a chance to spend time with a nice guy like me."

"You forgot modest," Romeo pointed out.

"That goes without saying."

"She's not available," Shane said firmly as he shifted his weight to his bad leg. Gritting his teeth against the initial shaft of pain, he waited for it to pass. Then he took one step, then another until he reached the armoire where he assumed his clothes were.

"What're you doing?"

Shane pulled the door open and saw his flight gear, bloody pants and only one boot.

"Leaving. I need clothes."

"Pretty sure you're not supposed to leave yet."

"I want out," he insisted. He wasn't going to humiliate himself by mentioning the linebacker with the needle. "I'm fine, the bullet is out, my leg works."

"The doctor said he wanted to keep you here a few days," Mr. Wizard said with a wicked smile. "You know, for observation and crap."

Shane stepped over to the window, looking past the Wizard's shoulder to gauge the distance to the ground. He glanced at the armoire with a frown, wondering why they'd left him one boot but not the climbing ropes he'd been hooked to.

"You're not jumping."

"I was thinking more along the lines of rappelling."

"Give the man his clothes." Romeo shook his head. "You know he'll go out the window otherwise."

Shane turned from the window, his gaze shifting from man to man. Nobody had clothes, though.

"We brought you flowers," Mr. Wizard reminded him with a grin.

"So, what? I'm supposed to wear posies over my—"

"Your clothes are with the flowers," Romeo interrupted, his grin even bigger than the Wizard's. "We figured it was easier to sneak them in and walk you out than the other way around."

Grateful beyond words to his pals, Shane dived for the flowers and some goddamn underwear.

Ten minutes and another reminder of rank from Irish, and Shane was free.

"Where do you want us to drop you?" Romeo asked as they settled into Irish's jeep. "Your place is gonna be a bitch with all those stairs."

"You can stay with Livi and I," Mitch offered.

"No." Shane shook his head. He knew he wasn't in good enough shape for anything physical—two flights of stairs included. But he knew what he wanted. Who he wanted. "You can drop me at Lark's hotel."

He might be low on blood, and seeing Lark was a guaranteed hard-on inducer. He didn't care. Seeing her, touching her, tasting her was worth any amount of dizziness.

8

LARK LAY IN the whirlpool tub, water jetting around her in what should have been relaxing waves. Instead, she felt as if she were sitting in a mixing bowl with the beaters on high—all churned up. The moist air was delicately scented with lavender essential oil—her favorite scent to help with sleep. But it wasn't working. Neither was the soothing melody of flutes and strings playing from her iPod.

The last time she'd slept in her own bed was two nights ago. She dropped her head back on the bath pillow, staring at the plants hanging over the tub. God, she needed to rest. She'd had to promise Sara that she'd crash in the bedside chair the previous night in order to convince Sara to go back to the hotel.

Instead, she'd spent the night sitting by Shane's bed, watching him sleep. The terror she'd carried through the trip to California and the hellish wait while Shane was in surgery had faded. But with that gone, she'd had to deal with the reality of Shane in that hospital bed. He'd been so pale.

Lark's eyes flew open as she remembered him there. She reached a trembling hand for the glass of wine on the edge of the tub. But the taste didn't do anything to wash away the fear that was trying to claw its way back into her heart.

She'd thought she'd lost him.

Lark rubbed her hand over her forehead, scented water

dripping down her cheek. It had been so much easier when she'd thought she'd lost him before. Her heart had been nicely insulated by the irritation and insult of his note.

Even after Sara had explained that Shane was a SEAL, even after Lark had researched enough to know what that actually meant, she hadn't really understood the reality of it.

He could have died. It wasn't one of those esoteric, *everyone dies sometime* issues. It was a very real job hazard. Every time he did his job, he was at risk.

Thinking about it was stupid. She took a choppy breath, her hands shaking as she pushed herself out of the tub. She was wrinkling to a prune here and not at all relaxed.

She'd packed so fast, she'd forgotten her robe and body lotion, so she made do with the ones the hotel provided. Her hair still pinned to the top of her head, her face flushed from the heat of the water, Lark looked around her hotel room. She should pack the few things she'd remembered to bring so she was ready to leave in the morning. She and Sara would have time for breakfast and one last visit to the hospital before they headed for the airport the following afternoon.

Instead, she dropped onto the bed, arms outspread.

The reality that she'd been studiously trying to ignore for the past two weeks could no longer be avoided. She didn't know what she was going to do about it, though.

Anger hadn't budged it. Distance hadn't changed it. Even scary reality wasn't shifting it.

She was in love with Shane.

Tears trickled down her face, pooling in her ears but Lark barely noticed them.

How had this happened? Sure, she'd gone to bed with him less than a day after they'd been introduced. But that should make her slutty, not in love.

She'd told herself she couldn't stop thinking about him because she was irritated over the way he'd left. And, of course, because leaving meant he'd taken away all that great sex.

She'd told herself that she'd tossed aside everything to fly to California because she was being a good friend and didn't want Sara to have to go alone.

But while she'd been sitting in the hospital last night watching him sleep, a bell had gone off in her head. Thankfully she'd been too shocked at the discovery to jump up and run all the way back to the airport. Then, just as the feeling was returning to her feet, he'd stirred. All it had taken was a kiss from him and she'd settled right back in the chair for the rest of the night.

And for the rest of the night she'd tried to come to grips with the fact that she was in love with a navy SEAL. Being in love was rough enough, but in love with a man like Shane?

Rolling to her feet, Lark scrubbed her hands over her face. If losing her mother had taught her anything, it was that lying around wallowing in self-pity wasn't going to help. So what if she loved Shane. Like grief, it'd eventually fade until it was more of an aching tug on her heart instead of this sharp stabbing pain.

Wouldn't it?

Anything is possible if you believe it. Her mother's words echoed through Lark's head with the comfort of a warm hug.

With that in mind, Lark pulled her nightgown out of the dresser. She was going to climb into bed and sleep, dammit.

Unknotting the robe, it was halfway down her arms when there was a knock at the door.

Frowning, she pulled it back on, retying the knot as she

crossed the room. She was sure it was Sara but she checked the peephole, anyway.

She looked, closed her eyes tight, then looked again.

No way.

It had to be a tear-induced hallucination.

Sure of it, Lark opened the door.

It wasn't a hallucination, though. It was Shane, in all his gorgeousness. Standing there in baggy khakis and a loose pullover, nobody would believe he'd been laid up in the hospital just a few hours ago.

"Hey," he greeted.

"Oh my God." She knew her mouth was hanging open, but she was too shocked to pull it shut. "What are you doing here?"

"Waiting for you to ask me in," Shane said with an easy smile.

"But you're supposed to be in the hospital. I was going to come see you in the morning." Hoping that didn't sound as stupid out loud as it did when she replayed it in her head, Lark rushed to add, "The nurse said you wouldn't be released for at least three more days."

"Fortunately, the time frame of my release wasn't up to the nurse."

"So you just up and left." Lark could only shake her head. "Then you, what? Walked here?"

She knew he couldn't drive. Not with the damage to his right leg.

"Nah." He tilted his head toward the end of the hallway.

Lark peeked out the door to see why. Eyes wide, she managed an awkward smile and a little finger wave before shifting back to the safety of her doorway, where the three men standing by the elevator wouldn't see her naked but for a bathrobe.

"What are Mitch, Gabriel and Taylor doing?" she asked,

her voice pitched as low. She didn't want them thinking her rude, but dammit, she wasn't asking four good-looking, incredibly built men into her hotel room. At least, not while she was bare-faced with her hair piled on top of her head and her too-large robe sliding off her shoulder.

"They were waiting to see if I need a ride." Shane glanced at his buddies before reaching out to tug the terry cloth closed. "Mitch said I could crash at his place."

"Where? In Morgan's room?" Lark asked, referring to Mitch's newborn baby daughter.

"I've gotta stay somewhere." He shrugged. "There are two flights of stairs to get to my own place. Mitch has an elevator and I can crash on his couch."

"You're hurt. You shouldn't be sleeping on a couch."

"Well, there are other options," he said slowly, his smile filled with wicked suggestions.

Eyes wide, Lark's brows almost hit her damp hair.

"You can't think that you're staying here," she said in a breathy whisper. "Why would you even consider it an option?"

"You do have an elevator." His smile was three shades of wicked as he reached out to slide his fingers over her robe again. This time instead of tugging the fabric closed, he ran his knuckles under the lapel, skimming her bare flesh.

Heat shot through her, desire curling in her belly. Her nipples rose to attention with an aching intensity.

"I don't think it would be a good idea," she murmured, wishing she could put some force behind her words.

"Hmm, but I think it would be a great idea," he countered, sliding his finger lower so it skimmed the sensitive flesh between her breasts.

Her breath a little uneven, Lark tried to shake her head.

But the aching need pulsing through her body was louder than her good sense.

"You should still be in the hospital."

"That depends on who you ask."

"Your doctor," Lark suggested, her gaze roaming over the sexy planes of his face. How had he got even better looking? He should be pale and worn looking. Instead, he was simply gorgeous.

"My commander outranks my doctor."

"What?"

His smile filled with charm, Shane wrapped his free hand on her waist, his fingers twisting around the robe's belt.

"It's a military hospital. Commander Green outranks me but Irish outranks him."

"So let me get this straight," Lark said, her eyes narrowed. "You got your friend to bust you out against doctors' orders?"

"Yep."

Lark's lips twitched. He wasn't even trying to fake remorse.

"Your sister's room is right over there." Lark pointed down the hall. Because Sara was a night owl and Lark an early bird, they'd got separate rooms. "I'm sure she's still up and she'd love to have you stay with her."

"That's mean." Shane gave her a pained look. "I'm injured, remember? Why would you subject me to an entire night of Sara babbling and worrying over me? I'd be better off in the hospital."

Lark knew she should say no. He'd left her with just a note. He had other places to stay. And being with him was only going to prolong the pain of saying goodbye.

Her heart wondered if it could be any more painful tomorrow, though than it was now. Figuring that was a good enough reason to give herself more time with him, Lark slowly stepped back, letting the door swing wide-open.

"You can come for a little while," she said, halting him with the flat of her hand before he could step over the threshold. "But you aren't sleeping here. If you won't stay with Sara, then you should let Mitch know to come back and get you soon."

"He's gone."

"What?" Risking showing her bedraggled face again, Lark peered around the edge of the doorway. The hall was empty. "He sprang you from the hospital and just left you here?"

"He sprang me but he didn't just leave. You gave him the signal."

"I what?" Her eyes widened. "When I waved? You knew I wasn't signaling for them to leave."

"They didn't know that." Shane grimaced, shifting his weight from one foot to the other, then back again. "Weren't you going to let me in?"

Her stomach dropping to her toes, Lark realized she'd been so busy freaking out that she'd made an injured man stand in the hallway.

"Yes, yes." She waved him inside. "Come in. Sit down. Rest your leg."

She held her breath as he walked into the room; her eyes narrowed as, after looking around, he crossed to sit on the bed.

The sight of Shane sitting on the covers already rumpled by her personal pity party brought to mind all of the reasons why Shane shouldn't be here. And all of the reasons he should. Of course, most of the shoulds included both of them naked.

Realizing she was almost there, Lark tightened the belt of her robe. Pushing one hand through her messy hair, she curled her bare toes into the carpet and tried desperately to think of an excuse to get dressed.

"Sit," Shane suggested, patting the mattress.

He looked so good, so tempting. He hadn't shaved in a couple of days, so his face was rougher than she was used to seeing. The dark stubble highlighted those dreamy eyes, just as the silver dog tags around his neck emphasized who he really was.

A warrior. A very sexy warrior.

She started to step forward, and then realized what she was doing. Nope, no way was she climbing in bed with him. The minute her body hit the blankets, she'd cave.

"Can I get you anything?" she offered instead, gesturing toward the minifridge. "I've got water, wine, soda. Um, cheese and crackers, cookies, some muffins, a couple of apples and some grapes."

"Is that all?" Looking amused at the rundown, he shook his head. "Thanks, but no."

She stood in the middle of the room, her hands knotted on her belt as if it would fly open on its own, waiting for him to say something else. Anything else.

But he simply sat watching her, completely at ease.

"Why are you here?" she blurted out. As soon as the words were spoken she wanted to grab them back. That was the sort of question that needed to be led up to, danced around. Or at the very least, politely stated.

Shane didn't seem upset or surprised, though. He looked pleased and just a little arrogant as he leaned back on his hands, his gaze sweeping up and down her body.

"Why were you at the hospital last night?" he countered smoothly.

"Sara wouldn't leave you alone, but she was totally exhausted. I told her I'd stay so she could get some sleep." There, that didn't sound as if she were looming over his bed, crying herself sick and worrying over his every breath.

"So you came for Sara?"

Lark wanted to say yes, that she'd only flown almost a thousand miles because she was a good friend. But she couldn't quite get the lie past her lips.

"Why did you leave?" she heard herself ask instead. This time she didn't wish the words back. Instead, she squared her shoulders, lifted her chin and stared him straight in the eye.

"I got called in," he said easily.

Nope, not good enough. Lark didn't say it aloud but she knew the message was clear.

For a second, his expression didn't change. Then he winced and shrugged. "You were asleep when I got the call. I could have woken you but if I did, I'd have had to explain."

"Explain what?" Lark asked, not giving either one of them an inch. Not him, because she deserved a real explanation. And not herself, because while the explanation could hurt like crazy, she had to know.

"Explain what I am, what I do. There are family issues." He hesitated, then shrugged. "But that's not the whole reason."

Deciding that she'd rather be sitting for this conversation, Lark glanced at the heavy chair in the corner, and then at the bed. Since struggling to push the chair closer would look petty, she took a deep breath, gave herself a quick lecture on keeping her hands to herself and gingerly settled on the edge of the bed.

"I know about the family issues." At his surprised look, she explained, "Sara told me the day you left. Not because she thought there was something between us. She was just venting about your mother."

At his questioning look, she shrugged.

"I think she'd hoped your visit would end in a reconciliation. She'd talked your mom around and came to get you but you were gone."

"I knew she was up to something," Shane murmured, shaking his head. "But I'd figured she was trying to hook us up, not that she was trying to mediate a cease-fire."

"You knew she was trying to fix us up?" Eyes wide with surprise, Lark drew one knee up and shifted so she was facing him.

"Please. Sara's anything but subtle." He shifted, stretching out sideways on the bed and bending his leg a couple of times. Figuring his wound was bothering him, Lark didn't comment. "She'd have done better to stick with that instead of shooting for the impossible."

"Because we did hook up?" Visions of the oh so many ways they'd hooked up flashed through Lark's mind. Her body warmed, heat pooling low in her belly at the memory. She was glad that the robe was thick enough to hide her nipples' reaction. "Maybe, but I'd think it was a lot more important to mend that bridge between you and the rest of the family. As much as I appreciate the idea that your sister thinks we're right for each other."

She waited with bated breath, but he didn't comment on that last part.

"She'd have more luck selling the Golden Gate than building that kind of bridge." For the first time since he'd walked in the door, Lark could see past his friendly poker face to the pain beneath.

"I can't imagine how hard it must be on you," she said softly, reaching out to lay a sympathetic hand over the back of his. Shane flipped his hand so their fingers entwined. "I've known your mom for over a year and I'd never have thought she could be hard enough to close out one of her children. It must be hard on her, too."

"You think?"

"Yeah." Lark nodded, her eyes distant as she tried to put herself in Molly O'Brian's place. "What you do is intense. Not just being in the military, although I'd imagine that's huge by itself. But you deliberately chose to join an elite group, one that takes on the most dangerous missions, the scariest challenges. She's got to be terrified about your safety. She must think it's easier to keep you at a distance."

"Is it?" Disappointment flashed in his eyes, then in a blink it was gone.

"No," she corrected, her words tumbling out in her haste to assure him. "I said that's what I imagine your mother thinks."

"What do you think?"

"What do I think?" Lark repeated, choosing her words with extra care. "I think that everyone deals with fear as best as they can, and their way might be difficult for others to understand. So your mother's way is hers. Mine wouldn't be the same."

"You wouldn't cut yourself off just because my career worried you?"

Lark desperately wanted to know if he was simply relating her words to the situation with his mother, or if he was asking a deeper, more personal question.

Without knowing, all she could do was be honest.

"I guess it would depend," she said slowly, thinking of how hard it had been waking up to find him gone. If they were in a relationship, that would become the norm. It might include a kiss and an actual goodbye, but the empty bed would be the same. Could she handle that? She didn't know, and wasn't willing to ask herself to even think about it.

Still, Shane wanted—needed—an answer.

"It must take an incredible amount of drive and discipline to become a SEAL in the first place, so it clearly means a lot to you. If I cared about someone who had that much passion and dedication to something, I'd find a way to support them. And if it were dangerous, as your job is, then I'd do my best to make sure my fear for them didn't make their job any harder."

Opening the door to temptation, Lark slid down on her side, resting her head on her elbow.

A hint of a smile playing over his gorgeous mouth, Shane reached out to unhook the clip holding her hair. It fell around her face like shaggy black silk before he scooped part of it with his fingers and tucked it behind her ear.

"Nobody's ever understood before," he said quietly. "At least, nobody outside of the team. Being a SEAL, it's what I've always wanted to do. I'm good at it. Damned good. It's not like we get through BUD/S, they hand us our trident and that's it. We train constantly. We work hard to continually improve. Our missions are meticulously planned, all contingencies considered and multiple backup plans put in place."

His eyes on his fingers as they played through her hair, Shane frowned.

"I wish my family would understand that."

Lark wanted to cry at the sorrow in his eyes. She knew it was rough feeling that you were going it alone, but at least she had her aunt's support. Shane, though, with most of his family living, had none. She couldn't imagine how hard it must be to do what he did, to train, serve, bust his butt like that. But to do it against the wishes of the people he loved? To know that they were so unsupportive of his choices that they'd rather cut him out of their lives than accept it? It was baffling. She'd have to give Sara a big, tight hug as soon as she saw her again. The younger woman was the only one who'd stood by Shane.

Lark vowed then and there that, no matter what happened between her and Shane, whether their relationship ended tonight or went on for an unforeseeable time that she'd never use his career against him.

An easy promise to make, the little voice in the back of her head mocked. She'd probably never see him after tonight. Still, it made her feel better to make it.

"You said your job was only one of the reasons you left?" Lark said, her voice whisper-soft. "What were the others?"

Shane's fingers skimmed through her hair, gently untangling the damp knots.

"I'm a SEAL," he said as he cupped his hand around the back of her neck to pull her closer.

"We covered that."

"SEALs are never afraid." His eyes locked on hers, he slowly brushed her mouth with his. When she caught her breath, he ran his tongue over her bottom lip.

"Never?" she asked, rolling to her back as Shane angled himself over her.

"Except with you."

Before Lark could answer, before she could even process what he'd said, he took her mouth. If the kiss had just held passion she could have resisted. She was sure she could. But his mouth was so sweet, that she had to lean in, open her mouth and seduce his tongue.

Next thing she knew, her robe was open and his hands were driving her crazy. Lark didn't know if it was because Shane was so good, or if it was all of that bottled-up fear exploding with relief knowing he was safe. But she got so hot, went up so fast at just his touch that she was afraid she'd come before he even got his pants off.

Needing to feel his body against hers, desperate to have him inside of her, Lark's hand made quick work of the buttons on his shirt.

She reveled in the rippled strength of his chest, her fingers combing through the soft hair and her body tightening even more. She'd been so scared, so worried seeing him lying in that hospital bed. Now he was here, alive. And she had to have him.

Shane's mouth took her deeper, his hands racing just as fast as hers, doing wickedly delicious things that sent her need for him flying even higher.

She ripped at his belt buckle, desperately fought his snap and zipper in order to shove his pants out of the way. She got them as far as his thighs, her hands skimming over the hair-roughened muscles, when her fingers grazed the edge of adhesive tape.

Ohmygod. Horrified, she tore her mouth from his to look down and see that she'd shoved his pants down so the waistband had a stranglehold over his wound.

"Oh God," she gasped. "You're hurt. We can't do this."

"Sure we can," he assured her, wrapping his hand around her wrist and bringing it back to his throbbing erection. "See, proof, I can do anything."

"That's not where you were hurt," she reminded him with a giggle.

"You're worried about me, you get on top."

Lark felt the smile spread, slow and satisfied, across her face as he made quick work of his laces and boots, shoved off his pants, then gestured to his body as if to say, "hop on."

Her body warring with her mind, Lark's gaze flew from his amused expression to his gauze-covered wound. Then took an appreciative trip back up with a long pause on the hard length of his erection, stiff and inviting.

"But—"

"Do you want me to feel better or not?" Shane asked as he cupped her breast, his thumb running dizzying circles around her nipple.

She could have resisted, she told herself. She'd have put his health first, she was sure. But then he gave her a puppy dog look and said in a low, seductive tone, "I need you."

She swore she actually felt her heart melt at his words. Unable to resist, Lark leaned over to kiss him. Then, as heat drowned out worry, she arranged her body over his, taking care not to bump his wound. A wicked smile played over his mouth as Shane angled her hips over his then, arching one brow, thrust.

Lark gasped, her body trembling as he filled her. Oh God, he was so big, so deep. Her hands braced on his shoulders, she slowly, achingly slid up until just the tip of his shaft was inside, then slid down again. Shane gave a low moan of approval. Confident now, wanting more, her knees gripped his waist and Shane's big hands worked her breasts as she straightened.

She rode him. Slowly at first, then faster, deeper, harder as sensation took over. She undulated, pressing tight against him before sliding up again, loving the feeling of power control gave her. Loving the feeling of delight Shane gave her.

Then he shuddered, a look of pleasure bordering on pain flashing across his face. Lark smiled. She'd never felt so good, so powerful.

Shane pinched her nipple with one hand while sliding his palm down her torso until he'd reached her wet, swollen bud. Then he pinched that, too.

Pleasure tore through her in waves so huge, so powerful

that her entire body shook. Back arched, Lark felt Shane's body jerk, his fingers digging into her as his own orgasm ripped through him.

She was dimly aware of collapsing against him, of Shane's quick cleanup before he tucked her into his arms. So right, she thought with a sigh. It felt so right here.

"Stay."

Her body lax and satisfied on its way to sleep, the word echoed through Lark's mind a few times before it registered.

"Huh?"

"Stay." His hand smoothed down her back, cupping her butt for a tempting moment before returning to wrap her in a tight hug. "You don't have to go back right away, do you?"

Go? He'd worn her out to the point that she wasn't sure she could move. Who knew that even injured, Shane was a wild sex machine? She shivered at the memory of that third orgasm, her fingers curling into the hair on his chest. Nope, no way she was moving.

It took her another moment to realize he meant that he wanted her to stay here in California. Her eyes flew open, her head jerking off Shane's chest so fast she was surprised she didn't get whiplash.

"Stay…?" she asked, just in case she'd jumped to a crazy conclusion.

"I'm on convalescent leave for the rest of the week."

Fear and delight tangled together, making Lark lightheaded. She wanted to say yes. She wanted every single second she could get with Shane.

"I really should go home." For oh so many reasons, not the least of which was that she was in love with him. "I need to run the coffeehouse. And Sara is expecting me to go with her. If I don't, she'll realize we're, you know."

She swept her hand up and down between their bodies to indicate what he knew.

"You're keeping our relationship a secret?" The words were calm and easy, but Lark felt his body tense under hers.

"I thought that's what you wanted." And after he'd left, she'd realized how smart it was to keep their relationship on the down low. The last thing she'd wanted were sympathetic pats on the head like the ones she'd got when Eric had dumped her.

"You think that I've got an issue with people knowing we're—"

Lark frowned.

"See," she said, jabbing her finger into his chest. "You don't know what we are, either."

He wrapped his hand around her hand, lifting it to his lips. He slid his tongue along her finger, nipping gently before laying it flat on his chest again.

"How about we take a few days to see if we can both figure that out?" The quiet suggestion held no pressure, no coercion. But Lark felt pressured all the same.

"Okay," she heard herself say. "But only if Heather is okay handling The Magic Beans for a more few days."

"Great." Shane brushed a kiss over her lips, the move so sweet it brought tears to her eyes. "We'll have fun."

Lark settled her head back against his shoulder, snuggling closer when his arms tightened around her.

Yeah, she thought as she slid into sleep. If Heather could handle the coffeehouse, she'd stay. She was already in love with him. So a few more days together couldn't hurt.

Much.

9

IN HIS USUAL FASHION, Shane woke, instantly aware of everything around him. That he was in an unfamiliar hotel bed. That it was sometime after 6:00 a.m. and before nine. That his leg was stiff and sore, the blood throbbing around the bullet wound.

And that he was holding a warm, delicious female. Which was the reason for an erection as hard as concrete.

Without opening his eyes, he shifted his head to brush a kiss over the flowery silk of Lark's hair. She gave a low murmur, snuggling closer. His dick pressed tight against the sweet curve of her butt where it met the smooth flesh of her upper thigh. He skimmed his hand up her torso to cup one of her lush, full breasts, loving the feel of her in his hand.

Apparently she loved it, too, he thought with a sleepy grin as she wiggled, her legs straightening to press back against his.

That got his eyes open. Biting back a grunt, he grimaced and wrapped his hand around her thigh and shifted it a little so it wasn't plastered against his wound. Then, because his hand was already there, he grazed his palm up her sleek thigh, over her luscious hip and in between her legs.

When his hand reached its target, he gently ran his finger along her delicate folds. He felt her slowly, gloriously awaken. First her nipple pebbled a greeting against his palm in an erotic *good morning*. Then her breath changed.

She clamped her thighs tight so they gripped his fingers, her hips gently undulating against him.

He slid a testing finger inside her, smiling at the damp welcome. God, she was hot.

Unable to resist, he reached behind to grab a condom.

"Good morning," he murmured into her ear as he slid into her from behind. Sensations hit him like a sledgehammer as he thrust deep, his hands gripping her breasts as she gasped a return greeting.

As long as *Oh God* was a greeting.

She tightened around him like a vise, her orgasm milking his before he'd thrust more than once.

His breath labored, his heart pounding as if he'd run a marathon, he lost himself in her. He thrust, shuddered, then thrust again until he came. The climax was like an explosion, so powerful that it rocked him inside and out.

Damn. His arms wrapped tight around her, he pulled Lark as close as he could as the power of the orgasm slowly waned.

His face buried in her hair, he gave a shuddering breath and wondered when he'd ever felt this good. Never, probably. But now that he did, he was going to make damned sure he felt this good on a regular basis.

AN HOUR LATER, Shane ate the last forkful of his scrambled eggs, then jerked his chin toward Lark's plate. "You going to finish those?"

"I guess you worked up quite an appetite this morning," Lark said, her voice light and amused as she handed him her plate.

"I can't think of a better way to wake up," he said, setting her plate on his empty one and digging in. "You make me hungry."

"You make me happy," she said in return. Then her

eyes widened, her lips clamped shut and color washed her cheeks.

Shane grinned. He loved it when she did that.

He backed against the pile of pillows and snagged a piece of bacon off the tray Lark had angled between them. He didn't think he'd ever had breakfast in bed before.

"Do you do this often?" he asked, pointing to the bacon on the tray.

"Breakfast in bed?" Lark smiled. "Once in a while. My mom had a tray she used for special occasions. You know, like birthdays or when I'd get all As on my report card, that sort of thing."

"So this is a special occasion?" Shane asked, liking the idea that she wanted to celebrate a night of hot sex. "Are we celebrating by the orgasm? Because I think we need more food for that."

"I don't think that was ever on my mom's list of things to celebrate," Lark said with a laugh, shaking her head at him.

"No?"

"Nope. She'd bring me breakfast in bed when I was sick, though." Her smile faltered, pain flashing in her eyes before she looked down. "Or I'd bring it to her."

Lark's face was calm, but the grief was pouring off her in waves big enough to drown in.

Despite being raised in the same house as six women, Shane was miserably uncomfortable with emotional displays. Or, well, emotions themselves.

He knew she'd lost her mother within the past couple of years. Should he ask if she was still missing her? Shane contemplated the last piece of bacon. If he asked, that'd open the door to talking about emotions and stuff.

He hated emotions and stuff.

Bacon in hand, he glanced at Lark's composed expression and sighed. Dammit.

"It's rough, losing a parent," he said. Hopefully she'd agree, and then change the subject to sports or sex or something.

"I'm okay," she said with a little shrug and a smile meant to reassure. Instead, it made his chest ache.

"The two of you were close?" he asked, the words a little painful as they left his throat.

"Yeah." Her smile was sweet as she shot him a grateful look. "We used to spend a lot of time together. After she moved and I stayed in California, we'd see each other a few times a year and usually talk every week. Well, up until I opened my studio. I was really busy that last year."

Her words trailed off. Shane didn't need to hear the rest; he could fill in the blanks from her expression.

"Survivor guilt," he said quietly, studying the choice of muffins before choosing the apple one.

"What?"

"It's pretty common. When we lose someone, we tend to run through a dozen mental scenarios. We beat ourselves up over what we should or shouldn't have done. List all the real or imagined mistakes we made, carry blame like chains around our neck." He took a big bite of the muffin.

"Is that so?" she asked, her tone warning him that she didn't think much of his assessment.

Shane swallowed as he contemplated the rest of his muffin. This was why talking about emotions was always a mistake. He could let it go. He *should* let it go.

But Lark wasn't happy. Oh, she flashed joy every once in a while. Especially when he was inside her, Shane thought with a grin. But he'd seen the pain on her face when she thought nobody was looking.

He recognized that pain. By nature and training, he was hardwired to fix things.

"Yeah. That's so. Guilt's a complicated thing that hits people in different ways. Sometimes it's right there in your face. Other times it's a sneaky bastard, worming its way in and screwing up your life."

"And you would be speaking from personal experience," she said. Then she wrinkled her nose and laid her hand on his wrist. "You are, aren't you? Is this what you went through with your father?"

"Not so much." Seeing the irritated twist of her lips, Shane realized that he was going to have to open up if he was going to help her feel better.

For a second, he debated just letting it go. He could offer her a muffin or move the food to the floor and give her enough orgasms that she forgot what they'd been talking about.

With anyone else, he'd do exactly that.

But this was Lark.

He didn't know what he felt for her, but he knew it was big. It was important. She was important.

So no matter how much it hurt, no matter how much he hated it, if opening up helped her, he'd do it.

He took a deep breath, tossed what was left of his muffin on the tray, then took her hand.

"Back when I first joined the SEALs I lost a team member on a mission." He shook his head before she could ask for details. He couldn't tell her, and that's not what this was about, anyway. "He had a wife, two kids. I took it hard. I didn't think about it, but I started volunteering for extra duty, looking for a side job to bring in more money so I could send it to his family."

Shane shook his head as he remembered the blurry pain of those months.

"What happened?" Lark asked quietly. He knew she wasn't asking about the mission.

"Captain Donovan, that's Irish's dad, he sat me down and laid it out. He opened my eyes to the realities, explained survivor guilt, helped me find a healthier way to deal with it."

Lark's fingers closed over his for a second before she let go and pulled back. He could see that she was pulling in, too. Her face closed up; she leaned back enough to break the feeling of intimacy between them. Shane almost sighed, because he knew what she was going to say before she even opened her mouth.

"That had to be rough, and I'm sorry you had to go through it. But while I understand why you felt guilty in your situation, that doesn't apply to me." She offered him a smile that would have been warm if not for the chill in her eyes. "I feel a lot of emotions over the loss of my mom, and yes, one of them is grief. But not because I'm alive. That'd be silly.

"Enough downer talk at breakfast, though," she said before he could respond. "Let's talk about something else."

She didn't get it. Or rather, Shane realized, she was deliberately refusing to get it. Still, there was more than one way to accomplish a mission. Some just hurt more than others. But he knew that some things were like a poison, ripping and destroying the insides before they showed on the outside.

He didn't know why, and he definitely wasn't willing to try to figure it out. But he hated seeing Lark suffer. He wanted her happy. Happy and whole.

And he was going to help get her there.

"So how long are you going to stay in Idaho?" he asked, retrieving the half muffin and taking a big bite.

"What?" Surprise flashed in her eyes, a tiny frown

working between her brows before she shrugged. "I don't have a timetable."

"You went to help take care of your mom, right?" He made it an offhand question, keeping his focus on the bowl of fruit he was poking through.

"Yes."

"That had to be rough. But you stayed after she was gone? You must love the place."

"Not really."

Sure he'd pushed all the chunks of banana aside—he hated banana—Shane had to work to keep from grinning. Usually it was him who answered in monosyllables.

"No? You don't love The Magic Beans? Or is it Little Lake you aren't fond of? I get that," he said, pointing a fork-speared strawberry her way. "The town has its charm but it's a pretty tight-knit community. Sometimes it's hard to fit in."

"I fit in fine." As if realizing how defensive she sounded, Lark smiled. Well, it was more a twist of her lips than a smile, but Shane got the intention. "Little Lake is a lovely town, and everyone has been really nice. My aunt's a long-time resident, and they all liked my mom a lot. Half the town gets coffee at The Magic Beans on a regular basis."

"Sounds like you're fitting in well." Finished with the fruit, Shane peered at the tray to see if he'd missed anything. Since he didn't do it much, talking always made him hungry. "But you said you didn't love it there. How come?"

"I said not really," she reminded him. "I like it fine, and everyone has been great."

"But?"

When she gave him an exasperated look, Shane countered it with a friendly smile.

"But it's a big adjustment to where I was before."

"How?"

"Everything, I guess. The weather, the fashion, the entertainment." She waved both hands in the air as if to indicate *everything*. "In my studio, I worked from late morning until whenever my hands cramped. And I usually did my best work at night. The coffeehouse opens at five, so more often than not, I'm too exhausted at night to do anything except sleep."

"Did your mom ask you to leave your studio so you could keep the coffeehouse running after she was gone? Like in her memory or something? My dad's death was an accident, so it wasn't like he had time to pass on that sort of thing," Shane admitted, sorta wishing he had. Then he'd feel as if he'd done something in his dad's name. Maybe that's what she was doing.

"My mom was really proud of my career," Lark admitted, watching her hands instead of looking at him. "She loved showing off the pieces I made or the news clippings of my shows. She'd never ask me to give that up."

"But you did." His words were as gentle as he could make them, but he still saw her wince. He hated doing it, but he had to know her reasons for the choices she'd made. Once he had a handle on her why, he could come up with a plan to counter it.

Once he'd fixed her problems, she'd be happy.

Shane didn't know why that was so important to him. He just knew that it was, that he wouldn't be satisfied until that joy he saw in her eyes every once in a while became the norm.

"I didn't give anything up," Lark countered, her chin set in stubborn lines. "I made a choice."

"You chose to give up a career you were passionate about?" Shane shook his head. "I couldn't do that. I can't do that. Even though it's a pain in the ass with my family, I can't give up what I am."

"I haven't given up anything," Lark snapped before her expression changed. She blinked quickly to clear her eyes, her lips trembling as she said, "Except my mom."

"It sucks," Shane said. Before he realized he was going to do it, he mimicked Lark's oft-used gesture of comfort. He reached out to take her hand. "But that's my point. It doesn't matter if it's war, cancer or a car accident. There's always an empty place when we lose someone. A place that sometimes fills with guilt. As long as that guilt is there, it's impossible to deal with letting go."

"I'm dealing with it." Lark pushed off the bed, grabbing the breakfast tray so fast he barely had time to snag the last muffin. After slapping it on the desk, she turned to face him with her hands fisted on her hips.

He'd always thought the phrase *you're beautiful when you're angry* was a lame cliché. Not anymore. Her cheeks were flushed, her eyes shining like diamonds. And that deep breath she took made her robe slip a little off her shoulder, giving him hope that a few more breaths would get rid of it altogether.

"Why are we talking about this?" she asked, her words clipped.

"I thought you wanted to talk about something else," he pointed out.

"This wasn't what I had in mind." Then her forced smile slowly changed, taking on a wicked edge.

"Why don't I pick the subject this time," she said, just before dropping her robe.

His eyes trailing over the delicious length of her, Shane couldn't fault her choice.

THAT BREAKFAST-IN-BED conversation with Shane lurked in the back of Lark's mind long after she'd distracted him with a sexier topic. He'd obviously got her message, because he hadn't brought it up again. Not that silly theory about guilt, no mention of their deceased parents, not a peep about Idaho.

So why couldn't she get it out of her mind?

Alexia could probably explain it, being a psychologist and all. Lark glanced around the darling art studio, looking for the other woman.

The place was a charming mix of oil paintings, ceramics and blown glass. Worrying about a few random words that really meant nothing was stupid, she decided. That, and it kept interfering with the inspiration she was soaking up everywhere she went. Who knew that Coronado and San Diego would give her a million ideas and make her fingers itch to be in clay?

"What do you think? Does this say Happy Ever After?"

Lark rounded the glass display shelf to carefully inspect the ceramic vase Alexia Landon was holding up, admiring the deep red of the etched roses and the slick use of glaze on the rim.

"It's beautiful," she said, smiling. "Romantic and sexy at the same time, with a feeling of durability."

"Perfect," Alexia decided. She looked around the small art studio with a happy sigh. "This place is great. I can't believe I've lived here for almost four years and had no idea it was here."

"I have a pottery fetish," Lark admitted with a laugh. "I used to search out galleries, ceramic studios and pottery venues anywhere I went looking for inspiration."

And she was finding it this week. Lark's mind was bubbling over with ideas, designs, colors and techniques she wanted to try. This was the fourth place she'd visited since Sara had returned to Idaho five days ago. She'd been shooting for one a day. But other than taking Sara to the airport, Lark and Shane had spent the entire day in bed experimenting with various sexual positions in the name of finding the ones that didn't bother Shane's wound.

They'd had tons of sex the other three days, too, of course. But Shane had made a point of showing her around the area. As if he had some sort of insider information as to everything she liked, he'd shown her galleries, ceramic studios, an incredible Thai restaurant and three cute coffeehouses.

He'd wined her, dined her, romanced her and sexed her up in ways she'd never imagined. He'd introduced her to Mitch's wife, Livi, and their baby daughter. They'd gone to the beach, which even though it was autumn, had been gorgeous. They'd gone to dinner with his friend Blake, which was where Lark had met Blake's wife, Alexia.

The two of them had become shopping and lunch buddies, a good thing since despite his claim to being on convalescent leave Shane had had to report to base for the past two days for light duty.

Lark should have used that as an excuse to leave. She knew staying was a mistake. She was falling in love with Shane and falling deeper every second she spent in his company. Except she wasn't falling any less in love with him when they were apart. For the past few days, she'd lunched with Alexia, met Mitch's wife and Gabriel's soon-to-be fiancé, Tessa, as well as a few of the other wives of Shane's SEAL friends.

Between how comfortable she felt with the women, how much she liked their husbands, the gorgeousness of Southern California and the depths of the feelings she was discovering for Shane she was in serious trouble.

Then again, she was in trouble, anyway.

Why not enjoy herself before she had to deal with the pain. She lifted a soda-fired bowl, the golds and purples so vivid and intense that her heart ached. Lark sighed, realizing she was going to have pain on more than one level to deal with when she got back to Idaho.

"I'm going to get this, too," Alexia said, holding up a covered soup tureen in muted shades of pumpkin and avocado. "It'll make a great Christmas gift for my mom."

"Is this the sort of thing you make?" Alexia asked as she set the tureen next to the vase on the checkout counter. She smiled at the clerk, then resumed wandering the displays.

"Some," Lark admitted, looking around. She stepped over to the wall of kitchenware and gestured. "I've done a lot of earthenware and stoneware like this. I have a lot of experience with hand-built sculpture. But my specialty was thrown porcelain with carved mythical motifs."

As she mentioned each style, she found a display to show Alexia so the other woman could see what she was talking about.

"I'm envious," Alexia remarked, running her finger around the edge of a fluted bowl so thin it looked like paper. "To have the talent and skill to make such beautiful things is a gift. You must love your work."

Lark's smile dimmed.

She had, when it had been her actual work. Now it felt more like a hobby she never had time for. But even knowing that, she'd been avoiding Carlo's calls all week because she couldn't bring herself to give him a definite no.

"We should get going," she said, making a show of looking at her watch. "Didn't you have to get ready for Tessa's engagement party?"

"I can't believe how fast the day's flown by." Alexia added the fluted bowl to the items on the counter, murmuring to the clerk that she was ready. After paying, Alexia took the heavy bag of gifts and one of the owner's business cards before she and Lark headed out of the store.

As Lark held it open, she took one last, wistful look around the shop.

"I'm so excited about tonight's party," Alexia said as they walked down the sidewalk toward where she'd parked. "Tessa is going to love the box you found them. What did you call it?"

"A memory box." The intertwined flowers and glossy hearts had caught her eye. She'd made a series of them herself for a wedding boutique when she'd first finished college and had always thought they were a wonderful idea for newlyweds.

She just hoped Tessa liked it. The other woman had a smooth sophistication that would have been intimidating if it wasn't for her wicked sense of humor and sweet nature.

Still, she'd only met her two days ago.

"Maybe you should drop me off at my hotel. I don't know if it's a good idea for me to go to the party. After all, Tessa and Gabriel just got engaged last night," she said. "I mean, it's a special occasion that I'm sure they'll want to share with their friends."

"You have to go," was all Alexia said before unlocking her car.

Nerves bouncing through her system with enough force to make her nauseous, Lark settled in the passenger seat of the sporty little BMW, fiddling with the braided leather strap of her belt.

"It's a surprise party. It's not as if Gabriel and Tessa have an expectation of the guest list," Alexia said, her words rounded because she was using the rearview mirror to touch up her lipstick. "Besides, there are so many people who still want to meet you. This is the perfect chance."

Catching Lark's frown in the mirror, Alexia laughed.

"Worried?" she asked, turning around to take Lark's

hands in hers. "It'll be fun. You'll finally get to meet everybody and get to know all of Shane's friends."

"They'll all be there, hmm?" That did nothing to dull the nerves jumping around in Lark's belly.

"Most of them." Alexia patted Lark's arm before starting the car. "It'll be fun. You'll see. Besides, Shane wants you to be there."

Pleasure seeped in, muting some of her nervousness. She knew it was silly, but the way she felt these days, she'd do absolutely anything Shane wanted.

10

THE FOLLOWING AFTERNOON Lark found herself relaxing in the passenger seat of Alexia's sassy little two-seater as they sped down the freeway from San Diego to Coronado.

"This has been such a wonderful week. I'm going to hate to go home." While she'd never utter those words to Shane in case it inspired another of his far-fetched guilt lectures, Lark felt comfortable saying them to Alexia.

Somehow, in just a few short days, the other woman had become a wonderful friend. Actually, Lark really liked the wives of Shane's friends. What an eclectic, fun, upbeat group they were.

"I'm glad you enjoyed visiting Livi. I know she appreciated us coming by since she had to leave the party early last night." Alexia laughed. "I'm surprised she stayed as long as she did last night. I know how hard it is for her to leave Morgan."

"Can you blame her? That little girl is probably the prettiest baby I've ever seen. She has the perfect combination of her parents' features." Lark reached over to touch Alexia's arm. "It was a great way to spend my last day here. I'm glad you didn't have patients."

What could be better than a day that included cuddling a baby, exploring another gorgeous pottery studio, then being pampered with a facial, body massage and pedicure? She was going to miss all of this when she got back to Idaho.

Not as much as she'd miss Shane, though. Her fingers twining together in her lap, Lark looked out the window but didn't see anything. Instead, she remembered the special moments with Shane. His smile when he'd seen her at the party last night and the feel of his arms around her while they danced. The way he held her at night as they slept. The way he looked in his uniform, so polished and sexy. Or the way he looked in a T-shirt and fatigues, so strong and powerful.

Or the look in his eyes when he was poised over her—or under her, beside her, any position they happened to be in when he was inside her. His gaze was so intent, so deep just before he came. He had a way of staring into her eyes that made her feel as if he could see all the way to her soul.

She'd never have that again, she realized.

Shane wasn't going to visit her in Little Lake. Or even if he did, there was so much family drama there for him that he'd regret it. And she couldn't come back here. She just couldn't. It was too fun, too inspiring, too perfect.

One more visit—hell, one more day—and she'd never be able to leave.

Let it go, she told herself. She'd had her week and she was grateful for it. Whining about not getting more was just childish.

Grabbing for something—anything—to say that would distract her from the misery she felt, Lark cast a desperate look around the car.

"You know, this car would never make it in the snow," she observed, sliding an appreciative hand over the leather armrest.

"Luckily we get more sunburns than snow here in Southern California," Alexia said with a laugh. "I'll bet you see a lot of it in Idaho, though, right? It must make fabulous skiing. Aren't you close to a resort?"

"Mmm, Kelly Canyon is closest, but Sun Valley and

Bogus Basin aren't far. Too bad I don't ski," she added with a shrug.

Alexia shot her a surprised sideways glance, but instead of commenting on what a waste it was or suggesting Lark get thee to a ski instructor, she simply nodded.

"I'll bet there's a lot of other fun nearby. I visited Idaho once. It's a gorgeous state."

"It is," Lark agreed, although she was pretty sure she preferred California. Wincing at how disloyal that sounded, even in her own head, she changed the subject. "Have you always lived in Southern California?"

"Oh, no. My father is an admiral, so I was raised a navy brat. I've lived just about everywhere there's a navy port."

Lark relaxed again while Alexia went on to describe the various places she'd lived.

"You must have been terrified," she said after Alexia had shared the story of how she and Blake had got together, including his rescuing her from the crazed terrorist who'd kidnapped her.

"I was for a while," Alexia admitted. "But Blake saved me. Even now when I remember it, when I think about what could have happened, he's there."

The smile she shot Lark was filled with an enviable combination of love, trust and confidence. What was it like to have that with a man? To know that he'd be there, no matter what.

"How do you deal with it?" Lark heard herself asking. "Isn't it hard being the wife of a military man?"

As soon as the words were out she wanted to grab them back. What a stupid question to ask. It wasn't as if she were ever going to be in that situation, would ever have to know how to deal with it. Besides, she was better off thinking it was impossible. Hearing hints, tips or encouraging ideas would only make her want more.

"Being married to a military man is a lot easier than being the daughter of one." Alexia grimaced, then waved her hand in the air as if to erase that comment. "No, I should say that I'm a better wife to a military man than I was the daughter to one."

"I'd think it was the opposite." Then, because it had been weighing heavily on her heart and mind for the past few weeks, Lark added, "Especially if the military man was a SEAL."

As much fun as she'd had this week with Shane and his friends, the reality of what they did was always there, like another guest in the room. How did they all deal with it?

As if seeing that the question was more important than even Lark had realized, Alexia shot her a quick look, then pulled off the freeway.

Wishing she hadn't said anything, Lark waited until Alexia pulled into a Starbucks lot, parked and turned off the car.

"That was a bad question, wasn't it," she said, trying to smile.

"No. That was an important question and one that I think requires enough attention that I'd rather not be driving while I give it." Alexia's tone and smile were easy and upbeat, but the look in her eyes was completely serious as she turned to face Lark.

"It's not easy," she started by saying. "I actually split up with Blake when I found out he was navy, that he was a SEAL. I'd promised myself at a young age that I'd never live with everything that entailed once I had a choice."

"But you changed your mind," Lark said, her words somewhere between a question and a fact.

"Not really." Alexia shook her head. "I loved Blake. That wasn't a choice, either. Once I realized that I'd love him whether we were together or not, that I'd worry no matter what, everything became easier to accept. As some-one pointed out to me, living is a risk in and of itself. So why not be as happy as I could be while doing so."

"Blake's lucky to have you," Lark said. "All of the team seems to be lucky to have women who are so supportive."

"It's a two-way street," Alexia pointed out. "Don't think the guys don't have to make their own adjustments."

"Well, that's only fair."

They both laughed as Alexia reached for the ignition again.

"Is it hard?" Lark asked, her words quiet enough to be drowned out by the sound of the engine when the other woman restarted the car. But Alexia heard her.

"Hard? Yes and no. It's hard to be apart. It's hard missing him. But knowing he's doing what he loves, what he's meant to do, that makes it easier. Knowing the world is safer because of what he does, that makes me feel better." She gave Lark an easy smile as she put the car in gear. "There aren't many who can do what the SEALs do. Not many who are that good, that dedicated. I'd love Blake even if he weren't a SEAL. But I'm proud that he is."

"That's so sweet." And it really was. Alexia was right—there was so much to be proud of with these guys. Lark had thought she'd clued in after she'd researched SEALs when Sara had told her what Shane did. But now that she'd had a glimpse of the real thing she knew that she'd actually been clueless. She was so impressed by it that she'd almost asked Shane to give her a civilian-approved tour of the base.

But she hadn't, and she didn't even know why.

Instead of trying to figure it out—because what difference did it make with her going home in the morning—Lark focused on the scenery. With the ocean on one side and gorgeous homes on the other, there was plenty to distract her. Especially when she started thinking about ways to glaze a bowl so it looked like the ocean. Something with ragged edges and a swirling body. She was debating glaze options when Alexia turned into a residential street.

"What a gorgeous area," she said when the other woman pulled up in front of a condominium complex. The Spanish architecture was striking with its arches and iron fencing. A wide expanse of lawn separated each building, lush flowering plants a vivid contrast to the creamy gold stucco. "Is this where Tessa lives?"

Alexia had mentioned stopping in to see the newly engaged woman, but Lark had thought they'd call first. The gorgeous brunette and her sexy husband-to-be had been all over each other at the party the previous night. So who knew, they could very well still be celebrating.

"No, this is a surprise." The engine still running, Alexia turned to Lark. "First, today was fun. Actually this entire week has been great. I hope we'll get to see a lot more of each other."

"I hope so, too." She really did. But she didn't see how it was possible. She flew home in the morning. Trying to avoid the disappointment of that realization, Lark looked at the condominiums again.

"So what's the surprise?"

"C'mon." Getting out of the car, Alexia waited for Lark to join her on the sidewalk before striding toward the buildings. Her stilettos made a quick rat-a-tat-tat as she walked. "I'm so excited about this. I hope you love it as much as I do."

"Give me a hint." About to burst with curiosity, Lark hurried to keep up with the other woman's long strides.

"Hmm, a hint." Alexia waltzed right up to the front door of one of the condos and knocked. "How's this? I think you'll get good use out of that sexy little nightie you bought the other day."

Huh? Before Lark could ask what that was supposed to mean, before she could even blink, the door opened.

"Shane?" she exclaimed, joy bubbling through her like an explosion of champagne at the sight of him. "I thought you had to report to base. What's up?"

Dressed casually, his jeans emphasizing the length of his legs and his blue T-shirt perfectly highlighting his broad shoulders and impressive biceps, he was a treat indeed.

"See ya," Alexia said before he could answer. She gave Lark a quick hug and Shane a thumbs-up before sauntering back toward her car. With a confused frown, Lark watched her for a moment, then looked back at Shane.

Was this some sort of going-away party? She hoped she didn't cry.

"So what's up? Are you my surprise?" Since she'd be more than thrilled if he was, she stepped forward to brush a kiss over his lips. "I've got a few surprises for you if that's the case."

He grinned at her teasing, but his smile quickly fell away.

"Come on in," he said instead of answering.

A little worried at the unreadable look in his eyes, Lark made sure her body brushed against his as she walked through the door. But when he grabbed her arms and pulled her up for his kiss desire took over, washing the worry away.

"Well, hello," she said, forcing her eyelids open when he released her mouth. "If that's the surprise, I'm all for it."

"Actually there's a little more to it than this." He pressed his mouth to hers again, his tongue sweeping over her bottom lip. Lark's body warmed, heat stirring low in her belly. She pressed closer to Shane, the hard planes of his chest delicious against her aching nipples.

"Mmm," he murmured as he slowly lifted his mouth from hers. "You taste so sweet."

"Want another taste?" Lark invited with a naughty smile.

His sea-green eyes glowing with desire, he started to lean down again, then stopped. Lark felt her mouth actually slip into a pout when he pulled away.

"This probably isn't the place for that sort of surprise."

"Oh my God. We're not alone?" Lark blinked once before her eyes went wide. Her cheeks burning, she peered past him, trying to see into the rest of the condo.

Shane grinned, brushing his forefinger over her cheek before pressing a soft kiss there.

"Nah, we're alone. But I'm not sure for how long. And you know how it is. As soon as I start kissing you, I can't stop until I hear that little sob you make when you come."

"Shane," Lark gasped, her entire body burning now.

"C'mon," he said, laughing. "Let's see the surprise."

Taking her hand, he led her up a flight of stairs to the main living area. A low wall separated the top of the staircase and the large open area that appeared to be the living room. Frowning, Lark looked around in surprise, not only to see it unfurnished but that there was no sign of her surprise.

"What's this?" she asked, turning to Shane.

"Check it out. What do you think?"

Lark glanced around. The hardwood floors gleamed like satin, a perfect contrast to the deep blue walls. Lark tilted her head to one side, noting that the blue was really close to the color of her apartment walls.

Curious, she crossed to the French doors, the glass on either side of them spanning the entire wall. Beyond that was a small balcony.

"Wow," Lark gasped, staring at the stunning view. "It's gorgeous."

"Pretty sweet, right."

"Can you imagine the view during a storm?" Turning

around, she gave him a wide-eyed look and gestured toward the view. "It'd be wild."

"You like storms?" he asked, pulling her against him as if that news turned him on.

"Ones in nature, yes. Ones in life?" she clarified. "Not so much."

"I'll bet the ones in life aren't so bad if you have someone there to hold your hand while you go through them," he murmured before his mouth took hers.

Lark gave herself over to the kiss, letting it wipe away the spark of fear his words caused.

"Mmm," she said when he released her mouth. Then, afraid he'd say another one of those heart-wrenchingly sweet things again, she gave him a bright smile. "You'd better show me that surprise of yours soon or I might just strip you naked and have my way with you."

The knot in her stomach loosened when Shane grinned.

"Come on," he said, tilting his head toward the next set of stairs. "Bedrooms are up there, but I want you to see this first."

Lark followed him through the archway, past what was probably the dining room with darling built-ins and a blown glass chandelier overhead. Lark was very impressed, until they stepped into the kitchen.

"Wow," she breathed.

The coral of the walls and teal of the trim were echoed in the Mexican tile floor. The rich colors melded perfectly with the sleek wood cabinets and black appliances.

"I wonder how much of the cooking in here would be edible," Lark wondered, skimming her fingers along the vivid teal windowsill. "You'd think the view would be so distracting that everything would end up burned."

"Maybe they have curtains or what are those things

called? The slats that open and close when you pull a string?"

"Blinds?"

"Okay," Shane said with a shrug that let her know that she could have told him they'd hang fish scales from the window and he'd have said the same thing.

"You're so cute," she said. Unable to resist, she rested her hands on his chest, stood on tiptoe and kissed him.

He really was. Despite her nerves over whatever he was up to, Lark knew she'd never forget how sweet and adorable Shane was.

"You think I'm cute? Wait till you check this out."

Taking her hand in his, he led her to the room off the kitchen. Flicking the light on, he gestured to the empty space. "It's wired for two-twenty, the plumbing is roughed in and there is plenty of natural light."

She could see that. Even as she looked around, admiring the space and imagining how she'd set up a studio if it were hers, she wanted to run. Edgy panic danced down her spine. Why was he showing her this?

Because she had a sick suspicion and desperately hoped she was wrong, she stepped over to the window. Instead of the ocean, this window overlooked a garden filled with a riotous show of flowers.

"Pretty nice place, don't you think?"

"It's lovely." Facing him again, Lark tried to smile. Fingers crossed behind her back, she asked, "Does it belong to a friend?"

"Nah, although Tessa's apartment is a block over and Cade's place is less than a mile away."

"Convenient," Lark said, making her way out of the temptation of this room. But the kitchen was just as tempting, so she moved on to the living room, careful to keep her back to the windows.

"So what's the surprise?" she asked when Shane joined her. Then, because waiting and wondering was driving her crazy, she added, "Are you thinking about renting this place?"

Please, oh, please, let him want to rent.

"Actually, I've put a deposit down on it."

"To buy?" Little black dots danced in front of Lark's eyes, the room contracting as black walls closed in on her vision. "You're going to buy this place? I thought you liked living on base."

"Living on base is great, but I'm looking for a change," he said, lifting her hand to his mouth to nibble on her knuckles. Even as the gesture stirred heat low in Lark's belly, fear stirred, too. She could see the expectation in his eyes but couldn't handle asking the question she saw there.

"Change is good," was all she could say, though. She wet her lips, cleared her throat and tried to smile.

But her mouth wouldn't cooperate.

Oh, please, let him have had a sudden urge for neighbors who didn't wear uniforms. But she could see it on his face. He wanted to talk about the house more. She was afraid if he did, he'd get to the part about why it was so perfect for her.

But she could already see that for herself. From the colors in the kitchen to the view of the ocean to the completely darling, right-size, well-thought-out potential studio. It was perfect.

Too perfect.

"Why?" she heard herself asking.

"Why, what?" He frowned.

"Why," she repeated, waving her hand to indicate the surprise, the condo, the, well, everything.

Shane's frown deepened.

"You like it here—you're having fun. We're good together," he said slowly. Lark could tell from his expression how difficult it was even to say that. "You know, we have fun. And that's outside of bed. When you add in sex as good, as hot and intense as ours? We can't just throw that away. You know?"

"Mmm," she said, nodding because she did know.

She knew that Shane thought that's all they had. Hot sex. Her chest ached, pain gripping her belly as the impact of his words rocked her back on her heels. Desperate for privacy, knowing there wasn't any to be had, she walked over to the French doors, pretending to look out in order to hide her tears.

"Did you want to check out the back?" he asked, stepping over to join her. "The stairs just beyond the fence lead to the beach. We'll take a walk by the water."

Lark's heart melted at the idea of a sunset walk on the beach. She and Shane could hold hands. They'd stand, arm in arm, watching the sky bleed into the sea. He'd pull her tight against his body, the temptation of his erection would press into her belly, making her hot and wet. Then he'd kiss her. A mind-melting, body-tingling, heart-singeing kiss.

It would be perfect.

Which was why she couldn't.

She couldn't handle any more perfection.

Because she knew it wasn't real. Knew that even great sex wouldn't keep it alive. Not for long.

"Actually, I'd rather go back to the hotel," she said quietly, wiping her eyes before turning and pressing her fingers against the throbbing in her temple. "I've got a headache. Maybe a nap will help."

"Sure." His face unreadable, Shane watched her for another second before gesturing toward the stairs. "I'll give you a ride back."

"Thanks."

Lark made sure she looked straight ahead as she descended the stairs and headed for the door. When she reached the walkway she froze, her escape hampered by the fact that she didn't know where he'd parked.

"Over here," Shane said when he joined her, tilting his head toward the driveway. "I'm in the garage."

When she got into the passenger seat of Shane's Camaro, Lark gave in to the need to grind her teeth. Even the garage was great. One wall was lined with shelves that would be fabulous for storing ceramics, the other opened to the condo's entry.

"So tell me about the area," she invited after he pulled out of the garage.

As Shane filled her in on all the fun to be had in the area, Lark tried to tune out her longing. It was a good distraction that helped keep her from bursting into tears.

Shane was offering her everything she hadn't let herself believe she wanted.

A gorgeous beachside home with the perfect ceramics studio.

A reason to live in California where it was warm year-round and filled with galleries and opportunities and chances to reclaim the career she loved.

And most of all, Shane himself.

Oh God, she wanted Shane.

But she couldn't walk away from her responsibilities, from the only family she had left, to move here because she had the hots for a guy.

Even if the hots meant that she was in love with him.

Lark wasn't sure how she kept from breaking down on the drive back to the hotel. She had no idea what they talked about or how she'd managed to fool Shane into believing that she was okay. But somehow, she did.

She even managed to keep a smile on her face until he

walked her to her door, gave her a sweet kiss and told her to get some rest.

As soon as the door clicked shut, her face crumpled.

She had to get back home.

Hot tears pouring over her cheeks, Lark stuffed her clothes in her suitcase, not bothering to fold them. She'd have the front desk call a cab to take her to the airport where she'd catch the first flight to Boise.

Once she was home, she'd be able to think straight. She was simply out of her element here. Overwhelmed by the supposed perfection of everything here.

California was the land of illusions.

She just had to remember that.

She'd only imagined that those pottery studios and galleries were perfect.

She'd only thought the weather and scenery were perfect because they were famous.

And she'd only imagined Shane was perfect for her because he was so sweet. So honorable. So dedicated.

And because he had such an incredible body. Or because he understood her. Or most likely because the sex was so great.

SHANE MOVED THE bouquet of flowers from one hand to the other, feeling like a complete ass as he waited for the elevator. He had no idea why he was bringing Lark roses, except that he remembered his dad always bringing flowers home when he apologized to Shane's mom.

Shane wasn't sure what he was apologizing for, but that wasn't the point. All he knew was that his surprise had upset her. So he'd give her the flowers to show her he hadn't meant to upset her. Then he'd seduce her to show her how much he wanted her.

After that, he'd simply ask what was up. She'd tell him

what had bothered her, he'd fix it and everything would be fine. He stepped into the elevator and grimaced. He was pretty sure fine didn't mean she'd move in with him, though.

That was okay. He'd get there sooner or later. He'd rather sooner, though. If she stuck with her plan to head back to Idaho in the morning, convincing her would be a lot more difficult.

So would sex.

He didn't mind working harder, he thought as he stepped off the elevator. Doing without the sex might be a problem, though.

The flowers tucked into the crook of one arm, Shane reached into his pocket for the keycard to open Lark's door and slid it into the slot.

The light stayed red.

He pulled it out and tried again.

Still red.

Frowning, he knocked.

Then he knocked again, pounding this time.

One thing Shane had never been was slow. After another thirty seconds, he realized she wasn't going to answer.

Because she wasn't there.

Snapping the flowers against his knee, he stared at the door until he could unclench his teeth. Then he turned on his heel and marched back to the elevator, dumping the flowers in the trash on his way.

He'd check the front desk. That was simple diligence.

But he knew what they'd say.

Lark had left.

He guessed this was her answer.

11

"This sucks," Shane said, shifting his long legs out of the way so Mr. Wizard didn't land on them while doing his burpees.

"I'd rather take a bullet to the butt than get a Dear John letter," Mr. Wizard tossed out as he jumped up from his push-up, then slid into a squat.

"Kiss ass," Shane muttered right back.

Shane, the exercising fool, Irish and Romeo had just finished off three large pizzas and were kicking back with their beers in his living room.

He'd figured it was the best he could do for distraction, given that there were no missions on the books, no danger to dive into. A little booze, a little time with his buds, that's all he'd figured he needed to forget what happened.

Except it wasn't working.

He couldn't get Lark out of his head.

He couldn't get the feeling of going to her hotel and finding her gone out of his gut.

He couldn't get the emptiness out of his chest.

"It's rough," Romeo agreed. "Nothing sucks worse than woman trouble."

Right. Like God's gift to women had ever had trouble with them? Shane almost rolled his eyes except in his impaired state, he was pretty sure Romeo could kick his ass.

"I don't get it," he said instead. "We were doing great.

She'd handled my injury—she liked the wives. She even tolerated your ugly faces. Why'd she bail?"

"She didn't leave a note? A message? All the gifts you ever gave her broken in a pile in the middle of the room?"

As one, the three men gave the Wizard arch looks.

"You've had women dump you like that?" Irish asked.

"Never been dumped, but I've learned the hard way that women don't take breakups well. Had my gifts broken, my clothes burned and in one memorable case, my bedroom window broken." Mr. Wizard pulled a face before dropping to the floor. "It was memorable because I happened to be in bed at the time. Entertaining."

"You're such a dog," Irish said. But he was grinning.

"Yo," Shane called in an aggravated voice. "Can we get back to my problem here? You're supposed to be the experts on women—burned clothes and broken windows aside."

"Your problem is you blew it." At Shane's dark look, Irish shrugged. "Okay, fine. Run us through it. We'll figure it out for you."

Despite feeling as sick as a green recruit on his first time at sea, Shane walked them through it.

"Lark and I had a thing when I was home for my sister's birthday. I got called to duty unexpectedly because someone—" he shot Irish a sneer "—was having a baby. I left a note, headed back."

Both Irish and Romeo grimaced.

"What?" Mr. Wizard asked. "He left a note."

"Never mind. Maybe we'll find time to educate the two of you later. But right now we've got a problem to solve."

Shane shared a frown with Mr. Wizard, then shrugged and at Romeo's gesture, got back to the subject at hand.

"Right, so I committed the unholy crime of leaving a note, then returned to duty. We successfully orchestrated operation sugar rush. I was ambushed by a moron on our return." He glared at Mr. Wizard. "I woke up in the hospital with Lark standing over me. We hooked up again. She met everyone, got cozy with the wives, slid right into the groove. We connected."

He paused, pain jabbing at his chest as he remembered how well they'd connected. Or, at least how well he'd thought they'd connected. Obviously he'd been wrong.

"She wowed everyone at Romeo's hook-through-the-nose celebration, seemed to get my career and enjoy the area. I figured we had a good thing. Good enough that I thought it would last. So I found a place, surprised her and she bailed."

There it was. Short, and painfully to the point. Just as miserable now that he'd relived it as he'd been when it happened, Shane pushed himself to his feet and headed for the kitchen and another beer.

"Did you make any emotional declarations before you presented her with her new home?" Mr. Wizard asked as soon as Shane was seated again.

"A what?" Shane glared at the Wizard. "Dude, you keep saying things like that and I'm going to burn your clothes."

Romeo and Irish exchanged looks, and out of the corner of his eye Shane saw the Wizard shake his head.

"What?" Shane asked, exasperated that they were all acting as if they knew everything about women and he was a freshly hatched moron.

"You were raised by your mom, right? And have, what, four sisters?"

"Five." Shane shot Romeo an aggravated look. It's not like he needed a reminder. After all, he'd just got rid of one of them. "Why?"

"When was the last time we went somewhere that a

woman didn't throw herself at you?" Romeo continued ignoring the question.

Rolling his eyes, Shane set down his beer and made a show of pulling out his cell phone, opening the calendar app and sliding through the dates.

"That'd be yesterday when we went to the exchange to get batteries," he said, referring to the store on base. "Do you have a point?"

"I think I see where he's going." Irish shifted, sliding his feet out in front of him and steepling his fingers on his flat belly.

"Catch up, Scavenger," Romeo suggested, tilting his beer bottle toward Shane. "You've spent your life surrounded by women. The ones who aren't related to you take one look at that sweet baby face of yours and fall all over you."

"You're the legend, not me."

"Does he lose his legendary status once he's married?" Taylor wondered, his voice muffled because he was doing sit-ups.

"Once a legend, always a legend," Romeo said comfortably, nudging the exercising Wizard with his boot.

"His point is that with all your experience with women, he's surprised you don't know what's going on."

Shane knew a dig when he heard it.

"Just because I'm not a legend doesn't mean I don't recognize what happened," he said with as much dignity as a guy who'd just been dumped could muster. "It's simple. Guy has girl, guy likes girl, guy loses girl. See, I know exactly what's going on."

As if they'd rehearsed, Irish and Romeo both gave a slow, pitying shake of their heads.

Frustrated, Shane tilted his head back and closed his eyes. Why the hell had he thought it was a good idea to have his buddies over to help drown his misery? So far all they'd done was rib him, drink his beer and, in the Wizard's case, sweat on his carpet while exercising.

"Hey, Scavenger, can I take over your place when you buy the condo? You've got more room than I do."

"Kiss my ass," Shane muttered.

"No, I'm serious. I could set up my own gym in your living room."

Peeling his eyes open, Shane forced his wavering gaze to focus. He saw that Taylor was serious.

"You can't have my living room, dude. Remember? She turned me down."

"No, she didn't."

Shane turned his head so fast that the room did a three-sixty before he could pin his gaze on Mitch.

"Did to."

"That's not what Blake said."

"Holy crap. You guys gossip like a bunch of giggly teenage girls."

"Nope." Romeo jutted out his chin while giving a slow shake of his head. "I don't recall giggling. Did you giggle, Mr. Wizard?"

"Nope. No giggling here. Irish?"

"Nah. I haven't giggled since my wedding night." Mitch shot Shane an easy smile. "There goes your theory."

"You are still gossips." Shane sent a smirk right back. "Don't you have anything better to discuss than my life? You know, something like training or our next mission or maybe whether you should wear flats or heels with your uniform?"

"Cut him a break," Romeo said with a sympathetic look. "He's new at this."

"At having a few drinks?" Shane shook his head. "I don't do it often, but I'm not a newbie."

"He means at being in love," the Wizard said, his words a huff as he angled up to touch his elbows to his knees.

"I'm not in love." Horrified, Shane let loose of his beer, then had to dive to catch it before the bottle hit the floor.

"Hell, you aren't," Irish said from his comfy slouch.

"Shit." Looking as horrified as Shane felt, Romeo leaned forward to plant his elbows on his knees. "You didn't know? You went house shopping. You put down a deposit. You planned on moving her here and living together. And you had no clue?"

Shane opened his mouth to reply, then closed it because he didn't know what to say. He wasn't used to feeling stupid, and he definitely didn't like it.

"Maybe it's just sex," Irish said with a let's-humor-him look in his face.

Shane nodded. Yeah. They had great sex. Mind-blowing sex. The kind of sex that he could happily spend the rest of his life exploring.

Then he frowned. He wasn't a total dog. No way he was after Lark because he wanted to roll on her body.

"Nah." Watching him carefully, Romeo shook his head. "Sex is good, but good sex isn't that hard to find. It's gotta be the connection. You know, that she's tight with your family. It's a way to reconnect with them without having to deal with the drama."

Before Shane could even dismiss that one as ridiculous, Irish shook his head, now addressing Romeo instead of Shane.

"I don't think so. It's more likely the way he can talk to her. You know how quiet Scavenger is. That's gotta be a major turn-on, finding a woman who he can communicate with."

"Nah. You guys are reading too much into it," Mr. Wizard threw in, sitting on the floor with both arms resting on his knees. "It's all about the fun. You know, sometimes a guy just wants to have a good time."

Or maybe, Shane realized as his gut sank to his toes, it was all of the above.

"Damn." His ears ringing as if someone had smacked him upside the head, Shane's eyes widened.

Watching closely, his friends all grinned.

"You know what you have to do, don't you?"

With the same stubborn resolve that had fueled his entire life, Shane studiously ignored Irish's question.

He tried to hide in his beer but when he tipped the bottle back, nothing came out. He shook it, peered inside, then sighed.

"Empty."

"That was the last one."

He frowned at the Wizard, who was now doing one-handed push-ups and barely breaking a sweat.

"You're sure?"

"Yep. Threw the empty case away when I got my bottle of water."

Shane sighed. Then, knowing he had no choice, he pushed himself to his feet, wandered into the kitchen, turned the faucet on cold and stuck his head in the sink.

"I blew it," he admitted when he came back in the room and sat down. "I never said anything about—" his throat closed up but he forced the word out "—feelings."

"Then you know what you're gonna do?" Romeo asked, his tone a little more sympathetic than Irish's had been earlier. Probably because he wasn't married yet so didn't take pleasure in the hoops unmarried men had to jump through.

"Yeah." Shane scrubbed the damp towel over his face, wishing it would wipe away the pain of admitting, "I'm gonna have to beg."

HOW DARE HE?

How freaking dare he?

What kind of jerk wowed a woman with mind-blowing sex, showed her a great time, and then offered her the world on a platter?

Had she asked him to walk away from his responsibilities? Had she uttered a single complaint when, after asking her to extend her stay to be with him, he'd gone to work?

No. Of course not.

Hot tears burned her eyes, but Lark stubbornly blinked them back. She'd be damned if she'd cry anymore. Not over Shane. Not over him changing the rules, changing the game.

Forget him, her mind counseled. *You've been home five days. If he cared, he'd have been in touch. So it's over, it's done. Focus on what's here and now.*

Lark tried, she really did.

"C'mon, baby. You can do it this time."

Maybe it was crazy to talk to a lump of clay, but given that this was her fifth time trying to shape the bowl, she was willing to try anything.

Hunched over her wheel, Lark used her thumb to drill down into the center of the ball of clay, then using her knuckles she pulled it up until it was shaped like a shallow, deep-lipped dish.

"Lark, sweetie, can we talk?"

Her hand jerked, the side digging into the clay. What she'd hoped would be a dish collapsed into itself in a sad sort of plopping motion. For a second, Lark wanted to do exactly the same thing.

Instead, she swallowed her frustration, sucked in a sharp breath, then looked up to meet her aunt's horrified gaze.

"I'm so sorry," Heather breathed, her hands out as if

she wanted to try to pat the clay back into shape. "I should have knocked."

"It's okay," Lark assured her, grabbing the towel to wipe her hands. "I'd have locked the door if things were going well."

"It looked okay until I walked in."

Lark just shook her head and turned off the wheel. No point keeping at it when it was going nowhere. Especially in front of Heather.

A trickle of guilt slid down her spine, making it impossible for Lark to look at her aunt. Instead, she rose to wash her hands. She took the time to slather on lotion, the lavender scent soothing her senses as much as her skin as she tried to figure out what to say.

First she'd run out, giving her aunt only a few hours' notice to cover for her at The Magic Beans. Then she'd called and asked her to remain for a whole week, lying about why she wanted to stay in Southern California. And because she'd claimed she was gathering supplies and inspiration for the Bellissimo order, the minute she'd returned, her aunt had shoved her up the stairs with orders that she get to work.

So Lark had used that as an excuse to hide.

Ashamed and ready to face the music, she turned toward her aunt. Before she could say a word, though, Heather wrapped her in a tight embrace.

"What was that for?" Lark asked with a laugh.

"I hate seeing you down."

"I'm not down," Lark lied.

"Sure you are. But I have just what you need to get up." Heather lifted the plate off the table. "Lemon sesame seed cookies. Your mom's favorite."

They were her favorite, too. Her hand froze before she could reach for the plate, though. Eyes wide, she saw how many cookies were on the plate. At least three dozen, and she'd eat every single one. Some things were too tempting to resist, too good to know when to stop.

But she already had a heartache to deal with because of her lack of willpower. She didn't need to compound the pain with a stomachache.

"You didn't have to do that," she said, slowly backing away from the plateful of temptation. "I'm okay."

"Well, I had to do something." Heather set the plate back on the table so she could throw her hands in the air. "I've been so stressed lately. I've tried yoga, meditation, *Magnum P.I.* reruns and mah-jongg. Nothing helped. So I gave up and baked."

The guilt pouring through her now, Lark heard herself offering, "Did you want to start making sexy snacks for the coffeehouse again?"

"Oh, wouldn't that be fun." Heather laughed before waving the idea away. "But, no. They were fun for a while, but you were right. People got weird—the mayor was whining, and Mr. Harris in the nursing home? He had a little heart blip after a cookie binge. Claimed his libido went into overdrive. Truth is he started chasing Misty Lane around the rec room when she was there visiting her granny. I don't know if it was the exertion or the shock when Misty called him a dirty old coot that caused his blip, but whatever it was, I figured it's time to put the aphrodisiac recipes aside."

Thank God. But Lark kept the gratitude to herself. Instead, she crossed the room to take her aunt's hands in hers.

"What's the matter?" she asked, more than willing to jump into fixing Heather's woes instead of wallowing in her own.

Her eyes sad, her face showing her age, Heather gave a deep sigh before squeezing Lark's hands.

"Can we sit?"

Terror grabbed her so tight that Lark couldn't move, couldn't breathe.

"Are you okay? Are you sick?"

"What?" Heather's eyes widened as she realized what Lark was thinking before filling with horror. "Oh, sweetie, I'm as healthy as a horse. I'm just going through a sort of midlife crisis I suppose you'd call it. That's what I want to talk to you about."

"Okay," Lark said, drawing the word out as she studied her aunt's face. She didn't see anything reassuring, but she didn't see anything worrying, either. Still, she steeled herself as they passed her pottery wheel with its lump of clay on the way to her small living area.

She gestured to the chaise to indicate her aunt sit there. Pretending her pouf—with all of its Shane-induced memories—didn't exist, she grabbed the extra ladder-back chair from her dining set that she kept in here.

As soon as Heather sat, Lark followed suit then leaned forward.

"What's going on?"

"I'm worried about you," Heather burst out, her words the last thing Lark had expected to hear. "You've been so unhappy, sweetie. I hate seeing you this way. Raine would be so mad at me for letting you stew in such misery."

"No." Appalled that Heather could think that, Lark jumped up and hurried over to sit on the chaise, wrapping her arm around her aunt. "You've been wonderful. I don't know what I'd have done after Mom died if I didn't have you."

"But you're not happy." Before Lark could offer up any sort of lie, Heather squeezed her hand. "Don't try to tell me otherwise, Lark Lavender Sommers. I've known you since the day you were born. I know you and I know happy. And you're not happy."

"Should I be?" On the verge of listing all of the lousy things that had happened, Lark clamped her lips shut. Because most of Heather's experiences had been just as lousy.

"Happiness is a choice," Heather said, reciting one of Raine's favorite sayings. "Of course, sometimes it's also elusive and we have to work hard to find it."

Lark frowned, remembering all of the rough times they'd had after her dad had died, the month they'd lived in the Bronco because they couldn't afford an apartment. She remembered the miserable cancer treatments, how sick her mom had been after each chemo session. And through it all, Raine had found things to smile about. Something she'd always told her daughter to do, too. Especially in the end.

"Mom wouldn't be angry with you. It's me she'd be disappointed with," Lark said, her words filled with shame.

"Oh, no. No no no, sweetie. You are doing your best to do what you think is right. But maybe it's time you tried rethinking some of your choices."

"What do you mean?"

"Three years ago, if you had to choose between pursuing the career you studied for and continuing to build a name for yourself or running a coffeehouse, which would you choose?"

"But—"

"No." Heather lifted her hand to stop Lark from speaking. "I'm not finished."

Lark wrinkled her nose and shut her mouth.

"In addition, ask yourself this. Do you prefer living in California or in Idaho? Or how about this, does spending hours a day with other people energize you or drain you?"

Lark grimaced, knowing she didn't have to answer since they both knew what she'd choose in all three cases.

Maybe Shane had been right.

"Someone suggested that I'm suffering from survivor guilt." Unable to meet her aunt's gaze, Lark looked at her pottery wheel and swallowed hard. "But that'd be crazy, wouldn't it?"

"Not as crazy as a ninety-year-old man thinking a cookie was going to get a twenty-three-year-old woman to jump in the sack with him."

Lark laughed as she knew Heather had intended, then met her aunt's eyes.

"I let her down."

"You never let her down. Your entire life, you were a joy to your mother. She was so proud of what you were doing. So thrilled with your success." Heather's smile shifted, her face becoming as stern as a woman with lavender hair and a nose ring could look. "She wouldn't expect you to take on her debt, to give up your dreams to live hers, though."

"I'm not…"

Her denial trailed off at the look on her aunt's face.

"I felt like I'd failed her," she admitted, the words coming out a hoarse whisper. "I should have come as soon as she said she wasn't feeling well. If I'd had more money, maybe we could have tried other treatments. I should have been able to find something—anything—that would help save her."

"And you think that was your responsibility? And that you should give up your own dreams to make up for that? That your mother would want that for you? And that somehow, in some way, that will make you happy?"

Lark wiped her wet cheeks and considered Heather's words. She couldn't think of any way to respond without sounding like an idiot, so she just shrugged.

"Good. Obviously you know how ridiculous that type of thinking is." Heather patted Lark's leg. "So let me say this, and please, Lark, believe that I know what I'm talking about. Your mother would be furious if she knew that you gave up your career, that you felt responsible for her debts—and more, that you feel in any way responsible for her death. She'd hate that."

"I loved her so much," Lark said, the words coming out in a hoarse whisper as she gave in to the grief and laid her head on her aunt's shoulder.

"I know, sweetie. I know."

Lark wasn't sure how long they sat there crying together. But finally her aunt pulled away, wiped her face and shook her head.

"Well, that's enough of that," she said. "At least it is as long as you'll stop this, what did you call it? Survivor guilt?"

Lark winced at having Shane's term thrown back at her. Just hearing it made her think of him, remember how sweet he'd been while showing her around the condo. How good he'd looked when she'd first opened her eyes in the morning to find him staring down at her. How sexy he'd been in his fatigues, the silver chain holding his dog tags glinting around his neck.

And she'd walked away from all of that.

Not that she'd have been able to enjoy it for long, she told herself. How had he put it? Sex as good, as hot and intense as theirs shouldn't be thrown away. But heat like that, it burned out eventually. And as painful as it had been to walk away from Shane and that gorgeous condo, it would have been even harder later.

"I'll quit feeling guilty if you quit stressing," Lark told her aunt as they both got to their feet.

"Oh, that reminds me." Heather clapped her hands together. "This was important, and I'm glad we talked. But it isn't what I came here to discuss."

"You didn't stop by to lecture and feed me cookies."

"I'm a multitasking wonder." Straightening her shoulders and putting on what Lark assumed was her most serious expression, Heather cleared her throat. "I'd like to take over The Magic Beans."

Lark shook her head, sure she'd misheard.

"You what?"

"I'd like to take over running the coffeehouse. Oh, I can't afford to straight out buy it," Heather said, waving her hand in the air to dismiss that craziness. "But I'd be happy to take your place. I'll take over the mortgage payments, manage The Magic Beans and work the shifts you've been working. That frees you to stay up here and work on that contract with Bellissimo. Or if you wanted, to move back to California and pick up where you left off."

Shock kept Lark mute. Just as well because apparently Heather wasn't finished.

"Now, don't think I'm trying to push you out, because I'm not. I would love nothing more than to have you stay here and I could work for you instead. But I think we both know that managing a coffeehouse isn't your life's path, sweetie."

A dozen thoughts sprang to mind, followed by another dozen doubts. But only one really mattered right now.

"Why?" Before Heather could answer, Lark frowned. "Is it because you think I'm unhappy? Because making yourself unhappy instead isn't the answer."

"Oh, no, I'm no martyr," Heather insisted, waving the suggestion away as she would an irritating fly. "I really want this. I didn't know how much I enjoyed running The Magic Beans until I had it all to myself while you were in California last week."

"But you'd worked there before. You and Mom ran it together for the first few months, didn't you?"

"We did, yes." Heather wrinkled her nose. "Well, actually Raine ran it and I worked for her. But as my many employers will attest, I don't do well as an employee. Besides, I was still working part-time doing massages, and Raine and I had so many differing ideas on what to do, on how to run things. It just seemed better that I go back to massage full-time and leave the business to her."

"You really liked running the place?" The very idea baffled Lark.

"I did, I really did. And that's without serving even one sexy muffin." Laughing, she reached over to pat her niece's cheek, heading out of the room. Lark followed a little more slowly.

"You think it over, sweetie. I'll cover your afternoon shift at the coffeehouse and give you time to decide what you want to do."

As much as Lark appreciated her aunt's offer, she knew she wouldn't be returning to California. There were too many memories, too much pain. Besides, even with the commission she'd make if she ever made anything for the Bellissimo job, she wouldn't receive payment for months and she had squat for savings. She simply couldn't afford to move back. But the rest, she'd definitely think about.

"I love you, Aunt Heather," Lark said quietly when her aunt reached the door.

"I love you right back." With that and a wave, Heather was gone.

Her easy declaration of love was still echoing through Lark's mind when she heard Heather greet someone on the landing. Lark stepped into her pottery room just as Sara was about to knock on the door.

"Oh, hey, hi," Sara said, her smile shining through the

screen. "I just saw Heather. Is everything okay? She was smiling big enough to be seen from the moon, but her face was splotchy like she was crying or something."

"She's okay." Lark motioned her friend in, figuring she could use her advice about Heather's suggestion. "Want a drink and a cookie?"

"Heather's cookies?" Sara practically bounced into the kitchen. Lark followed, a little slower. "Mmm, lemon sesame seed."

"What's up?" Lark asked, handing her friend a can of soda.

"I'm here on a mission." The pretty blonde giggled. "You know, like what Shane does? I figure you know all kinds of things he does, since you guys have a thing going on."

Knowing Sara would just keep talking, Lark took a drink of her juice instead of answering. It was hard to swallow past the knot in her throat, though.

"So, like, I told my mom that you and Shane were, you know, like sweethearts. She was so excited." Sara paused to take a swig of soda and missed Lark's stunned expression. By the time she'd resumed talking, Lark managed to close her mouth.

"Actually everybody is excited. Not surprised, though, since we all saw the two of you at my birthday party. Well, my mom was a little surprised, but that's because she was mad at Shane. She's not anymore, though. He called her the other day and they sorta made up over the phone. Not all the way, but it was a start. It'll get better when she can hug him in person. That'll be soon, I hope. If you guys are a couple, then Shane's sure to come visit, right?"

"Sara—" Lark started to explain that she and Shane weren't a couple but Sara had only stopped to take a breath, not to let anyone else speak.

"So, here's the thing. Carly had this idea. Mind you, this is from her, not me." Sara paused and bit her lip. Then she sat in the chair opposite Lark. "Um, so how much do you like Shane?"

Lark frowned. "That's Carly's thought?"

"No, that's my question. See, I'm not sure how I feel, exactly, about Carly's thought. I mean, I know she's thinking of Mom with her thought, and since she lives right next door to her, having a happy mom would definitely play into her thinking, you know?"

Lark rubbed her fingers against her forehead but it didn't help that make any better sense.

"Okay, what are your thoughts?" she asked, figuring that would cut through at least some of the confusion.

"Mine?" Sara bit her lip again. "Um, well, that's why I asked how much you like Shane. Because if you like him a lot, my thoughts are different than if you just want him for wild monkey sex."

"Wild…"

"Monkey sex," Sara finished with a nod. "See, if it's just sex, then Carly's idea will work great. But if it's more, you know, if you care about Shane for more than his love stick, then it's a totally crappy idea."

"Love stick?" Lark started to giggle, then laughed even harder when she imagined Shane's face if he'd heard his pride and joy being called a love stick. "Where do you come up with these things?"

"Just something I read on the internet." Sara shrugged. "Well?"

Laughter dying, Lark looked at her drink for a moment.

"Why don't you tell me what Carly thinks first," she countered.

"Fine." Sara heaved a huge sigh. "Carly thinks you should use your feminine wiles to convince Shane to leave the navy. That way he'll move back here, Mom will stop freaking and everyone will be happy."

"I couldn't do that," Lark protested. "He loves what he does and he makes a difference in the world. I'd never try to manipulate him into giving that up."

"But if you cared about him, wouldn't you worry?"

Lark stared at Sara for one long moment before she had to sit back down.

"My worrying isn't the issue. Neither is your mom's or yours or anyone else's. Shane has to follow his own heart and do what makes him happy. Caring about someone doesn't mean that they have to give up their life for you."

As she said the words, Lark felt as if she'd just got a big smack upside the head. Even more than Shane's comments about guilt or her aunt's argument about what her mom would want—those words made Lark see what she'd been doing.

Worse, what she'd done. She'd given up Shane because she was martyring herself to her mother's memory.

"Yep," Sara said. When Lark met her gaze, the younger woman gave a sage nod. But there was a hint of sadness in her eyes. "You do care about him. I knew it."

"I do." Lark took a deep breath, wet her lips and finally admitted what she hadn't even let herself believe. "I'm in love with him."

12

It HAD BEEN five hours after Sara had left, wide-eyed and silent, and Lark still couldn't get her own confession out of her head. She'd gone down to the coffeehouse and washed dishes. When Heather shooed her away after an hour, she'd come upstairs to look at the books to see if dumping the business on her aunt was realistic. But the numbers hadn't made any sense.

Then she'd turned to her once-tried-and-true method of finding peace of mind. Her pottery wheel. But as she watched her third attempt at a bowl sink flatter than a pancake, she gave up.

Glaring at the clay, Lark tugged a chunk loose and rolled it between her fingers until it resembled a long snake.

Why had she told Sara that she was in love with Shane?

And more to the point, what was she going to do about it.

She'd walked out on Shane. Sure, he seemed to think that all they had going on was great sex, but he'd liked it so much that he was willing to buy a condo so she could move in with him. He'd chosen a place that he'd realized she'd love, that had the perfect potential pottery studio. He'd introduced her to his friends and made her a part of his life.

Maybe he didn't love her, but he cared about her.

With time, caring could grow into love, couldn't it?

Except she'd run out on him without a word. Unless the lame words on that note counted. Since she'd guess Shane didn't consider them sufficient, going back and trying to convince him to give them another chance was probably useless.

Lark glanced down at the clay in her hand. Her frown faded when she saw that she'd wrapped the coils around themselves until she'd made a heart. That's what mattered, wasn't it?

Lark stared at it for a few moments before sighing.

She loved him.

So of course she had to try.

She just had to figure out how she was going to do it. Did she call him? Text a message? Send an email?

She didn't know what to do.

Lark set the heart on her wedging table, then looked around. She was too churned up to throw clay, so she got her cleaning caddy out from under the kitchen sink.

She'd use her mother's time-honored method of working off frustration by cleaning. Raine Sommers always said that busy hands made for a peaceful mind. And a peaceful mind was fertile ground for well-thought-out answers.

And Lark really needed some answers.

She figured by the time she'd cleaned the place from top to bottom, back to front, she'd either have a clue what to do or she'd be too tired to worry about it. Either way, the place would be clean and shiny.

Lark didn't let herself think about what to do with The Magic Beans or dream about how great it would be to live with Shane, even if it meant no emotional commitment.

Instead, she let her mind empty. *Focus on the positive*, she told herself as she finished wiping down the refrigerator shelves. *Be open to belief*, she chanted as she scrubbed the bathroom floor. *Have faith in the possibilities*, she thought as she washed the clay residue out of her wet box.

Screw it all. She wanted Shane.

Lark flipped off the water, gave the box a cursory shake and grabbed the lid. Just as she turned from the sink, there was a knock on the door.

Sara or Heather. Babbling or cookies.

Not wanting to deal with either, Lark debated ignoring it. But when the knock came again, she rolled her eyes, tucked the wet box under the wedging table and yanked the door open.

"Wha…"

Her words trailed off when she saw who it was. Lark blinked a couple of times, sure this was a cleanser-induced hallucination.

"Shane?"

"Lark," he returned, leaning against the door frame and grinning at her.

"What are you doing here?"

And why did he look so damned good.

"We didn't actually finish our conversation last week," he said before inclining his head. "Why don't I come inside and we can finish it now."

But she wasn't ready to finish it.

Lark looked down at herself, double-checking to make sure she was wearing her ratty jeans with the hole in the knee and a threadbare T-shirt so thin that her bra showed through.

No, she definitely wasn't ready.

She looked at Shane again, noting his easy smile at odds with the intense expression in his eyes. She realized that he was changing the rules again. But maybe that wasn't a problem if she was a part of making the new ones.

"Come in," she invited, her mind racing to find the right thing to say, the right way to say it so he didn't go running right back out.

She absently noticed how easily he crossed the room, not favoring his left leg at all. His jeans skimmed the length of his long legs with no ridges or bumps, so she assumed he'd had his bandages removed.

Lark tried to steady her breath, but her heart was pounding as if she'd just run a mile. So many emotions tangled inside her that she could barely identify them. Delight, pain and fear were clear, though.

Delight because he was close enough to touch, near enough that she could smell the warmth of his cologne, could simply reach out to slide her hand down the gloriously hard planes of his chest.

Pain because she'd missed him so much, and fear because she knew now that he was here, that they'd have to settle things. One way or another, they'd be over.

And fear of what he was going to say. Was he angry with her for leaving? Trying not to be obvious, she inspected his face. He didn't look angry.

Shane tossed her a friendly smile as he walked over to her wedging table to look over the only decent thing she'd made since coming home, a sculpture drying in readiness for the kiln.

"This is great." He pointed to the sailor cap-wearing seahorse she'd sculpted. "Is it for Morgan?"

Blinking with surprise at his perception, she stepped closer. She was careful to keep a little distance between them so she didn't forget her resolve and grab him.

"It'll be a piggy bank. Once it's leather hard, I'll cut a slot in the cap and the hole in the bottom, then glaze it. It'll be rich shades of teal and purple with mother-of-pearl accents." Lark's words trailed off as she shrugged. "Sorry, I'm babbling."

"You're kidding, right?" Shane laughed. "You do know my sisters, don't you?"

Lark's lips twitched.

"Livi will love it," he said. "Morgan, too, when she's old enough to know what it is."

"You think?"

"I do. You have a gift."

The look in his eyes was so intense, so sexy that Lark's stomach slid into her toes, nerves fizzling out in the wash of passion.

"Thank you." Swallowing to get the words past the knot in her throat, Lark nodded and pretended he hadn't uttered the big *L* word. "I was lucky to be good enough at it to make a living with it. Especially since it's something I really enjoy and was happy to focus my life on."

There were so many emotions tangling up inside her that Lark couldn't meet his eyes any longer. She looked away, her gaze landing on the heart she'd made earlier.

She'd promised herself that she'd try, that she'd do her best to give them a chance.

Shane had made it so easy for her. She didn't even have to pick up the phone. Now it was time to do her part.

"I really love pottery. And I loved devoting myself to making a living at it," she said, lifting her gaze to his, letting him see whatever he wanted in her eyes. "But I tried to set it aside. I told myself it was because I was being responsible. That I owed it to my mother."

Shane didn't speak, but his expression was so sweet and supportive. So she took a deep breath, reached out and took his hand.

"But you were right. I was so hung up on losing my mom, so angry and hurt and miserable without her, I was really just punishing myself." Lark paused, waiting to see what he'd say.

But Shane didn't gloat; he simply nodded with a look of understanding. That was one of the things she loved about him, she realized. He never spoke unless he had something to say. Instead, he watched; he absorbed. And he empathized. Because he did, it made it easier to finish her confession.

"I ran away because I was afraid," she said quietly. "Standing in that beautiful condo, you were offering me so much, almost everything that I could want. But taking it meant facing my pain. More, it meant giving up that pain. I couldn't do it."

His eyes so distant he could still be in California, Shane slowly nodded.

"You said *almost*," he pointed out.

"Okay." Confused as to why that one word was so important, Lark pushed her hand through her hair and shrugged.

"I'm just clarifying." His smile said he understood her confusion. Then he shifted his gaze to the shelf next to her wedging table where she stored the completed pieces of pottery.

"You do amazing work. I guess it's a gift, your talent." He ran his hand over the bowl she'd taken from the kiln that morning, the last thing she'd made before rushing to his hospital bed. His finger followed the swirls in the glaze but his eyes locked on hers.

"You know what else is a gift?"

He paused, lifting his brows as if waiting for Lark to respond. Totally confused by the change of subject, though, she didn't know what to say. So all she could do was shrug.

"Love."

Shock slammed through her so hard that Lark had to grip the table to keep from falling down. Legs trembling, heart pounding, she shook her head. She couldn't have heard him right.

"I suppose it's like your talent," Shane continued as if

he couldn't see her reaction. "You can nurture it, work with it and grow it. You know, really make something from it. Or you can ignore it. Just let it go and move on with your life. You can probably even convince yourself that you're okay without it."

What was he saying? She knew what she wanted him to be saying. But this was Shane. He didn't talk about emotions. She remembered his exact tone when he'd claimed that discussing feelings was a waste of time. So why was he talking about them now? Unless something had changed.

Terror and joy spun through her so fast that Lark was dizzy. Because terror was stronger, because her heart didn't have enough joy to waste, she didn't let herself read what she wanted in his words.

Instead, she shook her head.

"I don't understand what you're saying," she admitted, putting all of her hope, all of her love into those words. Because she knew what she wanted him to be saying, and she wanted to make it as easy as possible for him to say it. And now, she realized with a mental sigh, she was babbling in her head the way Sara babbled out loud.

SHANE GRIMACED AT the looks rapidly chasing each other across Lark's face.

Trust, shock, love, embarrassment.

It was the last one that hit him hardest as he realized that if he blew this, he'd never see that expression she made when she said something she wished she hadn't.

He'd been so afraid of his feelings that he'd hurt hers.

Damn, he'd been an ass.

"I'm trying to say that I'm in love with you," he told her.

He was pretty sure she couldn't have looked more surprised if he'd stripped naked, jumped on her pottery wheel and done the twist while singing "The Star Spangled Banner."

"I'm sorry," he said quietly, "I should have told you, but I didn't realize that what I felt for you was love. I just knew it was more than anything I'd experienced before."

"You think you love me?" she repeated, her words so faint that Shane felt as if he were reading her lips.

"No. I know I love you."

Instead of launching herself into his arms and stripping them both naked as he'd hoped, she just stared.

"At first, I thought it was just really hot sex," Shane said, rubbing his thumbs over her palms. "Because, well, it was really hot."

Her eyes warmed, amusement flashing for a second.

"Then when it hit me that you were going to leave, to come back to Idaho, I realized I couldn't let you go. I told myself it was still the hot sex, of course."

"Of course," she repeated, nodding.

Shane frowned for a second because she looked as if she'd done the exact same thing. He couldn't fault her for it, but his ego still recoiled at the hit.

"After you left, I realized it was more. I was going to wait until I could get a couple of weeks' leave, then come here and sweep you off your feet." He shrugged. "But Sara clued me in and I knew I couldn't wait any longer to tell you how I felt and how important you are to me."

"You wanted to sweep me off my feet?" She frowned. "I thought you'd be mad that I left like I did."

"I was, but not at you. I was mad at me. I wasn't willing to look at what I was feeling, and definitely wasn't ready to hear what you were feeling. So I tried to steamroll you with the condo surprise."

"It was a lovely surprise. If I hadn't been wallowing

in that guilt you mentioned, I'd have seen the gesture for what it was."

"And what's that?"

"A chance."

Even as Shane nodded, he knew that didn't sound right. But before he could pinpoint what was wrong, she stepped closer. Close enough for her body heat to wrap around him like a hug, for her perfume to fog his senses.

"You really love me?"

He grinned.

"Yeah. I really do."

"I love you, too." Her dark eyes were filled with a promise that made Shane feel warm inside. Then she frowned a little and shook her head. "Wait a second. What do you mean, Sara clued you in?"

"She called. Told me that I was a stubborn idiot and if I didn't get my dumb ass here and fix things that she'd make my life a living hell."

Lark's mouth dropped for a second before her eyes flashed.

"You came because your little sister called you?"

"No. I came to tell you I loved you. Instead of waiting for leave, I swapped duty with the Wizard. I was coming one way or the other. My little sister's kick in the ass just reminded me that time isn't to be wasted."

"You're right." Lark nodded. "When I realized I loved you, I thought that was it. I'd find a way to contact you, apologize for what I'd done and that then everything would be fine."

"But?"

"But I tried to tell myself that the problems I had were just me creating issues that would keep us apart because of the whole guilt thing."

Shane nodded.

"But they are real issues."

"Yeah. They are real." Lark wet her lips. Then, as if she couldn't handle touching him and telling him at the same time, she pulled her hands from his and stepped away.

"When you left that morning, I told myself that even though it hurt, that I had to be okay with it because you hadn't broken any rules."

"What?" Baffled, Shane shook his head and racked his brain. "What rules?"

"You know, relationship rules." Lark looked surprised at his blank expression. "You don't know about the rules of relationships?"

"I know about the rules of combat. You'll have to fill me on in the others."

"There are different rules for different situations. Like there are no rules about saying goodbye or keeping in touch in a one-night stand like there are in a relationship."

Shane scowled.

"We didn't have a one-night stand."

"Well, more like two nights in our case," Lark said with a laugh. Her smile disappeared at the look on his face. She threw up one hand as if that would keep him from being pissed. "Remember, I'm talking about that first time. The one when you left with just a note on my pillow."

Shane scrubbed his hand over his short hair and sighed.

"Yeah, okay. That was a stupid move. No wonder you're calling it a one-night stand."

"Hey, I thought we were done with the guilt stuff." Lark held up one hand again. "There was no reason for either of us to think otherwise."

"Okay," he said slowly. He frowned, but couldn't argue with her logic. He did vow to get hold of these rules of hers, though, so he could make sure he didn't break any in the future. "Do the rules have anything to do with your issues?"

"Kinda." Her expression was pained, as if she'd just been told she had to jump off a cliff. She knew she had to do it, but knew it was going to hurt, too.

Wanting to make it easy for her—and for him, since he had to know—Shane asked, "Is it my career?"

He held his breath.

"Kinda."

Pain jabbed him in the gut. Sara had warned him of Carly's bright idea, to get Lark to convince him to leave the navy. But he hadn't thought she'd do it.

"It comes back to that note," she said quietly, her eyes dark and sad. "I realized that if we were together that it'd always be that way. You'd always be leaving at the drop of a hat."

"Not always," Shane disagreed quickly. "There were extenuating circumstances on that mission. It's rare that I'm called to duty without warning like that."

He couldn't tell if his answer had made any difference because all she did was nod.

"But sometimes, even when you get that advanced notice, you're gone long periods of time, right?"

HE'D SEEN ENOUGH resentment and anger in his family's faces to easily recognize it. But it wasn't resentment he saw in her eyes.

It was fear.

Damn. Why hadn't he seen it? She was still grieving over losing someone she loved. And here he was asking her to open her heart again.

Needing to reassure her, Shane closed the space between them. Even though he knew she wanted distance, he needed to touch her. So in the spirit of compromise, he only took one of her hands in his instead of both.

"Lark, I'm a SEAL. We're the best for a reason. I'm not going to lie and say what I do doesn't have its dangers. But we train for every mission, we do everything we can to minimize the risks." He knew he was getting through; he could see it in her eyes. But he knew, too, that he couldn't fill her with hot air, either. "I won't promise you that nothing can ever happen. My leg is proof of that. And you're right. There will be times when I'm deployed that we might not see each other for weeks or even months. But there are upsides, too."

"The hot sex again?" she asked, smiling even though her eyes were gravely serious.

"Yeah, that. Most of the time we'd live in California. That's my PCS, my home base. You'd be able to hang out with a lot of the wives like Alexia and Livi. You'd—"

Lark gently pressed her hand to his mouth to stop him.

"I'd be with you as much as possible," she said. "That's what matters."

Damn. She was so perfect.

"I can't take away all of life's problems and I can't promise that there will never be another storm," he said, lifting both of her hands to his lips. "But I can promise to do my best to be by your side during the storms, and to try to protect you from them if I can."

Her eyes flashed with surprise before her face crumbled. Well versed in crying women thanks to his sisters, Shane pulled Lark into his arms, rubbing gentle circles over the small of her back while murmuring soothing noises.

"This is stupid," she murmured against his chest.

"Me loving you is stupid?"

"No." She raised her face to give him a shocked look. "I meant crying over you loving me was stupid."

Shane was pleasantly surprised to see that she didn't get all splotchy and swollen when she cried. Instead, those dark eyes were drenched like a midnight storm, her lashes spiky and her lower lip pouting just a little. Damn, she was sexy.

He'd had a very specific plan when he'd got on the plane.

Come here, tell Lark that he loved her, convince her to return to Southern California, where she'd resume her career, have lots of success and they'd have great sex.

He could see now that he wasn't going to be able to stick with that plan.

"I want us to be together," he told her quietly.

"I do, too," she said with a tremulous smile. "So, now that we've made those into nonissues, I'd love to live with you."

"Yeah, see that's the thing." Shane hesitated, checking for fear. But there was none. Everything about this felt good. Felt right. "I don't want to just live together."

"What?"

"I want to marry you."

He waited for the storm, but it never came. Instead, Lark's eyes rounded with shock, her lips trembling before they slipped into a wide smile. She shook her head but the smile didn't shift.

"We've only known each other for a month," she pointed out.

"Yeah, but look what happened in that month. I hurt you when I left you, and we got through it. You hurt me when you left me, but here we are, getting through it. I was shot—you handled it fine. I was called on a mission and you dealt with it. You've met my friends and they all love you. And most of all, you know my family and you still love me."

Pretty sure that was the longest he'd ever talked at one time, Shane took a deep breath, then let it out in a huff.

"We're great together, right?" Not giving her a chance to respond, he did the unthinkable. He talked about feelings. "I'm happy when I'm with you. I've never felt as good as when we're together. You make me laugh, you make me think. All I've had, all I've let myself care about since I became a SEAL was my job. You show me a world outside of the navy and make me want to be a part of it."

Tears welled in her eyes again, but Lark didn't let them fall. Instead, she reached out to press her hands to his cheeks, pulling his face down to meet her kiss. Her lips moved over his in that sexy way she had that drove him crazy.

When she finally released his mouth, Shane wasn't sure if he wanted to keep convincing her or simply drag her off to bed. Both options had merit, but he figured if he managed the former, he'd automatically get the latter.

"So what do you say?" he asked. "If you don't like the condo, we can find something else. If you don't want to move to California we can…"

"Move here?" she asked, her brows rising.

Looking at her face, the sweet curve of her cheek and the amused look in her eyes, Shane realized he'd do whatever it took to spend his life with her. Even if it meant living right down the street from his mother part of the time.

"Yeah," he said, leaning down to brush his lips over hers. "Anything you want."

"Okay. Because I know exactly what I want." Her arms wrapped around his neck, Lark nodded.

"Yeah? What?"

"You," she said simply. "I want to move wherever you're

based, so I can be near you when you're not on duty. I want to spend my life with you when you're home, and believing in you when you're not. I want to build my career again. I want to build our life together."

Shane's grin was so big it hurt.

"I want all that, too." Then, frowning, he tilted his head to one side. "But you know what I want right now?"

"What?"

"You. Me. In bed." He swept her into his arms, and as she laughed, headed for the bedroom. "Shall we?"

* * * * *

Look for another UNIFORMLY HOT! *story from* New York Times *bestselling author Tawny Weber.*
A SEAL'S TOUCH is on sale February 2016 from Harlequin Blaze.

*Gage Ringer: Powerful, fierce, unforgettable...
and temporarily sidelined from his MMA career
with an injury. Back home, he has one month
to win over the woman he could never forget...*

Read on for New York Times *bestselling author
Lori Foster's*

HARD KNOCKS

The stunning prequel novella for her Ultimate *series!*

HARD KNOCKS

Lori Foster

CHAPTER ONE

GAGE RINGER, better known as Savage in the fight world, prowled the interior of the rec center. His stride was long, his thoughts dark, but he kept his expression enigmatic to hide his turmoil from onlookers. He didn't want to be here tonight. He'd rather be home, suffering his bad mood alone instead of covering up his regret, forced to pretend it didn't matter. His disappointment was private, damn it, and he didn't want to advertise it to the world. Shit happened.

It had happened to him. So what?

Life went on. There would be other fights, other opportunities. Only a real wimp would sit around bellyaching about what could have been, but wasn't. Not him. Not publicly anyway.

Tonight the rec center would overflow with bodies of all shapes, sizes and ages—all there for different reasons.

Cannon Coulter owned the rec center. It was a part of Cannon's life, a philanthropic endeavor that, no matter how big Cannon got, how well-known he became in the Supreme Battle Championship fight world, would always be important to him.

Armie Jacobson, another fighter who helped run the rec center whenever Cannon had to travel for his career, had planned a long night of fun. Yay.

Not.

At least, not for Gage.

Earlier they'd had a party for the kids too young to stick

around and watch the pay-per-view event that night on the big screen. One of Cannon's sponsors had contributed the massive wall-mounted TV to the center.

So that they wouldn't feel left out, Armie had organized fun activities for the younger kids that had included food, games and some one-on-one play with the fighters who frequented the rec center, using it as a gym.

With the kiddie party now wrapping up, the more mature crowd would soon arrive, mixing and mingling while watching the fights.

The rec center had originally opened with very little. Cannon and some of his friends had volunteered to work with at-risk youths from the neighborhood to give them an outlet. They started with a speed bag, a heavy bag, some mats and a whole lot of donated time and energy.

But as Cannon's success had grown, so too had the rec center. Not only had Cannon added improvements, but his sponsors loved to donate anything and everything that carried their brand so that now the size of the place had doubled, and they had all the equipment they needed to accommodate not only a training camp for skilled fighters, but also dozens of boys, and a smattering of girls, of all ages.

Gage heard a distinctly female laugh and his gaze automatically went to Harper Gates.

So she had arrived.

Without meaning to, he inhaled more deeply, drawing in a calming breath. Yeah, Harper did that to him.

He watched as Harper assisted Armie in opening up folding chairs around the mats. Together they filled up every available speck of floor space. She stepped around a few of the youths who were still underfoot, racing around, wrestling—basically letting off steam with adult supervision, which beat the hell out of them hanging on street corners, susceptible to the thugs who crawled out of the shadows as the sun went down.

Gage caught one boy as he recklessly raced past. He twirled him into the air, then held him upside down. The kid squealed with laughter, making Gage smile, too.

"You're moving awfully fast," Gage told him.

Bragging, the boy said, "I'm the fastest one here!"

"And humble, too," he teased.

The boy blinked big owl eyes at him while grinning, showing two missing teeth. He was six years old, rambunctious and considered the rec center a second home.

"I need you to take it easy, okay? If you're going to roughhouse, keep it on the mats."

"'Kay, Savage."

Gage glanced at a clock on the wall. The younger crowd would be heading out in a few more minutes. Still holding the boy suspended, he asked, "Who's taking you home?"

"My gram is comin' in her van and takin' all of us."

"Good." Luckily the grandmother was reliable, because the parents sure as hell weren't. And no way did Gage want the boys walking home. The rec center was in a decent enough area, but where the boys lived…

The kid laughed as Gage flipped him around and put him back on his feet.

Like a shot, he took off toward Miles, who was already surrounded by boys as he rounded them up.

Grandma would arrive soon. She'd probably appreciate how the kids had been exercised in the guise of play, schooled on control and manners, and fed. The boys always ate like they were starving. But then, Gage remembered being that age and how he could pack it away.

Briefly, his gaze met Harper's, and damn it, he felt it, that charged connection that had always existed between them. She wore a silly smile that, despite his dark mood, made him want to smile, too.

But as they looked at each other, she deliberately wiped the smile away. Pretending she hadn't seen him at all, she got back to work.

Gage grunted. He had no idea what had gotten into her, but in his current frame of mind, better that he just let it go for now.

Very shortly, the most dedicated fight fans would arrive to catch the prelims. By the time the main card started, drawing a few high school seniors, some interested neighbors and the other fighters, there'd be bodies in all the chairs, sprawled on the mats and leaning up against the concrete walls. Equipment had been either moved out of the way or stored for the night.

This was a big deal. One of their own was competing tonight.

The high school guys were looking forward to a special night where they'd get to mingle more with their favorite fighters.

A dozen or more women were anxious to do some mingling of their own.

Armie, the twisted hedonist, had been judicious in handing out the invites: some very hot babes would be in attendance, women who'd already proven their "devotion" to fighters.

Gage couldn't have cared less. If he hadn't been fucked by karma, he'd be there in Japan, too. He didn't feel like celebrating, damn it. He didn't want to expose anyone to his nasty disposition.

The very last thing he wanted was a female groupie invading his space.

Actually, he'd been so caught up in training, he'd been away from female company for some time now. You think he'd be anxious to let off steam in the best way known to man.

But whenever he thought of sex...

Harper laughed again, and Gage set his back teeth even while sneaking a peek to see what she found so funny. Armie said something to her, and she swatted at him while smiling widely.

Gage did a little more teeth grinding.

Like most of the fighters, Armie understood Gage's pre-occupation and ignored him. Now if he would just ignore Harper, too, Gage could get back to brooding.

Instead, he was busy thinking of female company—but there was only one woman who crowded his brain.

And for some reason, she seemed irritated with him.

His dark scowl made the stitches above his eye pull and pinch, drawing his thoughts from one problem and back to another.

One stupid mistake, one botched move during prac-tice, and he had an injury that got him kicked out of the competition.

Damn it all, he didn't want to be here tonight, but if he hadn't shown up, he'd have looked sad and pathetic.

"Stop pacing," Harper said from right behind him. "It makes you look sad and pathetic."

Hearing his concern thrown right back at him, Gage's left eye twitched. Leave it to Harper to know his exact thoughts and to use them as provocation. But then, he had to admit, she provoked him so well...

He'd missed the fights. And he'd missed Harper.

The only upside to heading home had been getting to see her. But since his return three days ago, she'd given him his space—space he wanted, damn it, just maybe not from her. At the very least, she could have *wanted* to see him, instead of treating him like one of the guys.

Relishing a new focus, Gage paused, planning what he'd say to her.

She didn't give him a chance to say anything.

With a hard whop to his ass, she walked on by and sashayed down the hall to the back.

Gage stood there, the sting of her swat ramping up his temper…and something else. Staring after her, he suffered the sizzling clench of emotions that always surfaced whenever Harper got close—which, since he'd returned home with his injury, had been rare.

He'd known her for years—grown up with her, in fact— and had always enjoyed her. Her wit. Her conversation. Her knowledge of mixed martial arts competition.

Her cute bod.

They'd recently taken their friendship to the next level, dating, spending more private time together. He'd enjoyed the closeness…

But he'd yet to enjoy her naked.

Time and circumstances had conspired against him on that one. Just when things had been heating up with Harper, just when it seemed she was ready to say "yes" instead of "not yet," he'd been offered the fight on the main card in Japan. He'd fought with the SBC before. He wasn't a newbie.

But always in the prelims, never on the highly publicized, more important main card. Never with such an anticipated event.

In a whirlwind, he'd gone off to a different camp to train with Cannon, getting swept up in the publicity and interviews that went with a main card bout…

Until, just a few lousy days ago—*so fucking close*— he'd miscalculated in practice and sustained a deep cut from his sparring partner's elbow.

A cut very near his eye that required fifteen stitches.

It made him sick to think of how quickly he'd been pro

nounced medically ineligible. Before he'd even caught his breath the SBC had picked his replacement.

That lucky bastard was now in Japan, ready to compete.

And Gage was left in Ohio. Instead of fighting for recognition, he fought his demons—*and got tweaked by Harper.*

He went after her, calling down the empty hallway, "I am not pathetic."

From inside a storage room, he heard her loud "Ha!" of disagreement.

Needing a target for his turbulent emotions and deciding Harper was perfect—in every way—he strode into the room.

And promptly froze.

Bent at the waist, Harper had her sexy ass in the air while she pulled disposable cups off the bottom shelf.

His heart skipped a beat. Damn, she was so hot. Except for bad timing, he'd be more familiar with that particular, *very perfect* part of her anatomy.

Not sleeping with her was yet another missed opportunity, one that plagued him more now that he didn't have the draining distraction of an upcoming fight. His heart started punching a little too hard. Anger at his circumstances began to morph into red-hot lust as he considered the possibilities.

But then, whenever he thought of Harper, lust was the least confusing of his emotions.

Now that he was home, he'd hoped to pick up where they'd left off. Only Harper had antagonism mixed with her other more welcoming signals, so he had to proceed with caution.

"What are you doing?" he asked, because that sounded better than saying, *"Damn, girl, I love your ass."*

Still in that tantalizing position, she peeked back at

him, her brown hair swinging around her face, her enormous blue eyes direct. With her head down that way, blood rushed to her face and made her freckles more noticeable.

There were nights he couldn't sleep for wondering about all the places she might have freckles. Many times he'd imagined stripping those clothes off her, piece by piece, so he could investigate all her more secret places.

Like him, she was a conservative dresser. Despite working at a secondhand boutique clothing store she always looked casual and comfortable. Her jeans and T-shirts gave an overview of sweet curves, but he'd love to get lost in the details if he could ever get her naked.

She straightened with two big boxes in her hands. "Armie had small juice containers out for the kids, but of course adults are going to want something different to drink. Same with the snacks. So I'm changing up the food spread."

Due to her schedule at the boutique, Harper had been unable to attend the party with the youngsters, but she'd sent in snacks ahead of time. She had a knack for creating healthy treats that looked fun and got gobbled up. Some of the options had looked really tasty, but if she wanted to switch them out, he could at least help her.

She glanced at the slim watch on her wrist. "Lots to do before everyone shows up for the prelims."

Since pride kept him at the rec center anyway…

"What can I do to help?"

Her smile came slow and teasing. "All kinds of things, actually. Or—wait—do you mean with the setup?"

"I… What?" Was that a come-on? He couldn't tell for sure—nothing new with Harper. Clearly she'd been pissed at him about something, but now, at her provocative words, his dick perked up with hopes of reconciliation.

Snickering, she walked up to him, gave him a hip bump,

then headed out of the room. "Come on, big boy. You can give me a hand with the folding tables."

As confusion warred with disgruntlement, he trailed after her. "All right, fine." Then he thought to remind her, "But I'm not pathetic."

Turning to face him, she walked backward. "Hit home with that one, did I?"

"No." *Yes.*

"I can help you to fake it if you want."

Despite the offhand way she tossed that out, it still sounded suggestive as hell. "Watch where you're going." Gage reached out, caught her arm and kept her from tripping over the edge of a mat.

Now that he had ahold of her, he decided to hang on. Where his fingers wrapped around her arm just above her elbow, she was soft and sleek and he couldn't stop his thumb from playing over the warm silk of her skin.

"Thanks," she said a little breathlessly, facing forward again and treading on.

"So." Though he walked right beside her, Gage couldn't resist leaning back a bit to watch the sway of her behind. "How would we fake it? Not that I need to fake shit, but you've got me curious."

Laughing, she leaned into him, smiled up at him, and damn it, he wanted her. *Bad.*

Always had, probably always would.

He'd had his chance before he left for the new camp. Even with the demands of training, he'd wanted her while he was away. Now he was back and the wanting boiled over.

Her head perfectly reached his shoulder. He stood six-three, nine inches taller than her, and he outweighed her by more than a hundred pounds.

But for a slim woman, she packed one hell of a punch.

"Harper," he chided. She was the only person he knew who seemed to take maniacal delight in tormenting him.

Rolling her eyes, she said, "You are such a grouch when you're being pathetic." She stepped away to arrange the cups on a long table placed up against the wall. "Everyone feels terrible for you. And why not? We all know you'd have won. Maybe even with a first-round knockout."

Did she really believe that? Or was she just placating him? "Darvey isn't a slouch." Gage wouldn't want an easy fight. What the hell would that prove?

"No," she agreed, "but you'd have creamed him."

"That was the plan." So many times he'd played it out in his head, the strategy he'd use, how he'd push the fight, how his cardio would carry him through if it went all three rounds. Darvey wasn't known for his gas tank. He liked to use submissions, manipulating an arm or leg joint to get his opponent to tap before something broke. His plan was always to end things fast. But Gage knew how to defend against submissions, how to make it *his* fight, not anyone else's.

"Sucks that you have to sit this one out," Harper continued. "But since you do, I know you'd rather be brimming with confidence, instead of moping around like a sad sack."

Folding his arms over his chest, he glared down at her. "I don't mope."

She eyed his biceps, inhaled slowly, blew the breath out even slower.

"Harper."

Brows raised, she brought those big blue eyes up to focus on his face. "What?"

He dropped his arms and stepped closer, crowding her, getting near enough to breathe in her unique scent. "How do you figure we'd fake things?"

"Oh, yeah." She glanced to one side, then the other. "People are looking at us."

"Yeah?" Currently the only people in the gym were the guys helping to set it up for the party. Armie, Stack, Denver, a few others. "So?"

"So…" She licked her lips, hesitated only a second, then came up against him. In a slow tease, her hands crawled up and over his chest. Fitted against him, she went on tiptoe, giving him a full-body rub.

Without even thinking about it, Gage caught her waist, keeping her right there. Confusion at this abrupt turnaround of hers stopped him from doing what came naturally.

Didn't bother her, though.

With her gaze locked on his, she curled her hands around his neck, drew him down to meet her halfway and put that soft, lush, taunting mouth against his.

Hell, yeah.

Her lips played over his, teasing, again provoking. They shared breath. Her thighs shifted against his. Her cool fingers moved over his nape and then into his hair. The kiss stayed light, slow and excruciating.

Until he took over.

Tilting his head, he fit his mouth more firmly against her, nudged her lips apart, licked in, deeper, hotter…

"Get a room already."

Gasping at the interruption, Harper pulled away. Embarrassed, she pressed her face against his chest before rearing back and glaring at Armie.

Gage just watched her. He didn't care what his dipshit friends said.

But he'd love to know what Harper was up to.

"Don't give me that look," Armie told her. "We have high school boys coming over tonight."

"The biggest kids are already here!"

"Now, I know you don't mean me," Armie continued, always up for ribbing her. "You're the one having a tantrum."

Gage stood there while they fussed at each other. Harper was like that with all the guys. She helped out, gave as good as she got, and treated them all like pesky brothers that she both adored and endured.

Except for Gage.

From the get-go she'd been different with him. Not shy, because seriously, Harper didn't have a shy bone in her hot little body. But maybe more demonstrative. Or rather, demonstrative in a different way.

He didn't think she'd smack any of the other fighters on the ass.

But he wasn't stupid. Encouraged or not, he knew guys were guys, period. They'd tease her, respect her boundaries, but every damn one of them had probably thought about sleeping with her.

For damn sure, they'd all pictured her naked.

Those vivid visuals were part of a man's basic DNA. Attractive babe equaled fantasies. While Harper hustled around the rec center helping out in a dozen different ways, she'd probably been mentally stripped a million times.

Hell, even while she sniped back and forth with Armie, Gage pictured her buck-ass, wondering how it'd feel to kiss her like that again, but without the barrier of clothes in the way.

"You need a swift kick to your butt," Harper declared.

"From you?" Armie laughed.

Fighting a smile, she said, "Don't think I won't."

"You wanna go?" Armie egged her on, using his fingertips to call her forward. "C'mon then, little girl. Let's see what you've got."

For a second there, Harper looked ready to accept, so Gage interceded. "Children, play nice."

"Armie doesn't like *nice*." She curled her lip in a taunt. "He likes *kinky*."

In reply, Armie took a bow.

True enough, if ever a man liked a little freak thrown into the mix, it was Armie. He'd once been dropped off by a motorcycle-driving chick dressed in leather pants and a low-cut vest, her arms circled with snake tattoos. She'd sported more piercings than Gage could count—a dozen or so in her ears, a few in her eyebrows, lip, nose. The whole day, Armie had limped around as if the woman had ridden him raw. He'd also smiled a lot, proof that whatever had happened, he'd enjoyed himself.

Unlike Gage, Armie saw no reason to skip sex, ever. Not even prior to a fight. The only women he turned down were the ones, as Harper had said, that were too nice.

"Come on." She took Gage's hand and started dragging him toward the back.

"Hey, don't leave my storage closet smelling like sex," Armie called after them. "If you're going to knock boots, take it elsewhere!"

Harper flipped him the bird, but she was grinning. "He is so outrageous."

"That's the pot calling the kettle black." Just where was she leading him?

"Eh, maybe." She winked up at him. "But I just act outrageous. I have a feeling it's a mind-set for Armie."

Ignoring what Armie had said, she dragged him back into the storage closet—and shut the door.

Gage stood there watching her, thinking things he shouldn't and getting hard because of it. Heart beating slow and steady, he asked, "Now what?"

CHAPTER TWO

COULD A MAN look sexier? No. Dumb question. Harper sighed. At twenty-five, she knew what she wanted. Whether or not she could have it, that was the big question.

Or rather, could she have it for the long haul.

"Is that for me?" She nodded at the rise in his jeans.

Without changing expressions, Gage nodded. "Yeah." And then, "After that kiss, you have to ask?"

Sweet. "So you like my plan?"

Looking far too serious, his mellow brown gaze held hers. "If your plan is to turn me on, yeah, I like it."

As part of her plan, she forced a laugh. She had to keep Gage from knowing how badly he'd broken her heart.

Talk about pathetic.

Gage was two years older, which, while they'd been in school, had made him the older, awesome star athlete and popular guy that *every* girl had wanted. Her included.

Back then, she hadn't stood a chance. He'd dated prom queen, cheerleader, class president material, not collect-for-the-homeless Goody Two-shoes material.

So she'd wrapped herself in her pride and whenever they'd crossed paths, she'd treated him like any other jock—meaning she'd been nice but uninterested.

And damn him, he'd been A-OK with that, the big jerk.

They lived in the same small neighborhood. Not like Warfield, Ohio, left a lot of room for anonymity. Everyone knew everyone, especially those who went through school together.

It wasn't until they both started hanging out in the rec center, her to help out, him to train, that he seemed to really tune in to her. Course, she hadn't been real subtle with him, so not noticing her would have required a deliberate snub.

She was comfortable with guys. Actually, she was comfortable with everyone. Her best friend claimed she was one of those nauseatingly happy people who enjoyed life a little too much. But whatever. She believed in making the most of every day.

That is, when big, badass alpha fighters cooperated.

Unfortunately, Gage didn't. Not always.

Not that long ago they'd been dating, getting closer. Getting steamier.

She'd fallen a little more in love with him every day.

She adored his quiet confidence. His motivation and dedication. The gentle way he treated the little kids who hung out at the center, how he coached the older boys who revered him, and the respect he got—and gave—to other fighters.

She especially loved his big, rock-solid body. Just thinking about it made her all twitchy in private places.

Things had seemed to be progressing nicely.

Until the SBC called and put him on the main card for freaking other-side-of-the-world Japan, and boom, just like that, it seemed she'd lost all the ground she'd gained. Three months before the fight, Gage had packed up and moved to Harmony, Kentucky, to join Cannon in a different camp where he could hone his considerable skills with a fresh set of experienced fighters.

He'd kissed her goodbye first, but making any promises about what to expect on his return hadn't been on his mind. Nope. He'd been one big obsessed puppy, his thoughts only on fighting and winning.

Maybe he'd figured that once he won, his life would get too busy for her to fit into it.

And maybe, she reminded herself, she was jumping ahead at Mach speed. They hadn't even slept together yet.

But that was something she could remedy.

Never, not in a million years, would she have wished the injury on him. He'd fought, and won, for the SBC before. But never on the main card. Knowing what that big chance had meant to him, she'd been devastated on his behalf.

Yet she'd also still been hurt that the entire time he was gone, he hadn't called. For all she knew, he hadn't even thought about her. Ignoring him had seemed her best bet—until she realized she couldn't. Loving him made that impossible.

And so she decided not to waste an opportunity.

Gage leaned against the wall. "I give up. How long are you going to stand there staring at me?"

"I like looking at you, that's all." She turned her back on him before she blew the game too soon. "You're terrific eye candy."

He went so silent, she could hear the ticking of the wall clock. "What are you up to, Harper?"

"No good." She grinned back at him. "Definitely, one hundred percent no good." Locating napkins and paper plates on the shelf, she put them into an empty box. Searching more shelves, she asked, "Do you see the coffeemaker anywhere?"

His big hands settled on her waist. "Forget the coffeemaker," he murmured from right behind her. Leaning down, he kissed the side of her neck. "Let's talk about these no-good plans of yours."

Wow, oh, wow. She could feel his erection against her

tush and it was so tantalizing she had to fight not to wiggle. "Okay."

He nuzzled against her, his soft breath in her ear, his hands sliding around to her belly. Such incredibly large hands that covered so much ground. The thumb of his right hand nudged the bottom of her breast. The pinkie on his left hovered just over the fly of her jeans.

Temptation was a terrible thing, eating away at her common sense and obscuring the larger purpose.

He opened his mouth on her throat and she felt his tongue on her skin. When he took a soft, wet love bite, she forgot she had knees. Her legs just sort of went rubbery.

To keep her upright, he hugged her tighter and rested his chin on top of her head. "Tell me what we're doing, honey."

Took her a second to catch her breath. "You don't know?" She twisted to face him, one hand knotted in his shirt to hang on, just in case. "Because, seriously, Gage, you seemed to know exactly what you were doing."

His smile went lazy—and more relaxed than it had been since he'd found out he wouldn't fight. He slipped a hand into her hair, cupping the back of her head, rubbing a little. "I know I was making myself horny. I know you were liking it. I'm just not sure why we're doing this here and now."

"Oh." She dropped against him so she could suck in some air. "Yeah." Unfortunately, every breath filled her head with the hot scent of his powerful body. "Mmm, you are so delicious."

A strained laugh rumbled in his chest. "Harper."

"Right." To give herself some room to think, she stepped back from him. So that he'd know this wasn't just about sex, she admitted, "I care about you. You know that."

Those gorgeous brown eyes narrowed on her face. "Ditto."

That kicked her heart into such a fast rhythm, she almost gasped. *He cared about her.* "And I know you, Gage. Probably better than you think."

His smile softened, and he said all dark and sensuous-like, "Ditto again, honey."

Damn the man, even his murmurs made her hot and bothered. "Yeah, so…" Collecting her thoughts wasn't easy, not with a big hunk of sexiness right there in front of her, within reach, ready and waiting. "I know you're hammered over the lost opportunity."

"The opportunity to have sex with you?"

Her jaw loosened at his misunderstanding. "No, I meant…" Hoping sex was still an option, she cleared her throat. "I meant the fight."

"Yeah." He stared at her mouth. "That, too."

Had he somehow moved closer without her knowing it? Her back now rested against the shelving and Gage stood only an inch from touching her. "So…" she said again. "It's understandable that you'd be stomping around in a bad mood."

He chided her with a shake of his head. "I was not stomping."

"Close enough." Damn it, now she couldn't stop staring at his mouth. "But I know you want to blow it off like you're not that upset."

"I'm not *upset*." He scoffed over her word choice. "I'm disappointed. A little pissed off." His feet touched hers. "I take it you have something in mind?"

She shifted without thinking about it, and suddenly he moved one foot between hers. His hard muscled thigh pressed at the apex of her legs and every thought she had, every bit of her concentration, went to where they touched.

Casual as you please, he braced a hand on the shelf beside her head.

Gage was so good at this, at stalking an opponent, at gaining the advantage before anyone realized his intent.

But she wasn't his opponent. Keeping that in mind, she gathered her thoughts, shored up her backbone and made a proposal. "I think we should fool around." Before he could reply to that one way or the other, she added, "Out there. Where they can all see." *And hopefully you'll like that enough to want to continue in private.*

He lifted one brow, the corner of his mouth quirking. "And you called Armie kinky."

Heat rushed into her face. "No, I don't mean anything really explicit." But that was a lie, so she amended, "Well, I mean, I do. But not with an audience."

Again his eyes narrowed—and his other hand lifted to the shelving. He effectively confined her, not that she wanted freedom. With him so close, she had to tip her head back to look up at him. Her heart tried to punch out of her chest, and the sweetest little ache coiled inside her.

"I'm with you so far," he whispered, and leaned down to kiss the corner of her mouth.

"I figured, you know…" How did he expect her to think while he did that? "We could act all cozy, like you had other things on your mind. Then no one would know how distressed you are over missing the fight."

"First off, I'm not acting." His forehead touched hers. "Second, I am *not* distressed. Stop making me sound so damned weak."

Not acting? What did that mean? She licked her lips—and he noticed. "I know you're not weak." Wasn't that her point? "So…you don't like my plan?"

"I like it fine." His mouth brushed her temple, his tongue touched the inside of her ear—*Wow, that curled her toes!*—then he nibbled his way along her jaw, under her chin. "Playing with you will make for a long night."

"Yes." A long night where she'd have a chance to show him how perfect they were for each other. And if he didn't see things the same as she did, they could still end up sharing a very special evening together. If she didn't have him forever, she'd at least have that memory to carry her through.

But before she settled for only a memory, she hoped to—

A sharp rap on the door made her jump.

Gage just groaned.

Through the closed door, Armie asked, "You two naked?"

Puffing up with resentment at the intrusion, Harper started around Gage.

Before she got far, he caught her. Softly, he said, "Don't encourage him," before walking to the door and opening it. "What do you want, Armie?"

"Refreshments for everyone." Armie peeked around him, ran his gaze over Harper, and frowned. "Damn, fully clothed. And here I was all geared up for a peep show."

Harper threw a roll of paper towels at him.

When Armie ducked, they went right past him and out into the hall.

Stack said, "Hey!"

And they all grinned.

Getting back to business, she finished filling the box with prepackaged cookies, chips and pretzels, then shoved it all into Armie's arms, making him stumble back a foot.

He just laughed at her, the jerk.

"Where did you hide the coffeemaker?" Harper asked, trying to sound normal instead of primed.

"I'll get it." Armie looked at each of them. "Plan to join us anytime soon?"

Unruffled by the interruption, Gage said, "Be right there."

"Not to be a spoilsport, but a group of the high school

boys have arrived, so, seriously, you might want to put a lid on the hanky-panky for a bit."

"People are here already?" She'd thought she had an hour yet. "They're early."

Armie shrugged. "Everyone is excited to watch Cannon fight again." He clapped Gage on the shoulder. "Sucks you're not out there, man."

"Next time," Gage said easily with no inflection at all.

Harper couldn't help but glance at him with sympathy.

"If you insist on molesting him," Armie said, "better get on with it real quick."

She reached for him, but he ducked out laughing.

She watched Armie go down the hall.

Gage studied her. "You going to molest me, honey?"

Did he want her to? Because, seriously, she'd be willing. "Let's see how it goes."

His eyes widened a little over that.

She dragged out a case of cola. Gage shook off his surprise and took it from her, and together they headed back out.

A half hour later they had everything set up. The colas were in the cooler under ice, sandwiches had been cut and laid out. A variety of chips filled one entire table. More people arrived. The boys, ranging in ages from fifteen to eighteen, were hyped up, talking loudly and gobbling down the food in record time. The women spent their time sidling up to the guys.

The guys spent their time enjoying it.

"Is there more food in the back room?"

Harper smiled at Stack Hannigan, one of the few fighters who hadn't yet staked out a woman. "Yeah, but I can get it as soon as I finish tidying up here." Every ten minutes she needed to reorganize the food. Once the fights started, things would settle down, but until then it was pure chaos.

Stack tugged on a lock of her hair. "No worries, doll. Be right back." And off he went.

Harper watched him walk away, as always enjoying the show. Long-legged with a rangy stride, Stack looked impressive whether he was coming or going—as all of them did.

In some ways, the guys were all different.

Stack's blond hair was darker and straighter than Armie's. Denver's brown hair was so long he often contained it in a ponytail. Cannon's was pitch-black with a little curl on the ends.

She preferred Gage's trimmed brown hair, and she absolutely loved his golden-brown eyes.

All of the fighters were good-looking. Solid, muscular, capable. But where Stack, Armie and Cannon were light heavyweights, her Gage was a big boy, a shredded heavyweight with fists the size of hams. They were all friends, but with different fighting styles and different levels of expertise.

When Stack returned with another platter of food, he had two high school wrestlers beside him, talking a mile a minute. She loved seeing how the older boys emulated the fighters, learning discipline, self-control and confidence.

With the younger kids, it sometimes broke her heart to see how desperate they were for attention. And then when one or more of the guys made a kid feel special, her heart expanded so much it choked her.

"You're not on your period, are you?" Armie asked from beside her.

Using the back of her hand to quickly dash away a tear, Harper asked him, "What are you talking about?"

"You're all fired up one minute, hot and bothered the next, now standing here glassy-eyed." Leaning down to better see her, he searched her face and scowled. "What the hell, woman? Are you *crying*?"

She slugged him in the shoulder—which meant she hurt her hand more than she hurt him. Softly, because it wasn't a teasing subject, she said, "I was thinking how nice this is for the younger boys."

"Yeah." He tugged at his ear and his smile went crooked. "Makes me weepy sometimes, too."

Harper laughed at that. "You are so full of it."

He grinned with her, then leveled her by saying, "How come you're letting those other gals climb all over Gage?"

She jerked around so fast she threw herself off balance. Trapped by the reception desk, Gage stood there while two women fawned over him. Harper felt mean. More than mean. "What is he doing now?"

"Greeting people, that's all. Not that the ladies aren't giving it the old college try." He leaned closer, his voice low. "I approve of your methods, by the way."

"Meaning what?"

"Guys have to man up and all that. Be tough. But I know he'd rather be in the arena than here with us."

Than here—with her. She sighed.

Armie tweaked her chin. "Don't be like that."

"Like what?"

"All 'poor little me, I'm not a priority.' You're smarter than that, Harper. You know he's worked years for this."

She did know it, and that's why it hurt so much. If it wasn't so important to him, she might stand a chance.

"Oh, gawd," Armie drawled, managing to look both disgusted and mocking. "You're deeper down in the dumps than he is." He tipped up her chin. "You know, it took a hell of a lot of discipline for him to walk away from everyone, including you, so he could train with another camp."

She gave him a droll look rife with skepticism.

Armie wasn't finished. "It's not like he said goodbye to you and then indulged any other women. Nope. It was celibacy all the way."

"That's a myth." She knew because she'd looked it up. "Guys do not have to do without in order to compete."

"Without sex, no. Without distractions, yeah. And you, Harper Gates, are one hell of a distraction."

Was she? She just couldn't tell.

Armie leaned in closer, keeping his voice low. "The thing is, if you were serving it up regular-like, it'd probably be okay."

She shoved him. "Armie!" Her face went hot. Did everyone know her damn business? Had Gage talked? Complained?

Holding up his hands in surrender, Armie said, "It's true. Sex, especially good sex with someone important, works wonders for clearing the mind of turmoil. But when the lady is holding out—"

She locked her jaw. "Just where did you get this info?"

That made him laugh. "No one told me, if that's what you're thinking. Anyone with eyes can see that you two haven't sealed the deal yet."

Curious, eyes narrowed in skepticism, she asked, "How?"

"For one thing, the way Gage looks at you, like he's waiting to unwrap a special present."

More heat surfaced, coloring not only her face, but her throat and chest, too.

"Anyway," Armie said, after taking in her blush with a brow raised in interest, "you want to wait, he cares enough not to push, so he did without. It's admirable, not a reason to drag around like your puppy died or something Not every guy has that much heart." He held out his arms "Why do you think I only do local fighting?"

"You have the heart," Harper defended. But she added, "I have no idea what motivates you, I just know it must be something big."

Pleased by her reasoning, he admitted, "You could be right." Before she could jump on that, he continued. "My point is that Gage is a fighter all the way. He'll be a champion one day. That means he has to make certain sacrifices, some at really inconvenient times."

Oddly enough, she felt better about things, and decided to tease him back a little. "So I was a sacrifice?"

"Giving up sex is always a sacrifice." He slung an arm around her shoulders and hauled her into his side. "Especially the sex you haven't had yet."

"Armie!" She enjoyed his insights, but he was so cavalier about it, so bold, she couldn't help but continue blushing.

"Now, Harper, you know…" Suddenly Armie went quiet. "Damn, for such a calm bastard, he has the deadliest stare."

Harper looked up to find Gage scrutinizing them. And he did look rather hot under the collar. Even as the two attractive women did their best to regain his attention, Gage stayed focused on her.

She tried smiling at him. He just transferred his piercing gaze to Armie.

"You could go save him from them," Harper suggested.

"Sorry, honey, not my type."

"What?" she asked as if she didn't already know. "The lack of a Mohawk bothers you?"

He laughed, surprised her with a loud kiss right on her mouth and a firm swat on her butt, then he sauntered away.

CHAPTER THREE

GAGE LOOKED READY to self-combust, so Harper headed over to him. He tracked her progress, and even when she reached him, he still looked far too intent and serious.

"Hey," she said.

"Hey, yourself."

She eyed the other ladies. "See those guys over there?" She pointed to where Denver and Stack loitered by the food, stuffing their faces. "They're shy, but they're really hoping you'll come by to say hi."

It didn't take much more than that for the women to depart.

Gage reached out and tucked her hair behind her ear. "Now why didn't I think of that?"

"Maybe you were enjoying the admiration a little too much."

"No." He touched her cheek, trailed his fingertips down to her chin. "You and Armie had your heads together long enough. Care to share what you two talked about?"

She shrugged. "You."

"Huh." His hand curved around her nape, pulling her in. "That's why he kissed you and played patty-cake with your ass?"

She couldn't be this close to him without touching. Her hands opened on his chest, smoothing over the prominent muscles. What his chest did for a T-shirt should be illegal. "Now, Gage, I know you're not jealous."

His other hand covered hers, flattening her palm over his heart. "Do I have reason to be?"

"Over *Armie*?" She gave a very unladylike snort. "Get real."

He continued to study her.

Sighing, she said, "If you want to know—"

"I do."

Why not tell him? she thought. It'd be interesting to see his reaction. "Actually, it's kind of funny. See, Armie was encouraging me to have sex with you."

Gage's expression went still, first with a hint of surprise, then with the heat of annoyance. "What the hell does it have to do with him?"

No way could she admit that Armie thought they were both sad sacks. "Nothing. You know Armie."

"Yeah." He scowled darker. "I know him."

Laughing, she rolled her eyes. "He's lacking discretion, says whatever he thinks and enjoys butting in." She snuggled in closer to him, leaning on him. Loving him. "He wants you happy."

"I'm happy, damn it."

She didn't bother telling him how *un*happy he sounded just then. "And he wants me happy."

Smoothing a hand down her back, pressing her closer still, he asked, "Sex will make you happy?"

Instead of saying, *I love you so much, sex with you would make me ecstatic*, she quipped, "It'd sure be better than a stinging butt, which is all Armie offered."

"Want me to kiss it and make it better?"

She opened her mouth, but nothing came out.

With a small smile of satisfaction, Gage palmed her cheek, gently caressing. "I'll take that as a yes."

She gave a short nod.

He used his hand on her butt to snug her in closer. "Armie kissed you, too."

Making a face, she told him, "Believe me, the swat was far more memorable."

"Good thing for Armie."

So he *was* jealous?

"Hey," Stack called over to them. "We're ready to get things started. Kill the overhead lights, will you?"

Still looking down at her, Gage slowly nodded. "Sure thing." Taking Harper with him, he went to the front desk and retrieved the barrel key for the locking switches.

The big TV, along with a security lamp in the hallway, would provide all the light they needed. When Gage inserted the key and turned it, the overhead florescent lights clicked off. Given that they stood well away from the others, heavy shadows enveloped them.

Rather than head over to the crowd, Gage aligned her body with his in a tantalizing way. His hand returned to her bottom, ensuring she stayed pressed to him. "Maybe," he whispered, "I can be more memorable."

As he moved his hand lower on her behind—his long *fingers seeking inward—she went on tiptoe and squeaked, "Definitely."*

Smiling, he took her mouth in a consuming kiss. Combined with the way those talented fingers did such incredible things to her, rational thought proved impossible.

Finally, easing up with smaller kisses and teasing nibbles, he whispered, "We can't do this here."

Her fingers curled in against him, barely making a dent in his rock-solid muscles. "I know," she groaned.

He stroked restless hands up and down her back. "Want to grab a seat with me?"

He asked the question almost as if a big *or* hung at the end. Like… *Or should we just leave? Or should we find an empty room?*

Or would you prefer to go anywhere private so we can both get naked and finish what we started?

She waited, hopeful, but when he said nothing more, she blew out a disappointed breath. "Sure."

And of course she felt like a jerk.

He and Cannon were close friends. Everyone knew he wanted to watch the fights. Despite his own disappointment over medical ineligibility, he was excited for Cannon's competition.

Her eyes were adjusting and she could see Gage better now, the way he searched her face, how he...waited.

For her to understand? Was Armie right? Maybe more than anything she needed to show him that she not only loved him, but she loved his sport, that she supported him and was as excited by his success as he was.

"Yes, let's sit." She took his hand. "Toward the back, though, so we can sneak away later if we decide to." Eyes flaring at that naughty promise, he didn't budge.

"Sneak away to where?"

"The way I feel right now, any empty room might do." Hiding her smile, Harper stretched up to give him a very simple kiss. "That is, between fights. We don't want to miss anything."

His hand tightened on hers, and she couldn't help thinking that maybe Armie's suggestion had merit after all.

GAGE GOT SO caught up in the prefights that he almost— *almost*—forgot about Harper's endless foreplay. Damn, she had him primed. Her closeness, the warmth of her body, the sweet scent of her hair and the warmer scent of her skin, were enough to make him edgy with need. But every so often her hand drifted to his thigh, lingered, stroked. Each time he held his breath, unsure how far she'd go.

How far he wanted her to go.

So far, all he knew was that it wasn't far enough.

Once, she'd run her hand up his back, just sort of feeling him, her fingers spread as she traced muscles, his shoulder blades, down his spine…

If he gave his dick permission, it would stand at attention right now. But he concentrated on keeping control of things—himself and, when possible, Harper, too.

It wasn't easy. Though she appeared to be as into the fights as everyone else, she still had very busy hands.

It wasn't just the sexual teasing that got to him. It was emotional, too. He hated that he wasn't in Japan with Cannon, walking to the cage for his own big battle. He'd had prelim fights; he'd built his name and recognition.

He'd finally gotten that main event—and it pissed him off more than he wanted to admit that he was left sitting behind.

But sitting behind with Harper sure made it easier. Especially when he seemed so attuned to her.

If her mood shifted, he freaking felt it, deep down inside himself. At one point she hugged his arm, her head on his shoulder, and something about the embrace had felt so damn melancholy that he'd wanted to lift her into his lap and hold her close and make some heavy-duty spur-of-the-moment promises.

Holding her wouldn't have been a big deal; Miles had a chick in his lap. Denver, too.

With Harper, though, it'd be different. Everyone knew a hookup when they saw one, and no way did Gage want others to see her that way. Harper was like family at the rec center. She was part of the inner circle. He would never do anything to belittle her importance.

Beyond that, he wanted more than a hookup. He cared about her well beyond getting laid a single time, well beyond any mere friendship.

Still, as soon as possible, he planned to get her alone and, God willing, get her under him.

Or over him.

However she liked it, as long as he got her. Not just for tonight, but for a whole lot more.

Everyone grimaced when the last prelim fight ended with a grappling match—that turned into an arm bar. The dominant fighter trapped the arm, extended it to the breaking point while the other guy tried everything he could to free himself.

Squeezed up close to his side, peeking through her fingers, Harper pleaded, "Tap, tap, tap," all but begging his opponent to admit defeat before he suffered more damage. And when he did, she cheered with everyone else. "Good fight. Wow. That was intense."

It was so cute how involved she got while watching, that Gage had to tip up her chin so he could kiss her.

Her enthusiasm for the fight waned as she melted against him, saying, "Mmm…"

He smiled against her mouth. "You're making me a little nuts."

"Look who's talking." She glanced around with exaggerated drama. "If only we were alone."

Hoping she meant it, he used his thumb to brush her bottom lip. "We can be." His place. Her place. Either worked for him. "It'll be late when the fights end, but—"

"I really have to wait that long?"

Yep, she meant it. Her blue eyes were heavy, her face flushed. She breathed deeper. He glanced down at her breasts and saw her nipples were tight against the material of her T-shirt.

Okay, much more of that and he wouldn't be able to keep it under wraps.

A roar sounded around them and they both looked up

to see Cannon on the screen. Gage couldn't help but grin. Yeah, he wanted to be there, too, but at the same time, he was so damn proud of Cannon.

In such a short time, Cannon had become one of the most beloved fighters in the sport. The fans adored him. His peers respected him. And the Powers That Be saw him as a big draw moneymaker. After he won tonight, Gage predicted that Cannon would be fighting for the belt.

He'd win it, too.

They showed footage of Cannon before the fight, his knit hat pulled low on his head, bundled under a big sweatshirt. Keeping his muscles warm.

He looked as calm and determined as ever while answering questions.

Harper squeezed his hand and when she spoke, Gage realized it was with nervousness.

"He'll do okay."

Touched by her concern, he smiled. "I'd put money on it."

She nodded, but didn't look away from the screen. "He's been something of a phenomenon, hasn't he?"

"With Cannon, making an impact comes naturally."

"After he wins this one," she mused, "they'll start hyping him for a title shot."

Since her thoughts mirrored his own, he hugged her. Her uncanny insight never ceased to amaze him. Then again, she was a regular at the rec center, interacted often with fighters and enjoyed the sport. It made sense that she'd have the same understanding as him.

"Cannon's earned it." Few guys took as many fights as he did, sometimes on really short notice. If a fighter got sick—or suffered an injury, as Gage had—Cannon was there, always ready, always in shape, always kicking ass. They called him the Saint, and no wonder.

Gage glanced around at the young men who, just a few

years ago, would have been hanging on the street corner looking for trouble. Now they had some direction in their lives, the attention they craved, decent role models and a good way to expend energy. But the rec center was just a small part of Cannon's goodwill.

Whenever he got back to town, he continued his efforts to protect the neighborhood. Gage had enjoyed joining their group, going on night strolls to police the corruption, to let thugs know that others were looking out for the hardworking owners of local family businesses. Actual physical conflicts were rare; overall, it was enough to show that someone was paying attention.

It didn't hurt that Cannon was friends with a tough-as-nails police lieutenant and two detectives. And then there was his buddy at the local bar, a place where Cannon used to work before he got his big break in the SBC fight organization. The owner of the bar had more contacts than the entire police department. He influenced a lot of the other businesses with his stance for integrity.

Yeah, Cannon had some colorful, capable acquaintances—which included a diverse group of MMA fighters.

Saint suited him—not that Cannon liked the moniker. It wasn't nearly as harsh as Gage's own fight name.

Thinking about that brought his attention back to Harper. She watched the TV so he saw her in profile, her long lashes, her turned up nose, her firm chin.

That soft, sexy mouth.

He liked the freckles on her cheekbones. He liked everything about her—how she looked, who she was, the way she treated others.

He smoothed Harper's hair and said, "Most women like to call me Savage."

She snorted. "It's a stupid nickname."

Pretending great insult, he leaned away. "It's a fight name, not a nickname. And it's badass."

She disagreed. "There's nothing savage about you. You should have been named Methodical or Accurate or something."

Grinning, he shook his head. "Thanks, but no thanks."

"Well," she muttered, "you're not savage. That's all I'm saying."

He'd gotten the name early on when, despite absorbing several severe blows from a more experienced fighter, he'd kept going. In the end, he'd beaten the guy with some heavy ground and pound, mostly because he'd still been fresh when the other man gassed out.

The commentator had shouted, *He's a damn savage*, and the description stuck.

To keep himself from thinking about just how savage Harper made him—with lust—he asked, "Want something to eat?"

She wrinkled her nose. "After those past few fights? Bleh."

Two of the prelim fights were bloody messes, one because of a busted nose, but the other due to a cut similar to what Gage had. Head wounds bled like a mother. During a fight, as long as the fighter wasn't hurt that badly, they wouldn't stop things over a little spilled blood. Luckily for the contender, the cut was off to the side and so the blood didn't run into his eyes.

For Gage, it hadn't mattered. If only the cut hadn't been so deep. If it hadn't needed stitches. If it would have been somewhere other than right over his eye. If—

Harper's hand trailed over his thigh again. "So, *Savage*," she teased, and damned if she didn't get close to his fly. "Want to help me bring out more drinks before the main event starts?"

Anything to keep him from ruminating on lost opportunities, which he was pretty sure had been Harper's intent.

"Why not?" He stood and hauled her up with him.

They had to go past Armie who stood with two very edgy women and several teenagers, munching on popcorn and comparing biceps.

Armie winked at Harper.

She smiled at him. "We'll only be a minute."

The idiot clutched his chest. "You've just destroyed all my illusions and damaged Savage's reputation beyond repair."

Gage rolled his eyes, more than willing to ignore Armie's nonsense, but he didn't get far before one of the boys asked him about his cut. Next thing he knew, he was surrounded by wide eyes and ripe curiosity. Because it was a good opportunity to show the boys how to handle disappointment, he lingered, letting them ask one question after another.

Harper didn't complain. If anything, she watched him with something that looked a lot like pride. Not exactly what he wanted from her at this particular moment, but it felt good all the same.

He didn't realize she'd gone about getting the drinks without him until Armie relieved her of two large cartons of soft drinks. Together they began putting the cans in the cooler over ice. They laughed together, and even though it looked innocent enough, it made Gage tense with—

"You two hooking up finally?"

Thoughts disrupted, Gage turned to Denver. Hard to believe he hadn't noticed the approach of a two-hundred-and-twenty-pound man. "What?"

"You and Harper," Denver said, while perusing the food that remained. "Finally going to make it official?"

"Make what official?"

"That you're an item." Denver chose half a cold cut sandwich and devoured the majority of it in one bite.

Gage's gaze sought Harper out again. Whatever Armie said to her got him a shove in return. Armie pulled an exaggerated fighter's stance, fists up, as if he thought he'd have to defend himself.

Harper pretended a low shot, Armie dropped his hands to cover the family jewels, and she smacked him on top of the head.

The way the two of them carried on, almost like siblings, made Gage feel left out.

Were he and Harper an item? He knew how he felt, but Harper could be such a mystery.

Denver shouldered him to the side so he could grab some cake. "Gotta say, man, I hope so. She was so glum while you were away, it depressed the hell out of everyone."

Hard to imagine a woman as vibrant as Harper ever down in the dumps. When he'd left for the camp in Kentucky, she'd understood, wishing him luck, telling him how thrilled she was for him.

But since his return a few days ago, things had been off. He hadn't immediately sought her out, determined to get his head together first. He didn't want pity from anyone, but the way he'd felt had been pretty damned pitiful. He'd waffled between rage at the circumstances and mind-numbing regret. No way did he want others to suffer him like that, most especially Harper.

He knew he'd see her at the rec center and had half expected her to gush over him, to fret over his injury, to sympathize.

She hadn't done any of that. Mostly she'd treated him the same as she did the rest of the guys, leaving him confused and wallowing in his own misery.

Until tonight.

Tonight she was all about making him insane with the need to get her alone and naked.

"You listening to me, Gage?"

Rarely did another fighter call him by his given name

That Denver did so now almost felt like a reprimand from his mom. "Yeah, *Denver*, I'm listening."

"Good." Denver folded massive arms over his massive chest, puffing up like a turkey. "So what's it to be?"

If Denver expected a challenge, too bad. Gage again sought out Harper with his gaze. "She was really miserable?"

Denver deflated enough to slap him on the back. "Yeah. It was awful. Made me sad as shit, I don't mind telling you."

"What was she miserable about?"

"Dude, are you that fucking obtuse?"

Stack stepped into the conversation. "Hell, yeah, he is." Then changing the subject, Stack asked, "Did Rissy go to Japan with Cannon?"

Denver answered, saying, "Yeah, he took her and her roommate along."

Merissa, better known as Rissy, was Cannon's little sis. A roommate was news to Gage, though. "If you have ideas about his sister, you're an idiot."

Stack drew back. "No. Hell, no. Damn man, don't start rumors."

Everyone knew Cannon as a nice guy. More than nice. But he was crazy-particular when it came to Merissa. For that reason, the guys all looked past her, through her or when forced to it, with nothing more than respect. "Who's the roommate?"

"Sweet Cherry Pie," Denver rumbled low and with feeling.

Stack grinned at him.

Gage totally missed the joke. "What?"

"Cherry Payton," Denver said, and damn if he didn't almost sigh. "Long blond hair, big chocolate-brown eyes, extra fine body…"

"Another one bites the dust," Stack said with a laugh.

"Another one?"

"Obtuse," Denver lamented.

Stack nodded toward Harper. "You being the first, dumb ass."

"We all expect you to make her feel better about things."

Confusion kicked his temper up a notch. "What *things*?"

Slapping a hand over his heart, Stack said, "How you feel."

Striking a similar pose, Denver leaned into Stack. "What you want."

Heads together, they intoned, *"Love."*

"You're both morons." But damn it, he realized that he did love her. Probably had for a long time. How could he not? Priorities could be a bitch and he hated the idea that he'd maybe made Harper unhappy by not understanding his feelings sooner.

He chewed his upper lip while wondering how to correct things.

"Honesty," Stack advised him. "Tell her how the schedule goes, what to expect and leave the rest up to her."

"Harper's smart," Denver agreed. "She'll understand."

It irked Gage big-time to have everyone butting into his personal business. "Don't you guys have something better to do than harass me?"

"I have some*one* better to do," Stack told him, nodding toward one of the women who'd hit on Gage earlier. "Butting in to your business was just my goodwill gesture of the day." And with that he sauntered off.

Denver leaned back on the table of food. "We all like Harper, you know."

Gage was starting to think they liked her a little too much. "Yeah, I get that."

"So quit dicking around, will you?" He grabbed up another sandwich and he, too, joined a woman.

Gage stewed for half a minute, turned—and almost ran into Harper.

CHAPTER FOUR

GAGE CAUGHT HER ARMS, steadying them both. "Why does everyone keep sneaking up on me?"

She brushed off his hands. "If you hadn't been ogling the single ladies, maybe you'd be more aware."

She absolutely had to know better than to think that, but just in case... "How could I notice any other woman with you around?"

She eyed him. "Do you notice other women when I'm not around?"

Damn, he thought, did she really *not* know how much he cared? Worse, had she been sad while he was away?

The possibility chewed on his conscience. "No, I don't." He drew her up to kiss her sweetly, and then, because this was Harper, not so sweetly.

To give her back a little, he shared his own complaint. "You spend way too much time horsing around with Armie."

Shrugging, she reached for a few chips. "I was trying not to crowd you."

"What does that mean?"

While munching, she gestured around the interior of the rec center. "This is a fight night. You're hanging with your buds. When I see you guys talking, I don't want to horn in."

Whoa. Those were some serious misconceptions. To help clear things up, he cupped her face. "You can't."

"Can't what?"

"Horn in. Ever."

Brows pinching in disgruntlement, she shoved away from him. "I just told you I wouldn't."

He hauled her right back. "I'm not saying you shouldn't, honey, I'm saying you can't because there's never a bad time for you to talk to me. Remember that, okay?"

Astonished, she blinked up at him, and he wanted to declare himself right then. Luckily the first fight on the main card started and everyone went back to their seats, saving him from rushing her.

This time, Gage had a hard time concentrating. He saw the fight, he cheered, but more of his attention veered to Harper, to how quiet she was now.

Thinking about him?

The fight ended in the first round with a knockout.

Instead of reacting with everyone else, Harper turned her face up to his. As if no time had passed at all, she said, "That's not entirely true."

Damn, but it was getting more difficult by the second to keep his hands off her. He contented himself by opening his hand on her waist, stroking up to her ribs then down to her hip. "What's that?"

"There are plenty of times when I can't intrude."

She was still stewing about that? "No."

Like a thundercloud, she darkened. Turning to more fully face him, she said low, *"Yes."* Before he could correct her, she insisted, "But I want you to know that I understand."

Apparently she didn't. "How so?"

Leaning around him, she glanced at one and all to ensure there were no eavesdroppers. As if uncertain, she puckered her brows while trying to find the right words. "I know when you're in training—"

"I'm pretty much always in training."

She looked like she wanted to smack him. "There's training and then there's *training.*"

True enough. "You mean when I go away to another camp."

"That, and when you're close to a fight."

Should he tell her how much he'd enjoy coming home to her—every night, not just between fights? Would she ever be willing to travel with him? Or to wait for him when she couldn't?

He had a feeling Harper would fit seamlessly into his life no matter what he had going on.

Being as honest as he could, Gage nodded. "There will be times when my thoughts are distracted, when I have to focus on other stuff. But that doesn't mean I don't care. It sure as hell doesn't mean you have to keep your distance."

The next fight started and though a few muted conversations continued, most in attendance kept their comments limited to the competition. Beside him, Harper fell silent. Gage could almost feel her struggling to sort out everything he'd said.

Again, he found himself studying her profile; not just her face, but her body, too. Her breasts weren't large, but they fit her frame, especially with her small waist and the sexy flare of her hips. She kept her long legs crossed, one foot nervously rocking. She drew in several deep breaths. A pulse tripped in her throat.

By the second the sexual tension between them grew.

The end of the night started to feel like too many hours away. They had at least three more fights on the main card. Cannon's fight would be last. It wasn't a title fight, but it'd still go five rounds.

The current match went all three rounds and came down to a split decision. Gage no longer cared; hell, he'd missed more of the fight than he'd seen.

Around him, voices rose in good-natured debate about how the judges had gotten it right or wrong.

"What do you think?" Gage asked Harper.

She shrugged. "Depends on how the judges scored things. The guy from Brazil really pushed the fight, but the other one landed more blows. Still, he didn't cause that much damage, and the Brazilian got those two takedowns—"

Gage put a finger to her mouth. "I meant about us."

Her wide-eyed gaze swung to his. "Oh." She gulped, considered him, then whispered, "I like it."

"It?"

"There being an 'us.'"

Yeah, he liked it, too, maybe more than he'd realized before now. "I missed you while I was away."

She scoffed. "You were way too busy for that."

"I worked hard, no denying it. But it wasn't 24/7. I found myself alone with my thoughts far too often."

She forced a smile. "I'm sure at those times you were obsessed about the SBC, about the competition, about winning."

"All that—plus you." When it came to priorities, she was at the top. He'd just made too many assumptions for her to realize it.

She looked tortured for a moment before her hand knotted in his shirt and she pulled him closer. With pained accusation, she said, "You didn't call."

Hot with regret, Gage covered her hand with his own. "I was trying to focus." Saying it out loud, he felt like an ass.

But Harper nodded. "That's what I'm saying. There will be times when I need to stay out of your way so I don't mess with that focus."

He hated the idea of her avoiding him.

Almost as much as he hated the thought of ever leaving her again. Yet that was a reality. He was a fighter; he would go to other camps to train, travel around the country, around the world.

He'd go where the SBC sent him.

"You have to know, Gage. I'd never get in your way, not on purpose."

He almost groaned.

"I'm serious! I know how important your career is and I know what a nuisance it can be to—"

Suddenly starved for the taste of her, for the feel of her, Gage took her mouth in a firm kiss.

But that wasn't enough, so he turned his head and nibbled her bottom lip until she opened. When he licked inside her warm, damp mouth, her breath hitched. Mindful of where they were, he nonetheless had a hell of time tempering his lust.

Damn it.

The next fight started. Cannon would be after that.

In a sudden desperate rush, Gage left his chair, pulling her up and along with him as he headed toward the dimly lit hallway. He couldn't wait a second more. But for what he had to say, had to explain, he needed the relative privacy of a back room.

Luckily she'd seated them at the end of the back row. In only a few steps, and without a lot of attention, he had them on their way.

Tripping along with him, Harper whispered, *"Gage."*

"There are high school boys out there," he told her. He glanced in the storage room, but no, that was too close to the main room and the activity of the group.

"I know. So?"

He brought her up and alongside him so he could slip an arm around her. "So they don't need to see me losing my head over you."

She stopped suddenly, which forced him to stop.

Looking far too shy for the ballsy woman he knew her to be, she whispered, "Are you?"

This time he understood her question. "Losing my head over you?" Gently, he said, "No."

Her shoulders bunched as if she might slug him.

Damn, but he adored her. "I lost it a long time ago. I just forgot to tell you."

Suspicious, she narrowed her eyes. "What does that mean exactly?"

Not about to declare himself in a freaking hallway, he took her hands and started backing up toward the office. "Come along with me and I'll explain everything." This particular talk was long overdue.

She didn't resist, but she did say, "The fight you should have been in is next. And Cannon will be fighting soon after that."

"I know." At the moment, seeing the fight he'd missed was the furthest thing from his mind. As to Cannon, well, he'd be in a lot of fights. This wasn't his first, wouldn't be his last. If all went well, Gage would get her commitment to spend the night, and more, before Cannon entered the cage. "The thing is, I need you."

She searched his face. "Need me...how?"

In every way imaginable. "Let me show you."

Her gaze went over his body. "Sounds to me like you're talking about sex."

Did lust taint his brain, or did she sound hopeful? They reached the office door and he tried the handle. Locked, of course. Trying not to think about how the night would end, he said, "Seriously, Harper, much as I love that idea, we're at the rec center."

"So?"

Damn, she knew how to throw him. He sucked in air and forged on. "I thought we'd talk." Digging in his pocket, he found the keys he'd picked up earlier when he shut off the lights.

Sarcasm added a wicked light to her beautiful blue eyes. "Talk? That's what you want to do? Seriously?"

"Yeah. See, I need to explain a few things to you and it's better done in private." The door opened and he drew her in.

Typical of Harper, she took the initiative, shutting and locking the door, then grabbing him. "We're alone." Her mouth brushed his chin, his jaw, his throat. "Say what you need to say."

"I love you."

She went so still, it felt like he held a statue. Ignoring her lack of a response, Gage cupped her face. "I love you, Harper Gates. Have for a while now. I'm sorry I didn't realize it sooner. I'm especially sorry I didn't figure it out before I took off for Kentucky."

Confused, but also defending him, she whispered, "You were excited about the opportunity."

She made him sound like a kid, when at the moment he felt very much like a man. "True." Slowly, he leaned into her, pinning her up against the door, arranging her so that they fit together perfectly. She was so slight, so soft and feminine—when she wasn't giving him or one of the other fighters hell. "I thought it'd be best for me to concentrate only on the upcoming fight, but that was asinine."

"No," she said, again defending him. "It made sense."

"Loving you makes sense." He took her mouth, and never wanted to stop kissing her. Hot and deep. Soft and sweet. With Harper it didn't matter. However she kissed him, it blew his mind and pushed all his buttons.

He brushed damp kisses over to the side of her neck, up to her ear.

On a soft wail, Harper said, "How can you love me? We haven't even had sex yet."

"Believe me, I know." He covered her breast with his hand, gently kneading her, loving the weight of her, how her nipple tightened. He wanted to see her, wanted to take her in his mouth. "We can change that later tonight."

"I'll never last that long." She stretched up along his body, both hands tangled in his hair, anchoring him so she could feast off his mouth.

No way would he argue with her.

Everything went hot and urgent between them.

He coasted a hand down her side, caught her thigh and lifted her leg up alongside his. Nudging in against her, knowing he could take her this way, right here, against the door, pushed him over the edge.

Not what he would have planned for their first time, but with Harper so insistent, he couldn't find the brain cells to offer up an alternative.

"Are you sure?" he asked, while praying that she was.

"Yes. Now, Gage." She moved against him. "Right now."

HARPER GRABBED FOR his T-shirt and shoved it up so she could get her hands on his hot flesh, so she could explore all those amazing muscles. Unlike some of the guys, he didn't shave his chest and she loved—*loved, loved, loved*—his body hair.

God, how could any man be so perfect?

She got the shirt above his pecs and leaned in to brush her nose over his chest hair, to deeply inhale his incredible scent. It filled her head, making her dazed with need.

When she took a soft love bite, he shuddered. "Take it easy."

No, she wouldn't.

"We have to slow down or I'm a goner."

But she couldn't. Never in her life had she known she'd miss someone as much as she'd missed him when he'd left. Now he was back, and whether he really loved her or was just caught up in the moment, she'd worry about it later.

She needed him. All of him.

She cupped him through his jeans and heard him groan. He was thick and hard and throbbing.

He sucked in a breath. "Harper, baby, seriously, we have to slow down." Taking her wrist, he lifted her hand away. "You need to catch up a little."

"I'm there already." She'd been there since first deciding on her course of action for the night.

"Not quite." Gage carried both her hands to his shoulders before kissing her senseless, giving her his tongue, drawing hers into his mouth.

She couldn't get enough air into her starving lungs but didn't care. Against her belly she felt his heavy erection, and she wanted to touch him again, to explore him in more detail.

He caught the hem of her T-shirt, drawing it up and over her head. Barely a heartbeat passed before he flipped open the front closure on her bra and the cups parted.

Taking her mouth again, he groaned as his big hands gently molded over her, his thumbs teasing her nipples until she couldn't stop squirming. She wasn't one of the overly stacked groupies who dogged his heels, but she didn't dislike her body, either.

She'd always considered herself not big, but big enough. Now, with his enormous hands on her, she felt delicate—even more so when he scooped an arm under her behind and easily lifted her up so he could draw one nipple into his hot mouth.

Harper wrapped her legs around his waist, her arms around his neck. He took his time, drawing on her for what felt like forever, until she couldn't keep still, couldn't contain the soft cries of desperate need.

From one breast to the other, he tasted, teased, sucked, nibbled.

"Gage..." Even saying his name took an effort. "Please."

"Please what?" he asked, all full of masculine satisfaction and a fighter's control. He licked her, circling, teasing. "Please more?"

"Yes."

Back on her feet, she dropped against the door. He opened her jeans and a second later shoved them, and her panties, down to her knees.

Anticipation kept her still, kept her breath rushing and her heart pounding. But he just stood there, sucking air and waiting for God knew what.

"Gage?" she whispered with uncertainty.

One hand flattened on the wall beside her head, but he kept his arm locked out, his body from touching hers. "I should take you to my place," he rasped, sounding tortured. "I should take you someplace with more time, more privacy, more—"

Panic tried to set in. "Don't you even *think* about stopping now." No way could he leave her like this.

His mouth touched her cheek, the corner of her lips, her jaw, her temple. "No, I won't. I can't."

A loud roar sounded from the main part of the room. Knowing what that meant, that Cannon's fight was about to start, guilt nearly leveled Harper. "I forgot," she admitted miserably.

"Doesn't matter," he assured her.

But of course it did. He was here to watch Cannon compete, to join in with his fight community to celebrate a close friend.

She was here to show him she wouldn't interfere and yet, that's exactly what she'd done. "We
could—"

"No, baby." Need made his short laugh gravelly. "Believe me when I say that I *can't*."

"Oh." Her heart started punching again—with excitement. "We'll miss the fight."

"We'll catch the highlights later. Together." He stroked her hair with his free hand, over her shoulder, down the side of her body.

"You're sure?"

Against her mouth, he whispered, "Give or take a bed for convenience, I'm right where I want to be." His kiss scorched her, and he added, "With you."

Aww. Hearing him say it was nice, but knowing he meant it multiplied everything she felt, and suddenly she couldn't wait. She took his hand and guided it across her body.

And between her legs.

They both groaned.

At first he just cupped her, his palm hot, his hand covering so much of her. They breathed together, taut with expectation.

"It seems like I've wanted you forever," he murmured at the same time as his fingers searched over her, touching carefully. His forehead to hers, he added, "Mmm. You're wet."

Speaking wasn't easy, but he deserved the truth. "Because I *have* wanted you forever."

"I'm glad, Harper." His fingers parted her swollen lips, stroked gently over her, delved. "Widen your legs a little more."

That husky, take-charge, turned-on tone nearly put her over the edge. Holding on to his shoulders, her face tucked into his throat, she widened her stance. Using two fingers, he glided over her, once, twice, testing her readiness—and he pressed both fingers deep.

Legs stiffening, Harper braced against the door.

"Stay with me," Gage said before kissing her throat.

She felt his teeth on her skin, his hot breath, those oh-so-talented fingers.

"Damn, you feel good. Tight and wet and perfect." He

worked her, using his hand to get her close to climax. "Relax just a little."

"Can't." Her fingernails bit into his shoulders. "Oh, God."

"If we were on a bed," he growled against her throat, "I could get to your nipples. But you're so short—"

"I'm not," she gasped, unsure whether she'd be able to take that much excitement. "You're just so damn big."

"Soon as you come for me," he promised, "I'll show you how big I am."

Such a braggart. Of course, she'd already had a good idea, given she often saw him in nothing more than athletic shorts. And she'd already had her hands on him. Not long enough to do all the exploring she wanted to do, but enough to—

He brought his thumb up to her clitoris, and she clenched all over.

"Nice," he told her. "I can feel you getting closer."

Shut up, Gage. She thought it but didn't say it, because words right now, at this particular moment, would be far too difficult.

He cupped her breast and, in keeping with the accelerated tempo of the fingers between her legs, he tugged at her nipple.

The first shimmer of approaching release took her to her tiptoes. *"Gage."*

"I've got you."

The next wave, stronger, hotter, made her groan in harsh pleasure.

"I love you, Harper."

Luckily, at that propitious moment, something happened in the fight because everyone shouted and cheered—and that helped to drown out the harsh groans of Harper's release.

CHAPTER FIVE

GAGE BADLY WANTED to turn on lights, to strip Harper naked and then shuck out of his own clothes. He wanted to touch her all over, taste her everywhere, count her every freckle while feeling her against him, skin on skin, with no barriers.

Even with her T-shirt shoved up above her breasts and her jeans down around her knees, holding Harper in his arms was nice. Her scent had intensified, her body now a warm, very soft weight limp against him. He kept one hand tangled in her hair, the other cupping her sexy ass.

He let her rest while she caught her breath.

If he'd found a better time and place for this, he could stretch her out on a bed, or the floor or a table—didn't matter as long as he could look at every inch of her, kiss her all over.

Devour her slowly, at his leisure.

But they were in an office, at the rec center, with a small crowd of fighters and fans only a hallway away.

He kissed her temple, hugged her protectively.

His cock throbbed against her belly. He badly wanted to be inside her, driving them both toward joint release.

But this, having Harper sated and cuddling so sweetly… yeah, that was pretty damn special.

"Mmm," she murmured. "I lost my bones somewhere."

"I have one you can borrow."

He felt her grin against his throat, then her full-body rub as she wiggled against him. "Yes," she teased. "Yes, you do."

"I like hearing you come, Harper." With small pecks, he nudged up her face so he could get to her mouth. "Whatever you do, you do it well."

That made her laugh, so the kiss was a little silly, tickling.

She drew in a deep breath, shored up her muscles, and somewhat stood on her own. "The fight is still going on?"

"Sounds like."

"So all that excitement before—"

"You coming?"

She bit his chest, inciting his lust even more. "No, I meant with everyone screaming."

"Probably a near submission. Cannon is good on the ground, good with submissions." Good with every facet of fighting. "But let's not talk about Cannon right now."

"You really don't mind missing his fight?"

"Jesus, woman, I'm about to bust my jeans. Cannon is the furthest thing from my mind."

Happy with his answer, she said, "Okay, then, let's talk about you." She nibbled her way up to his throat. "There is just so much of you to enjoy."

"You could start here," he said, taking one of her small, soft hands down to press against his fly.

"I think I will." With her forehead to his sternum, she watched her hands as she opened the snap to his jeans, slowly eased down the zipper. "I wish we had more light in here."

Because that mirrored his earlier thought, he nodded. "You can just sort of feel your way around."

"Is that what you did?" Using both hands, she held him, so no way could he reply. She stroked his length, squeezed him. "You are so hard."

"Yup." He couldn't manage anything more detailed than that.

"You have a condom?"

"Wallet."

Still touching him, she clarified, "You have a condom in your wallet?"

"Yup."

She tipped her face up to see him, and he could hear the humor in her voice. "A little turned on?"

"A *lot* turned on." He covered her hand with his own and got her started on a stroking rhythm he loved. *"Damn."*

Harper whispered, "Kiss me."

And he did, taking her mouth hard, twining his tongue with hers, making himself crazy by again exploring her, the silky skin of her bottom, the dampness between her thighs, her firm breasts and stiffened nipples.

Harper released him just long enough to say, "Shirt off, big boy." She tried shoving it up, but Gage took over, reaching over his back for a fistful of cotton and jerking the material away. Anticipating her hands, her mouth, on his hot skin, he dropped the shirt.

She didn't disappoint. Hooking her fingers in the waistband of his jeans, she shoved down the denim and his boxers, too, then started feeling him all over. His shoulders to his hips. His pecs to his abs. She grazed her palms over his nipples, then went back to his now throbbing cock.

"You are so impressive in so many ways."

He tried to think up a witty reply, but with her small, soft hands on him, he could barely breathe, much less banter.

"I've thought about something so many times…" And with no more warning than that, she sank to her knees.

Oh, God. Gage locked his muscles, one hand settling on top of her head.

Holding him tight, Harper skimmed her lips over the sensitive head, licked down the length of his shaft.

Never one for half measures, she drew her tongue back up and slid her mouth over him.

A harsh groan reverberated out of his chest. "Harper."

Her clever tongue swirled over and around him—and she took him deep again.

Too much. Way too much. He clasped her shoulder. "Sorry, honey, but I can't take it."

She continued anyway.

"Harper," he warned.

She reached around him, clasping his ass as if she thought she could control him.

But control of any kind quickly spiraled away. Later, he thought to himself, he'd enjoy doing this again, letting her have her way, giving her all the time she wanted.

Just not now, not when he so desperately wanted to be inside her.

"Sorry, honey." He caught her under the arms and lifted her to her feet, then set her away from him while he gasped for breath. As soon as he could, he dug out his wallet and fumbled for the condom.

Sounding breathless and hot, she whispered, "You taste so good."

He'd never last. "Shh." He rolled on the condom with trembling hands. Stepping up to her in a rush, he stripped away her shirt and bra, shoved her jeans lower. "Hold on to me."

Hooking her right knee with his elbow, he lifted her leg, opening her as much as he could with her jeans still on, his still on. He moved closer still, kissing her until they were both on the ragged edge.

"Now," Harper demanded.

He nudged against her, found his way, and sank deep in one strong thrust.

More cheers sounded in the outer room, but neither of them paid much attention. Already rocking against her, Gage admitted, "I'm not going to last."

She matched the rhythm he set. "I don't need you to… *Gage!*"

Kissing her, he muffled her loud cries as she came, holding him tight, squeezing him tighter, her entire body shimmering in hot release. Seconds later he pinned her to the door, pressed his face into her throat, and let himself go.

For several minutes he was deaf and blind to everything except the feel of Harper in his arms where she belonged.

Little aftershocks continued to tease her intimate muscles, and since he remained joined with her, he felt each one. Their heartbeats danced together.

Gradually he became aware of people talking in the outer room. They sounded happy and satisfied, telling him the fight had ended.

Harper came to the same realization. "Oh, no. We missed everything?"

"Not everything." After a nudge against her to remind what they hadn't missed, he disengaged their bodies. Slowly he eased her leg down, staying close to support her—which was sort of a joke, given how shaky he felt, too.

"Do you think Cannon won?"

"I know he did."

Her fingers moved over his face, up to the corner of his eye near his stitches. "You're sure?"

"Absolutely." He brought her hand to his mouth and kissed her palm. "I was sure even before the fight started."

Letting out a long breath, she dropped her head. "I'm sorry we missed it."

"I don't have any regrets."

She thought about that for a second, then worried aloud, "They'll all know what we were doing."

"Yeah." There was barely enough light to see, but he located paper in the printer, stole a sheet, and used it to wrap up the spent condom. He pitched it into the metal waste can.

"I hope they didn't hear us."

Gage tucked himself away and zipped his jeans. "Even if they did—"

She groaned over the possibility. "No, no, no."

Pulling her back into his arms, he teased, "They won't ask for too many details."

Her fisted hands pressed against his chest. "I swear, if Armie says a single word, I'll—"

Gage kissed her. Then touched her breasts. And her belly.

And lower.

"Gage," she whispered, all broken up. "We can't. Not now."

"Not here," he agreed, while paying homage to her perfect behind. "Come home with me."

"Okay."

He'd told her that he loved her. She hadn't yet said how she felt. But while she was being agreeable… "I'll fight again in two months."

Gasping with accusation, she glared at him. "You knew you'd fight again—"

"Of course I will." He snorted. "I got injured. I didn't quit."

"Yeah, I know. But…" Her confusion washed over him. "I didn't realize things were already set. Why didn't you tell me?"

"Didn't come up." He kissed the end of her nose. "And honestly, I was too busy raging about the fight I'd miss to talk about the next one."

He felt her stillness. "You're not raging anymore?"

"Mellow as a newborn kitten," he promised. "Thank you for that."

Thinking things through, she ran her hands up his chest to his collarbone. "Where?"

"Canada."

Gage felt her putting her shoulders back, straightening her spine, shoring herself up. "So when you leave again—"

Before she could finish that thought, he took her mouth, stepping her back into the door again, unable to keep his hands off her ass. When he came up for air, he said, "If you can, I'd love it if you came with me."

She was still all soft and sweet from his kiss. "To Canada?"

"To wherever I go, whenever I go. For training. For fighting." He tucked her hair behind her ear, gave her a soft and quick kiss. "For today and tomorrow and the year after that."

Her eyes widened and her lips parted. "Gage?"

"I told you I love you. Did you think I made it up?"

In a heartbeat, excitement stripped away the uncertainty and she threw herself against him, squeezing tight. With her shirt still gone, her jeans still down, it was an awesome embrace.

A knock sounded on the door, and Armie called, "Just about everyone is gone if you two want to wrap it up."

"He loves me," Harper told him.

Armie laughed. "Well, duh, doofus. Everyone could see that plain as day."

Gage cupped her head in his hands, but spoke to Armie. "Any predictions on how she feels about me?"

"Wow." The door jumped, meaning Armie had probably just propped his shoulder against it. "Hasn't told you yet, huh?"

"No."

"Cruel, Harper," he chastised her. "Really cruel. And here I thought you were one of those *nice* girls."

Lips quivering, eyes big and liquid, she stared up at him. "I love you," she whispered.

"Me or Gage?" Armie asked with facetious good humor.

Harper kicked the door hard with her heel, and Armie said, "Ow, damn it. Fine. I'm leaving. But Gage, you have the keys so I can't lock up until—"

"Five minutes."

"And there go my illusions again."

The quiet settled around them. They watched each other. Gage did some touching, too. But what the hell, Harper was mostly naked, looking at him with a wealth of emotion.

"I should get dressed."

"You should tell me again that you love me."

"I do. *So much*," Harper added with feeling. "I have for such a long time."

Nice. "The things you do to me…" He fumbled around along the wall beside the door and finally located the light switch.

She flinched away at first, but Harper wasn't shy. God knew she had no reason to be.

Putting her shoulders back, her chin up, she let him look. And what a sight she made with her jeans down below her knees and her shirt gone. He cupped her right breast and saw a light sprinkling of freckles decorating her fair skin.

"Let's go," he whispered. "I want to take you home and look for more freckles."

That made her snicker. As she pulled up her jeans, she said, "I don't really have that many."

"Don't ruin it for me. I'll find out for myself."

By the time they left the room, only Armie, Stack and Denver were still hanging around.

With his arm around Harper, Gage asked, "You guys didn't hook up?"

"Meeting her in an hour," Stack said.

"She's pulling her car around," Denver told him.

Armie shrugged toward the front door. "Those two are waiting for me."

Two? Everyone glanced at the front door where a couple of women hugged up to each other. One blonde, one raven-haired.

"Why does she have a whip in her belt?" Harper asked.

"I'm not sure," Armie murmured as he, too, watched the women. "But I'm intrigued."

"Are they fondling each other?" Gage asked.

"Could be." Armie drew his gaze back to Harper and Gage, then grinned shamelessly. "But I don't mind being the voyeuristic third wheel."

The guys all grinned with amusement. They were well used to Armie's excesses.

A little shocked, Harper shook her head. "One of these days a nice girl will make an honest man of you. That is, if some crazy woman doesn't do you in first."

"At least I'd die happy." Leaning against the table, arms folded over his chest, Armie studied them both. "So. You curious about how your match went?"

"Wasn't my match," Gage said.

"Should have been. And just so you know, Darvey annihilated your replacement."

"How many rounds?"

"Two. Referee stoppage."

Gage nodded as if it didn't matter all that much. Darvey had gotten off easy because Gage knew he'd have won the match.

Then Armie dropped a bombshell. "Cannon damn near lost."

Because he'd been expecting something very different, Gage blinked. "No way."

Armie blew out a breath. "He was all but gone from a vicious kick to the ribs."

"Ouch." Gage winced just thinking of it. If the kick nearly took Cannon out, it must have been a liver kick, and those hurt like a mother, stole your wind and made breathing—or fighting—impossible.

Stack picked up the story. "But you know Cannon. On his way down he threw one last punch—"

"And knocked Moeller out cold," Denver finished with enthusiasm. "It was truly something to see. Everyone was on their feet, not only here but at the event. The commentators went nuts. It was crazy."

"Everyone waited to see who would get back on his feet first," Stack finished.

And obviously that was Cannon. Gage half smiled. Every fighter knew flukes happened. Given a fluke injury had taken him out of the competition, he knew it better than most. "I'm glad he pulled it off."

"That he did," Armie said. "And if you don't mind locking up, I think I'll go pull off a few submissions of my own."

Harper scowled in disapproval, then flapped her hand, sending him on his way.

A minute later, Denver and Stack took off, too.

Left alone finally, Gage put his arm around Harper. "Ready to go home?"

"My place or yours?"

"Where doesn't matter—as long as you're with me."

She gave him a look that said *"Awww!"* and hugged him tight. Still squeezed up close, she whispered with worry, "I can't believe Cannon almost lost."

Gage smoothed his hand down her back. "Don't worry,

about it. We fighters know how to turn bad situations to our advantage."

"We?" She leaned back in his arms to see him. "How's that?"

"For Cannon, the near miss will only hype up the crowd for his next fight." He bent to kiss the end of her freckled nose. "As for me, I might have missed a competition, but I got the girl. There'll be other fights, but honest to God, Harper, there's only one *you*. All in all, I'd say I'm the big winner tonight."

"I'd say you're *mine*." With a trembling, emotional smile, Harper touched his face, then his shoulders, and his chest. As her hand dipped lower, she whispered, "And that means we're both winners. Tonight, tomorrow and always."

* * * * *

Want more sizzling romance from
New York Times *bestselling author Lori Foster?*
Pick up every title in her Ultimate *series:*

HARD KNOCKS
NO LIMITS
HOLDING STRONG
TOUGH LOVE

Available now from HQN Books!

COMING NEXT MONTH FROM

HARLEQUIN® Blaze®

Available September 15, 2015

#863 TEASING HER SEAL
Uniformly Hot!
by Anne Marsh
SEAL team leader Gray Jackson needs to convince Laney Parker
to leave an island resort before she gets hurt—and before his
cover is blown. But as his mission heats up, so do their nights...

#864 IF SHE DARES
by Tanya Michaels
Still timid months after being robbed at gunpoint, Riley Kendrick
wants to rediscover her fun, daring side, and Jack Reed, her
sexy new neighbor, has some wicked ideas about how to help.

#865 NAKED THRILL
The Wrong Bed
by Jill Monroe
They wake up in bed together. Naked. And with no memory. So
Tony and Hayden follow a trail of clues to piece together what—
or *who*—they did on the craziest night of their lives.

#866 KISS AND MAKEUP
by Taryn Leigh Taylor
Falling into bed with a sexy guy she met on a plane is impulsive
even for Chloe. But when Ben's client catches them together,
she does something even more impulsive: she pretends to be
his wife!

YOU CAN FIND MORE INFORMATION ON UPCOMING HARLEQUIN® TITLES
FREE EXCERPTS AND MORE AT WWW.HARLEQUIN.COM.

HBCNM09

REQUEST YOUR FREE BOOKS!
2 FREE NOVELS PLUS 2 FREE GIFTS!

Ⓗ HARLEQUIN®

Blaze®

red-hot reads!

YES! Please send me 2 FREE Harlequin® Blaze® novels and my 2 FREE gifts (gifts are worth about $10). After receiving them, if I don't wish to receive any more books, I can return the shipping statement marked "cancel." If I don't cancel, I will receive 4 brand-new novels every month and be billed just $4.74 per book in the U.S. or $5.21 per book in Canada. That's a savings of at least 14% off the cover price. It's quite a bargain. Shipping and handling is just 50¢ per book in the U.S. and 75¢ per book in Canada.* I understand that accepting the 2 free books and gifts places me under no obligation to buy anything. I can always return a shipment and cancel at any time. Even if I never buy another book, the two free books and gifts are mine to keep forever.

150/350 HDN GH2D

Name _____ (PLEASE PRINT)

Address _____ Apt. #

City _____ State/Prov. _____ Zip/Postal Code

Signature (if under 18, a parent or guardian must sign)

Mail to the **Reader Service:**
IN U.S.A.: P.O. Box 1867, Buffalo, NY 14240-1867
IN CANADA: P.O. Box 609, Fort Erie, Ontario L2A 5X3

Want to try two free books from another line?
Call 1-800-873-8635 or visit www.ReaderService.com.

* Terms and prices subject to change without notice. Prices do not include applicable taxes. Sales tax applicable in N.Y. Canadian residents will be charged applicable taxes. Offer not valid in Quebec. This offer is limited to one order per household. Not valid for current subscribers to Harlequin Blaze books. All orders subject to credit approval. Credit or debit balances in a customer's account(s) may be offset by any other outstanding balance owed by or to the customer. Please allow 4 to 6 weeks for delivery. Offer available while quantities last.

Your Privacy—The Reader Service is committed to protecting your privacy. Our Privacy Policy is available online at www.ReaderService.com or upon request from the Reader Service.

We make a portion of our mailing list available to reputable third parties that offer products we believe may interest you. If you prefer that we not exchange your name with third parties, or if you wish to clarify or modify your communication preferences, please visit us at www.ReaderService.com/consumerschoice or write to us at Reader Service Preference Service, P.O. Box 9062, Buffalo, NY 14240-9062. Include your complete name and address.

HBI5

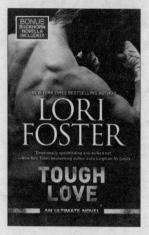

Blaze®

Red-Hot Reads

A hot shade of lipstick calls for a hot, sexy guy...

Falling into bed with a sexy guy she met on a plane is impulsive even for Chloe. But when Ben's client catches them together, she does something even more impulsive: she pretends to be his wife!

✂- -

SAVE $1.00

on the purchase of **KISS AND MAKEUP** by Taryn Leigh Taylor {available Sept. 15, 2015} or any other Harlequin® Blaze® book.

Redeemable at participating outlets in the U.S. and Canada only. Not redeemable at Barnes & Noble stores. Limit one coupon per customer.

52612884

Canadian Retailers: Harlequin Enterprises Limited will pay the face value of this coupon plus 10.25¢ if submitted by customer for this product only. Any other use constitutes fraud. Coupon is nonassignable. Void if taxed, prohibited or restricted by law. Consumer must pay any government taxes. Void if copied. Inmar Promotional Services ("IPS") customers submit coupons and proof of sales to Harlequin Enterprises Limited, P.O. Box 3000, Saint John, NB E2L 4L3, Canada. Non-IPS retailer—for reimbursement submit coupons and proof of sales directly to Harlequin Enterprises Limited, Retail Marketing Department, 225 Duncan Mill Rd., Don Mills, Ontario M3B 3K9, Canada.

U.S. Retailers: Harlequin Enterprises Limited will pay the face value of this coupon plus 8¢ if submitted by customer for this product only. Any other use constitutes fraud. Coupon is nonassignable. Void if taxed, prohibited or restricted by law. Consumer must pay any government taxes. Void if copied. For reimbursement submit coupons and proof of sales directly to Harlequin Enterprises Limited, P.O. Box 880478, El Paso, TX 88588-0478, U.S.A. Cash value 1/100 cents.

COUPON EXPIRES DEC. 15, 2015

Available wherever books are sold, including most bookstores, supermarkets, drugstores and discount stores.

www.Harlequin.com

and ™ are trademarks owned and used by the trademark owner and/or its licensee. HBCOUP0915
© 2015 Harlequin Enterprises Limited